A
Mosaic
of
Grace

A Novel

NINA NAVISKY

Cover design by Teddi Black

ISBN-13: 978-1518820335
ISBN-10: 1518820336

CHAPTER 1

"What name this one is it?" asks Luke, in his unmistakable, stilted voice. He's pointing at an older woman walking towards him, on the opposite side of the trail. He doesn't take his eyes off her, this woman in the distance, even when he addresses Tim. "What name this one is it, Grandpa?"

Tim struggles to close the gap that separates him from Luke, his hurried footsteps spraying gravel and dust. He squints as he tries to bring the woman's blurry outline into focus, swallows flecks of dirt as they mingle with the humid Texas air. *I shouldn't have let him get this far ahead of me. Gracie told me to stay right next to him at all times. But what does she expect? She knows what a nightmare a walk with her son can be.*

1

He can't help but feel defensive, having spent the last half hour suppressing his frustration as Luke zigzagged from one side of the path to the other, scratching his nails along the coral granite, pricking his fingers on the low-lying cacti, and eating bits of dehydrated brush. The walk to the lake should take fifteen minutes at most, but they've never made it in less than thirty-five. *A straight line. That's all I'm asking for. For once, just walk in a straight line.*

They follow this same trail every Saturday, but have yet to fall into stride with one another. Luke can't walk more than several steps without stopping to tap the ground with his hand or sit in the dirt. Sometimes his face darkens, and he tilts his head as if straining to hear a faint noise. Other times he laughs, his giggling pure and infectious, but the joke is never shared. "What's so funny, Luke?" Tim always asks, as hope, foolish and obstinate, whispers to him: maybe this time.

It's useless to try and set the pace by walking ahead. Luke doesn't try to catch up. "Come on, Luke, we're almost there. You can do it," Tim will say, using the exaggerated inflection typically reserved for toddlers. Or, using Luke's substitute phrase for *swimming*, "Don't you want to go to the water?" But Luke holds his ground without fail, waits for Tim to double back and push from behind.

On straightaways, Tim doesn't mind. It's fun, watching Luke run, then stop short, giggling in anticipation of the next push. But uphill is exhausting. Luke makes him do all the work, makes it harder even, by leaning backwards, stiff and uncooperative, as if he were a dolly that could be rolled. Downhill is problematic as well. Luke doesn't understand why Tim won't push him as hard, will scream "more push" until he's hoarse. "But you'll trip. I don't want you to get hurt," Tim will say, pantomiming a fall, but this explanation never satisfies Luke.

Once, Luke's screaming wore Tim down, and he gave the boy a shove. Not too hard, just enough to prove his point. But Luke, caught unprepared, tripped over a rock and skinned his hands and knees. He'd looked up at his grandfather, tears welling, and Tim, choking on guilt, had wanted to wrap him up in his arms, ease his pain, and yell "I told you so" all at the same time.

"That's Miss Wendy, Grandpa! That's Miss Wendy!" Luke is pointing at the woman with certainty, barely able to contain his delight.

Tim doubts that Luke knows her, but hopes his instinct is wrong. He knows what's coming next, and sees that he won't reach Luke in time to stop him. Luke steps right in front of the woman, forcing her to come to an abrupt halt.

"Hi, Luke! Hi, Luke!" Luke says, his hands flapping in excitement. He leans in and sniffs the collar of her lime-colored sweatshirt, his nose reaching her collarbone.

Tim catches up in time to see a combination of confusion and fear on the woman's face. It's clear that she doesn't know Luke, although his enthusiasm hasn't been lessened by her expression. He's still standing far too close to the woman, who has backed up several steps and is now attempting to walk around him. Tim guides Luke away as he begins the delicate process of apologizing.

He starts to explain Luke's odd behaviors, incompatible with those of a typical eight-year-old, but she waves away his explanations. "Someone needs to teach that child some manners. My goodness, no one teaches young ones how to behave anymore." She flashes both of them a disapproving look and continues on her way.

Rage courses through Tim, disproportionate to the woman's mild intolerance. He knows that Luke is at fault; he's yet again failed to follow the social rules learned by all though never taught. Gracie has told Tim that he needs to develop a thicker skin, but he still can't seem to staunch this primal response the way his daughter can. Or *says* she can. He still sees her flinch at judgmental stares and bruising words. At any rate, he isn't convinced that Gracie is right. It's almost comforting to focus all of his anger on this stranger for a moment, to define the enemy. An enemy can be defeated.

He turns to Luke, knows that his grandson is unaware of the emotion that this small exchange has dredged up from within him. Once again he's struck by the relative insignificance of words. Until they're draped in gestures, expressions, and inflections they're worth little, like a Christmas tree without ornaments and lights. The most critical information is conveyed without words, he's come to realize, and all of it eludes Luke. He aches for how much his grandson will never understand.

"I don't think that was Miss Wendy. Is Miss Wendy someone you know from school?" Not a teacher—none of the staff in his class photo look a day over thirty—but maybe an administrator, a therapist, a nurse?

"Yes."

Tim wonders if this answer is reliable. Luke defaults to "yes" when he doesn't understand the question. *Sort of like being in a foreign country. Sometimes it's easier to just agree. People will leave you alone if you agree with them.*

They walk in silence for a moment, and then Luke offers, "Miss Wendy green shirt Burton School."

Tim pounces on this jumbled bit of information, and fishes for more. "Did that woman have the same green shirt as Miss Wendy?"

"Yes."

He knows their conversation will end here, that he doesn't know enough of the specifics of Luke's daily life to fill in the blanks. There's something he's supposed to say now, some type of choice he's supposed to offer Luke to keep him engaged. Gracie even reminded him about it this morning, but for the life of him he can't—

"Water," Luke says.

"Yes, Luke, we're going to the lake. You can go swimming with Amanda. Are you excited?"

"Yes. Luke's going water Amanda. And?"

"And we'll see Josephine, too," he says, although he knows that Amanda's much older sister holds far less appeal. To be fair, Luke thinks of Amanda as family. He probably can't remember a time before he and his mother shared a roof with her childhood friend. But Tim doubts that Luke would have felt this rare connection with Josephine even if the situation had been reversed, and Amanda had been the able sister.

"And?"

"And that's it. Just Luke, Grandpa, Josephine, and Amanda."

"We're gonna go to?"

"We're going to the water, Luke."

"With?"

"You know who we're going to see." Tim's voice is bright, but he dreads how often he'll have to answer these same questions on their walk. Most days, he continues this circular conversation with Luke eight or nine times before giving up and ignoring him. He longs to connect with his grandson, to answer the same questions Gracie asked him when she was young, to tell him stories, to explain the rules of football. But this repetitive back-and-forth isn't really conversation.

"Grandpa." It's a comment, not a question. Luke isn't even looking Tim's way. There's no upwards tilt of the head, no curious gaze, no look of anticipation.

"Yes, Luke?"

"Grandpa."

"What?"

"Grandpa."

"Do you need something?"

"Grandpa."

Tim says nothing, hopes that Luke will be appeased, at least for the moment, with these four "Grandpas." There are rare days when four or five rounds of this nonsense will be enough for him. Not responding is risky, though, because more often Luke will react to silence by repeating himself louder and faster, like an engine revving, gritting his teeth and clenching his fists. Sometimes he'll lean into Tim, pushing him off balance, or grab his forearm and pinch him hard enough to leave a bruise. Tim gives in then, every time, and lets Luke drag him back into the loop to keep the peace.

Luke spies a lizard and stops, watches it scurry across the path and disappear behind a rock. He picks up a chewed piece of gum next to the rock and puts it in his mouth before Tim is able to wrest it away from him.

"No, Luke, no! That's yucky." He forces his grandson's mouth open, removes the gum, and throws it far into the brush. He wipes the spit off on the sides of his bathing suit, cringing at the thought of the germs that Luke has just swallowed.

Luke looks up to the sky and giggles, and, as usual, Tim can't pinpoint why. Is it the lizard that's so funny? Or being naughty by eating the gum? He follows Luke's gaze, looks upward into the cloudless sky for a clue, but finds none. He can hear the giggles turn to hiccups, but in between the spasms Luke still manages to ask, "We're gonna go to?"

Tim doesn't answer. Instead, he sighs and waits, wishing they were already there. He can feel the sun burning the tops of his ears and the back of his neck. Every Saturday Gracie lectures him about his fair skin, but he doesn't even own a tube of sunscreen. He hates the gluey feeling of it on his skin. *At least I still have my hair. I can't imagine having to glop that stuff over my whole head.*

Luke's hiccups are subsiding, and he's focused on breaking twigs off of a branch as the spasms become farther apart and his breathing begins to steady. Then, without warning, he screams, "Water! More water! *More water!*"

Tim feels a bolt of adrenalin surge through him, jarred by this unexpected outburst. "We're going to the water, Luke," he says, irritated. *You're the one holding things up, not me. If you didn't stop for every rock, lizard, and chewed up piece of gum, we'd be there already.*

Luke grits his teeth so hard that Tim worries that he'll chip a tooth. "Luke, stay calm." He tries to keep his voice neutral, like Gracie has told him to, but he can hear how shrill it is. Luke stops for a beat, and Tim holds his breath, wondering if he's been able to deescalate the situation.

Luke lets out a lone earsplitting shriek. "Let's keep walking to the water," Tim says, his voice and steps cautious, but he can see by the expression on Luke's face that he's somehow made a mistake.

The screams become louder still, interrupted only by the necessity of inhaling. Luke's face is red with fury, and he begins hitting his head on either side with both hands. The sound is almost comical, quick *rat-a-tat-tat*s, like a harried teacher clapping her hands for attention. Tim wrestles with him, tries to hold his hands down, but Luke manages to break free. He picks up a rock and throws it, just missing an oncoming jogger, and then flops to the ground, all four limbs flailing.

Tim doesn't apologize to the runner, who has averted his gaze and picked up his pace. He has bigger fish to fry. He grabs Luke by the hands and tries to pull him up, but is no match against the combination of his grandson's uncooperative seventy-five pounds and gravity. Gracie has told him that showing anger during one of Luke's tantrums only gets him more riled up, that it's essential to remain composed. But he's aggravated, tired, and hot, and doesn't care that he isn't following her stupid, endless rules. And isn't it important that the boy learns to respect authority? "Luke," he hisses. "Get up *now*. We can't go to the water if you won't get up. You're too big for me to carry."

Luke is covered in dirt, still struggling, and Tim releases him and sinks to the ground next to him. His screams are replaced by whimpers as he tries to clear dirt from his right eye.

Tim softens. "Here, let me help you." He pulls out a tissue and opens his thermos to dampen it. Luke bolts up, lunges for the thermos, and guzzles down its contents in one extended gulp.

Remorse floods Tim as he realizes his mistake. The poor kid. No wonder he screams and throws rocks. "Luke, I'm sorry, I didn't understand. I didn't know you were thirsty. I thought you were talking about swimming." He stops, realizing clarification will get him nowhere. "Are you hungry, too? Do you want a snack?"

"Snack."

Is he really hungry, though? Or just repeating what I say? He decides that it's safer to assume hunger, and walks over to a low boulder to rest his backpack on it. As he hands an apple to Luke, he hears the familiar ding of a text:

Running 15 min late. Don't want D-Day #2. Take the long route.

He smiles, grateful that Josephine understands. Every contingency must be planned for with Luke.

* * *

"D-day," or "Dock Day," as Josephine has dubbed it, occurred the one time that she and Amanda were late. Tim had followed Luke to the old, wooden dock, thinking they would spend the time looking at fish and dipping their toes in the water while they waited. But Luke had sprinted down the dock before Tim could stop him, picking up speed as he reached the end rather than slowing. "Get him! He can't swim by himself!" he'd yelled to the lifeguard, who blocked Luke just as he reached the edge. The result was a full-blown tantrum, far worse than he'd ever seen.

Luke had flopped down on the dock, his screams putting an abrupt end to the cheerful splashes and chatter of surrounding families and causing three lifeguards to come running. Pulling him back into a sitting position without wrenching his shoulder, risking splinters, or dragging him through bird droppings was impossible. The only solution was to pick him up, each person holding a thrashing limb, as he tried to hit and kick whoever was closest.

As they reached the shore, he turned his head towards the lifeguard supporting the right side of his torso, and bit her arm. She pulled it away, an instinctive withdrawal, and looked down in shock at the circle of white indentations etched in her inflamed skin. His shoulder slammed into the packed sand, causing him to cry out. The pain fueled his rage further, and he writhed and screamed for another twenty minutes before giving up, spent. Tim had just finished wiping sand from his tear-stained cheeks when Josephine and Amanda arrived. Luke heard them first, and ran to Amanda, laughing, as if nothing had happened.

Tim knew that he shouldn't allow Luke to go swimming afterwards, but what could he do? Four people had struggled to carry him from the dock to the beach. There was no question that Luke would melt down again if he were to attempt to take him home now, and there was no way that he could get him all the way down the trail to the car, even with Josephine's help. Besides, Luke was finally calm. Tim didn't have the energy to deal with a second round.

"How did it go?" Gracie asked over her shoulder, when he dropped Luke off late that afternoon. Already she was on patrol, following Luke as he discarded sandals in different rooms, turned on the TV, and rummaged through the freezer for a Popsicle. She squatted to pull his wet bathing suit down, and as she did, he ripped open the wrapper and let it fall, the syrupy residue clinging to her hair as the plastic floated past her. He wobbled as she tried to lift his foot from the mesh lining, then regained his balance and pushed by her. Bathing suit around his ankles, he shuffled over to the table and dropped his Popsicle onto it before she could slide a plate underneath.

Tim bent over and pulled Luke's bathing suit up again, hid behind him so she couldn't see his face. He'd planned on telling the truth. She deserved to know. But if he did, she wouldn't allow their Saturdays to continue. She'd have no choice, which left him with none, either. He couldn't let her give them up. "He was great."

She'd paused, and Tim could tell that she was deciding if she should believe him. But then the creases in her forehead had released, and she'd turned her attention to Luke, smoothed his hair and told him how proud she was of him as he stared out the window and wiped his sticky hands on his bathing suit.

* * *

Tim unscrews the thermos, hopes Luke has left behind a sip or two. He can feel his shirt sticking to his back, and he peels it from his skin, fans it to let the air dry him. He wonders, now, if he's made the right decision. The past few weeks have been peaceful, so much so that he'd begun to dismiss D-Day as a one-time incident. But maybe not. Today has gotten off to a rocky start, that's for sure. He can't take Josephine's suggestion, though. The long route isn't an option. What she forgets is that it involves passing Hornsby's Peak, the summit of a massive outcropping of rock that juts out over a deeper portion of the lake. It's a popular hangout for teenagers on the weekend, filled with boys diving in to impress their bikini-clad girlfriends.

"You *can not* take him there, Dad, for any reason," Gracie had said, prior to their first Saturday outing. She'd enunciated each word, as if he was a child. "He's fast, he's strong, and he could kill himself." Her condescension had irritated him, but he'd bit his tongue because he knew that she wasn't exaggerating. The boy had no concept of danger.

His attention turns to Luke, who's eating the apple's core, flinging away its stem. He has an insatiable appetite, and the sturdy frame to prove it. Tim digs through his backpack, and settles on a huge bag of carrots. *Better to stall him with more snacks than continue.* He passes them to Luke, who crunches into them as he stares at the surrounding hills, green and incongruous with the parched shrubs on the trail.

Now that Luke's occupied, Tim can feel his heartbeat return to normal. He musses Luke's hair, the once-blonde waves that refuse to be tamed, and is consumed by the torrent of emotions that overwhelm him every time he's with his grandson. Love, of course: fierce, primal, and boundless. But enmeshed within are frustration, anger, and above all, fear. Although he's only fifty, he already feels the constraints of time, knowing that he'll leave this world long before Luke.

He remembers Shayla's words when Gracie was tiny, maybe one or two. "Isn't it amazing, that all of our hopes and dreams are tied up in that tiny body of hers?" Those words had stuck with him all of these years, even though it was an offhand comment made on an uneventful day. He can't even remember where they were when she said it. But the memory is laced with innocence, with the unflagging optimism of youth. Back then there was no reason to expect that any of their dreams would be buried. After all, they'd confessed their sins; they'd accepted Christ as their almighty Lord and Savior. Tim had even received the calling to spread His Word, and they'd dedicated their lives to serving Him.

It wasn't until Shayla was gone that fear first snaked its way into Tim's thoughts. *Who will help me take care of Gracie?* he worried, and he prayed every day that God would forgive him his failings and provide him with the wisdom to guide Gracie towards a life devoted to Jesus.

It was the chaos of everyday life that allowed him to keep the fear in check for so many years. There wasn't time to be paralyzed by it. There were Bible study groups to be led, sermons to be written, church members to counsel; there were meals to be cooked, bills to be paid, dance recitals and soccer games to attend. There was never enough to time to think further ahead than the next Sunday.

Then he realized that the fear was simply biding its time, content to wait seventeen years to strike. One chilling word—autism—forced him to feel the weight of his mortality for the first time. *Lord, when I'm delivered to your glorious kingdom, I pray that it will be Your Will to send Gracie a husband who will cherish her and Luke, and that they, in turn, will serve you selflessly.* These words became an unconscious refrain that ran through his mind so often that he sometimes felt his lips moving before he realized what he was saying.

During difficult times he'd find himself bargaining, just as Jacob had when he ventured eastward to his Uncle Laban's home. Of course, God sets the terms of an agreement, not man; this he knew. Yet he couldn't control the immature, feral urgency that would leak into his prayers. *Please Lord, I beg of you, give me a sign that you'll take care of Luke after Gracie and I are gone, and I'll do whatever you ask of me in this life and the next. Anything. There is nothing You can ask for that I won't do, I promise you.*

And the Lord had responded and provided Keith, the gentle Christian man who loves his daughter and, remarkably, his grandson. His pleas had been heard, his lifetime of service had been rewarded. Or so he had believed until recently.

How to tell her? Over the countless weddings he's officiated, he's always thought of Gracie, of the enormous blessing it would be to preside over hers. But now that the time has come, he finds himself unready. How can he, a pastor without faith—a fraud—sanctify the union?

Already he's waited too long. Telling her now would cast a shadow over her wedding day, just two weeks from now. Unburdening himself at the expense of her happiness would be selfish. *She should be worrying about seating charts and florists, not about how to explain to her guests that her father isn't leading the ceremony.*

But keeping his secret would be selfish, too. What kind of father would be willing to invalidate his daughter's wedding in the eyes of God in order to spare himself rejection? What possible explanation could he give her for sullying her wedding, should she find out?

He thinks of Paul's admonishment to the Corinthians, words he's used when counseling many times over the years: "Do not be yoked together with unbelievers. For what do righteousness and wickedness have in common?"

His second wife, Jane. His friends. His flock. He'll lose them all if he admits that he no longer believes, because a biblical response is the only one a true evangelical is allowed. He'll lose his life's work, and then what will he do? How will he support himself?

It's exhausting, though. The lying. It isolates him, strips all that is genuine from his relationships. He's desperate to be done with it. But every time he musters up his courage, every time he convinces himself that he'll manage, he's stopped by the thought of the one loss that's intolerable: Gracie's. What if she were to shut him out of her life, out of Luke's? Just thinking about having to spend his days near them but without them is enough to make him feel bitterness at the back of his throat.

Tim is pulled out of his fevered thoughts by the sound of Luke digging through his backpack, looking for more snacks. He wipes away the remnants of carrot left on Luke's face with a gentle swipe of his thumb and lets him continue, knowing that his best course of action at this point is no action. Josephine and Amanda will catch up with them soon enough.

CHAPTER 2

Where the hell are they? thinks Josephine.

She's standing in the parking lot at the main entrance to Trent Lake State Park, scanning the license plates of the incoming cars. She's looking for the one that reads "WALLIS," and she smiles at the thought of her proper, unassuming mother driving a car that broadcasts the family name. *Poor Mom. Twenty-seven years later, and she's still paying the price for bringing* Anne of Green Gables *to the DMV.*

Josephine had been ten at the time, and had spent a sweltering Saturday afternoon waiting in line with her mother at a stale, non-air-conditioned DMV branch office. "I've read that book already," she said, pushing her mother's hand away, "and I hate it." She'd repaid her for this poor selection by whining for the next hour and a half. When they reached the front of the line, she noticed a sign on the desk advertising custom plates, and she'd begged her mother for them, sensing that guilt would give her the upper hand. "WALLIS" was her consolation prize for the wasted afternoon.

Once she was in her teens, she begged her parents again, although this time her goal was to get rid of the plates. "It's embarrassing. Everyone knows that I'm driving a *station wagon*." She didn't win the negotiation the second time around. Her father had refused, saying that it was a good safety measure for Amanda. What if she were to get separated from them in a public place? It made sense to have a license plate that she could remember. The station wagon was replaced by a sedan twelve years later, an SUV a decade after that, but "WALLIS" survived the switch both times, for Amanda's sake.

Josephine turns her back to the sun, shading her phone while she checks to see if Tim has texted her back. Nothing, although her initial one is marked delivered. Now that she thinks about it, she doesn't think she's ever received a text from him. *Maybe he's a caller only, like Mom. She's never sent a text in her life.*

"Why on earth would I text someone?" Ellen had asked, as Josephine demonstrated how to launch the Messages app, tap the Compose icon, enter a contact, and type in the dialogue box.

"Because you can leave someone a message and not have to talk to them."

"But I can do that by email. Besides, why wouldn't I want to talk to someone that I'm trying to get in touch with?"

"I don't know… maybe you don't have time for a whole conversation, or maybe you need to do something else at the same time." As soon as the words had left her mouth, she realized what a foreign argument this was to her mother. Ellen didn't multi-task. She didn't email while watching TV, didn't call while driving. As a rule her phone was left off, turned on only when an outgoing call was a necessity.

Tim surprises her, though, and her phone lights as he replies:

Can't go by Hornsby. Near the end of the short route now. We'll wait for you.

Josephine scolds herself as she realizes her mistake. *Hornsby's Peak. What was I thinking?* She wonders whether Gracie warned Tim in advance or whether he foresaw the danger on his own. If he did, she's impressed, as well as embarrassed that she suggested such a risky alternative. No one can keep up with Luke when he decides he wants to do something, especially something that he shouldn't be doing. And Tim isn't much of an athlete, despite his misleading runner's build.

She considers calling her mother again, then decides against it, knowing that she dislikes multiple check-ins. *Maybe I should just pick up Amanda at her apartment from now on.*

* * *

Josephine had driven to her parents' home, their usual meeting place due to its location between her house and Amanda and Gracie's apartment, to find it empty. She called her mother on her cell, and was surprised to hear her pick up.

"Sorry honey, we're running a little late."

"Really busy at Kroger today?

"No, we did all of Amanda's shopping and we dropped off her groceries at her apartment. But we had to turn around after we got halfway home because she remembered she left something behind."

"But, Mom, I made her that checklist. This is *exactly* the reason why I made it for her. You told me you put it on her fridge."

Ellen's voice turned icy. "It wasn't something on your *checklist*, Josephine. We went back for Luke's goggles. Amanda remembered that she saw them on his bureau this morning after he left with Gracie. So it's *Gracie* who forgot, not Amanda."

The Amanda voice. Josephine hated being spoken to in the tone that her mother saved for defending her sister. She had to admit, though, that her immediate response was to fault Amanda. She deserved her mother's clipped tone, which made it much harder to swallow. She took a deep breath, and counted to eight as she exhaled. "Okay. Fair enough. So where are you now?"

"We're just coming up to the light at North Gaynor."

Josephine glanced at the clock on the microwave. "There's no time for you to come home now. Take the left and head to the park instead. I'll meet you there."

"I'm sure Tim will understand if you're a little late. I'll just be a bit, and then you and Amanda can go together."

"Mom, Luke will *freak out* if we're too late. Don't you remember what happened last month? On the dock?"

"Oh, honey, all kids get fussy from time to time."

"*Fussy?* We're not talking about a spoiled toddler. That's like calling a peptic ulcer a tummy ache."

"What does that mean?"

"It means that it's not the same at all."

"No, Josephine, I mean 'peptic.' I assume it means stomach?"

"Yes, but that's not the point."

"*My* point is that you need to remember that not everybody knows these fancy medical terms that you throw around. You don't want to sound snooty. No one likes a know-it-all."

"Just turn left, okay, Mom?"

* * *

Josephine replays this conversation in her head as she sits on the top rail of the weathered fence surrounding the park entrance. *Fussy. Honest to God, Mom is the queen of denial. Does she really think that downplaying scary labels somehow fools people? Maybe calling Amanda "a little slow" isn't too far off the mark, but at a certain point people figure it out. And what's the benefit in hiding it, anyway? People cut you some slack if they know.*

A lanky teenager makes his way over to her, and she moves aside to let him pass. But instead of opening the gate, he stops in front of her, and waits for her to look at him.

"Hi. I'm Matt. I'm taking an opinion poll today and was hoping you could help me out." He offers her an easy, confident smile.

She supplies the quickest excuse, which happens to be the truth. "Sorry, I can't. I'm meeting my family here. They'll be here any minute."

"It won't take very long. How about we get started, and when your family shows up, we'll stop?"

A good comeback. I kind of like this cocky kid. "Okay. I guess."

"Great!" He looks down at his clipboard. "All right, first question: Who's the greatest person you know?"

She thinks for a moment, and pushes the lock of hair that has escaped her ponytail back behind her right ear. "That I know personally? Or know *of?*"

Matt nods his head as if she's given him an answer, and continues. "You know what? Let's just move on. Let's see… question two: Do you consider yourself a spiritual person?"

A slow smile spreads across her face. "Jesus."

"Uh, what?"

"That's the answer you were fishing for with your first question, right? Pardon the pun."

He flushes, caught, and his Adam's apple bobs up and down with repeated swallows. She can tell that he's trying to determine where she lands on the flow chart he's been told to memorize, and she feels a sudden empathy for the kid. *Come on, Matt. I hinted at Jesus' call for his disciples to become fishers of men. It's a safe bet that I'm a Christian. Go from there.*

"Well, *do* you have a personal relationship with our Lord and Savior?" he asks, recovering.

She's pleased with him despite herself. "Look, I know what you're doing, and I know you're doing it for the right reasons, but I'm not the right person to witness to," she says, using church lingo in place of the secular translation, *convert.* "There are lots of other people here. Good luck." She nods a curt goodbye, and walks a couple of steps further into the parking lot.

To her surprise, he follows her. "Why do you say that?"

"Because I don't believe… what you believe." She was planning on saying "in God," and is surprised to hear the amended version that comes out instead. *Why is it that I still find myself apologizing?*

"Can I ask what's happened in your life that's caused you to turn away from God?" His voice is soft, concerned.

"Listen, there was no major trauma. I know that you think you're saving me from hell, and I respect the fact that you're willing to put yourself out there for your beliefs, but I'm *really* not interested in having this discussion anymore." She walks a few more determined steps away from him, but they both know that she's trapped. Someone who's waiting for her family doesn't decide to go for a walk in the park by herself all of a sudden, and she doesn't get in her car and go home, either. *Damn it.*

Matt raises his hands to his chest, palms out, gesturing that he means no harm. "I don't want to bother you. Just one last question, I promise: When you die, do you think you'll go to heaven or hell?"

She knows that he's lying, that it's not the last question, and it pisses her off. If she answers "heaven," he'll point out the impossibility of her answer, since she's already admitted that she hasn't been saved. If she answers "hell," then he'll try to convert her. Either way the conversation will continue. She knows his next steps because she learned the same script, or at least a variation of it, when she was his age. The pretext of an opinion poll is new, though. That's what threw her off at first.

Hasn't she asked him, two times now, to leave her alone? She's been polite, even complimentary, and it's a pretty safe bet that he's been treated far worse today. She hasn't ignored him, or laughed, or yelled—and this is what she gets for being considerate. Enough.

She feigns remorse, looks down at the ground and shuffles her feet. "Hell, I guess. I know that I've sinned."

Matt's face brightens. "Then I have good news! God loves you, and He made the ultimate sacrifice by sending His Son to die on the cross so that all of our sins may be forgiven. All you need to do is confess your sins and let Jesus into your heart. Would you like to pray together?"

She sidesteps the question. "I don't think God made the ultimate sacrifice."

"What?" Enthusiasm vanishes from his voice.

She relishes watching him squirm. "You heard me. I think God cut himself a pretty sweet deal. How about I ask *you* a couple of questions. It's Matt, right?"

"Yeah." He glances to either side of him nervously.

"Don't worry, it's an easy one. Ready? What's the Holy Trinity, Matt?"

"The Father, the Son, and the Holy Spirit." His answer is automatic, but he still doesn't look her in the eye, looks everywhere but, like a student caught unprepared for a pop quiz.

"Exactly. And they're all different forms of the one God, correct? Just like water—it can be seen as a solid, a liquid, or a gas, but it's all the same thing, right?"

He nods.

"Jesus is the Son of God, but he's not actually a son, is he? At least not in the way humans have sons. He's not a completely separate being. Jesus is a part of the one God."

Matt is silent, has settled on looking at the park regulations sign to her left.

"Let me ask you one last question. Is God omniscient?" Then, thinking of her mother's earlier reprimand, she rephrases: "Is God all-knowing?"

"Yes."

"So then it would follow that when God the Father sent Jesus to die on the cross, he already knew that Jesus would rise from the grave and ascend to heaven on the third day."

"Well, I guess, but—"

"So God gives up part of himself, knowing it'll only be a few days, and in exchange he can save billions of people from hell for generations. That doesn't seem like such a big sacrifice to me."

"But... but Jesus suffered for our sins."

"He suffered terribly. But no more so than the thousands of others who died the same horrific death before him. And not one of them was resurrected. Not one of them had the comfort of knowing that their death had a purpose." She pauses, waits for him to meet her eyes. "You know that Christ wasn't the first person to be crucified, don't you? That it wasn't an uncommon way for slaves and traitors to be killed for centuries before him?"

He doesn't answer or counter. He looks deflated, and she feels a twinge of guilt for meddling with his placid, unchallenged beliefs. She considers apologizing to this well-meaning kid, but doesn't need to entertain the unpleasant thought for long. She's saved by the crunching of tires on the gravel behind her, and she spins around to see the familiar plate as her mother's SUV slows to a stop. *Finally. WALLIS.*

CHAPTER 3

"Manda! Manda! Manda!" chants Luke, his face bright with anticipation. He hovers next to Amanda, his gaze moving back and forth between her and the lake. Unable to resist the beckoning water, he runs full speed into it, squealing with pleasure and splashing those unfortunate enough to be caught in his wake. Just as the waters calm, and the swimmers surrounding him wipe the spray from their faces, he turns around and splashes his way back to Amanda, drenching them a second time and leaving Tim to contend with their dirty looks and rude comments.

"Manda's wearing blue bathing suit!" he says, as she pulls her t-shirt over her head. "Manda's wearing blue bathing suit, that's right, Grandpa, that's right!" He presses his cheek against her stomach, grazing her breasts as he leans down, and she flinches in surprise. He tickles her waist, and then her hip, while her face is still covered with her shirt.

"Luke, no hands," Tim says, but Amanda laughs and tickles Luke on his neck. He tilts his head to the side and raises his shoulder, trapping her hand, and giggles until he's out of breath.

Tim shakes his head and turns towards Josephine. "The two of them."

She smiles. "Lycra is hard to pass up."

He's relieved that she understands that Luke's inappropriate touching isn't sexual. The lycra in Amanda's bathing suit, the velour in Mommy's sweatshirt, the silk in Jane's blouse—the common denominator seems to be texture. But some pieces of clothing captivate Luke for reasons Tim doesn't understand. Like his black jacket. It's not fleece, it's not plush on the inside. It's just regular cotton. But every time he wears it Luke runs to him and tickles him on his neck and shoulders. He's taken to wearing it as soon as the temperature dips below seventy-five, even though he knows he'll be sweaty and uncomfortable, just to see Luke smile.

They set their towels down on the small strip of beach surrounding the lake. Luke sprints towards the water again the moment he's freed from his shirt, this time with Amanda following him, her steps cautious and lumbering.

"So where's Gracie today?" asks Josephine.

"First Baptist."

"You know that only pastors having a working knowledge of where every church within a ten-mile radius is located, right?"

He laughs. "Sorry. It's in Cutler. She'll be home on the earlier side."

"So she's teaching four more special needs workshops this summer?"

"Yep. Not sure about the fall yet. Things always get hectic for her at the beginning of the school year." He shades his eyes from the sun, but keeps them trained on Luke, who has waded in farther than Amanda.

Luke is wet from the chest down, while Amanda has allowed the water no higher than her knees. He's still for a moment, then turns back and runs towards her as fast as the water will allow him. She staggers back a few steps as he barrels into her, then grabs onto him as she tries to right herself. "Manda!" he squeals. "Manda's going water with Luke!"

Tim puts his face in his hands. "Part hug, part tackle."

"And part bath. That's exactly how Wes helps me get used to the water," Josephine says, her fingers air-quoting the word *helps*.

"What about Wes? Do you think you could talk him into skipping soccer one week and joining us?"

She shakes her head. "It'd be nice, but I can't see it happening. He says that he needs it to stretch out after a week of sitting in front of a computer. He's super religious about it." She flushes. "Sorry. Poor choice of words."

"Not when you're talking about sports, it's not. Excellent choice of words, actually." He can feel the corners of his lips pulling up into a smile, and bites his bottom lip to keep a straight face. "Not in the case of soccer, of course, but certainly in the case of *real* sports."

She rolls her eyes. "Hilarious. I'll be sure to tell him that one."

Wes. Try as he might, he can't figure Wes out. Not once has he joined them. Doesn't it bother Josephine that he has no interest in spending time with her sister? Sometimes Tim wonders if Wes is ashamed of Amanda. Or Luke, maybe? After all, Wes joined the soccer league *after* their Saturday outings had begun. It's not as if he already had a commitment that he had to honor. And even before soccer began, he'd had a different excuse every week as to why he couldn't make it.

Something about Wes just rubs Tim the wrong way. Like the time he introduced Wes to the wife of a board member several Easters ago. He'd fumbled his way through the introduction. "Marie, this is Wes. Do you know Josephine Wallis? Ellen and Chuck's daughter? No? I thought you did. Well, anyway, Wes and Josephine are… um… " Wes jumped in and put his spluttering to a stop. "Together. Pleasure to meet you, Marie.

I've heard so much about you." Wes clasped her chunky hand, enclosed it within his.

Tim doubted this was true. He'd never mentioned Marie to Wes, and she'd just said that she didn't know Josephine. It chafed at him, that Wes thought nothing of lying on the holiest day of the year. But sin or not, Marie had fallen for his act, reddening and mentioning him in passing the following Sunday.

But maybe Marie saw through him, and just hadn't cared, he thinks. She's an older lady, and, truth be told, an unattractive one. False or not, flattery works. *But with Josephine? The straightest shooter I know?*

He glances at Josephine, who is wiping smudges off of her sunglasses with her shirt. *Together.* Wes and Josephine have lived with each other for six or seven years now, haven't they? There's no reason to be suspicious of Wes. The guy likes soccer, it works out schedule-wise, end of story.

Luke lets out a short, piercing screech. He's struggling to sit upright while Amanda tries to position him in a back float. Tim feels a spike of panic, knows that the clock is ticking. Luke will only tolerate a few more moments of this tug-of-war. "He's getting frustrated," he says to Josephine, his voice shaky. "What else does she need to practice?"

She nods, jumps up and takes a few quick steps closer to the shore-line. She cups her mouth to tunnel the sound. "Amanda. Pick something else."

Amanda looks up, still trying to get Luke to lay flat. "But all that's l-left is back float. He needs to l-learn the back float or he can't move up to Guppy."

"I know, but Luke doesn't like it. You need to pick something else."

"But—"

"Blowing bubbles. Try that."

"Uh-uh," Tim says, shaking his head no. He mimics swallowing, reminds her that Luke always drinks the water.

"I mean kicking." She simulates kicking with her hands, alternately moving them up and down.

"But he knows how to kick," Amanda argues.

"Yeah, but he needs to learn how to practice breathing at the same time. He still holds his breath while he kicks. Rotary breathing, isn't that what it's called?"

Amanda relaxes her hold on Luke as she considers Josephine's suggestion. He disentangles himself, dog paddles towards the shore, and stands in the shallows. He coughs several times, then leans over and angrily slaps the water with his hands, spraying it into the air. Then, an abrupt stop.

Tim holds his breath. *Here it comes.* But Luke surprises him by sinking back down into the water, propping himself up on his arms and resting his stomach on the lake's bed.

Josephine follows Tim's gaze to Luke, and he nods in response to her questioning look. "He's okay now. Close one." She gives him a reassuring pat on his shoulder, and then jogs over to Amanda.

He watches her as she pantomimes breathing on either side with a kickboard. *They look so alike.* The same hazel eyes, the same thin lips, the same thick black hair. Amanda's has always been cut to her chin, though, with chunky bangs that graze her eyelashes. Ever since Gracie's "friend down the street" was a toddler, she's had the same haircut. The only stark difference between the two sisters is Josephine's wiry frame and Amanda's doughy one.

He smiles and thinks of how he and Shayla used to refer to Amanda as "Dawn" when it was just the two of them. Gracie and Amanda must have been around three when the nickname was coined.

Gracie had refused lunch one day after coming home from preschool, demanding that she see her "fwend dawn dastwee" first, which Shayla had misinterpreted as "friend, Dawn Dustry." Shayla had called him an hour later, near tears, as Gracie howled in the background.

"I can't find anyone on the class list with a name even close to Dawn Dustry. I have no idea who she's talking about. She's trying to unlock the front door now, but we can't go roaming all over Loring Point looking for this mystery kid."

"Just take a walk with her. Let her blow off some steam."

"Where? We have to go to the dentist. We only have time to go down the street." There had been a brief pause on both ends of the line, and then they both burst into laughter.

Josephine walks back towards Tim, rolling her eyes now that her back is to Amanda. "Sorry. She just wants to do it right, you know?" She brushes sand off of her towel before sitting down again. "There's no way the Y can hire her as a swim instructor," she says, lowering her voice. "It'd be a huge liability."

"Has she asked to take the CPR course again?"

"Not yet. Honestly, I don't know what my mom was thinking, taking her to that course. There's no way Amanda could pass the test. Mom made all these phone calls, arranged for her to take an oral exam instead of a written one, and then Amanda didn't even make it past the first class. Sometimes I think Amanda's a better judge of what she can handle than my mom."

Tim shades his eyes from the glare, keeps Amanda and Luke in sight. They're back at work, Amanda holding the kickboard out for Luke, who grabs it and places it under his stomach rather than holding it straight out in front of him. "How did she get it in her head that she wants to be a swim instructor? Gracie never told me that part. She just told me that Amanda's been feeling down."

"I guess she's gotten bored at her job over the past couple of years. Running the concession stand was perfect at first. She was really proud of herself, and after work she could stay at the Y and go swimming. She loves kids and she loves swimming, so it makes sense that she'd be drawn to it, but my mom's delusional if she thinks Amanda's going to be able to get CPR, First Aid and AED-certified. Any employer is going to be looking for someone who's able to make crucial decisions quickly. Does that sound like Amanda to you?"

"No," he says, unable to think of a counter argument. "I think this set-up is a good consolation prize, though. A way to build up her confidence. Although Luke's not the easiest student."

"A tough test case, I'll give you that. But a charming one."

He smiles. "It's good for Amanda, good for Luke, and definitely good for Gracie. Babysitting, free swimming lessons, and a doctor as a lifeguard. Hard to beat."

"True."

"Doesn't Amanda have someone helping her? I think you called him a job coach?"

"Yeah, but he doesn't see her that often anymore because she knows how to work the concession stand so well now. Don't get me wrong—he's great. When Amanda first started, she was having problems making the right change, so he convinced the management to change all the menu items to be on the dollar or fifty-cent mark. My mom's going to see if he can arrange some way for her to bring snacks to the after-school kids. Maybe get her involved in story time or arts and crafts."

"Is there an opening in child care? She could switch to that."

She shakes her head. "Same thing. She'd need CPR and First Aid certification. The room has to be staffed appropriately, but I think there's no harm in her being an extra set of hands for an hour a day. So we'll see what happens."

"She's determined."

"Stubbornness runs in the family." She points to Amanda, who's trying to coax Luke out of his belly-down position at the shoreline. "Determination in action right over there."

Tim watches as Amanda's tickles win Luke over, and he follows her back to deeper water. "He's going to miss her. Gracie's trying to prep him, but it's not going to be easy."

"I know."

"How about Amanda? Do you think she's ready for the move?"

She nods. "She's more than ready. She's *really* excited." Her eyes widen, and she covers her mouth with her hand. "That didn't come out right. Living with Gracie and Luke has been great for her. But she's twenty-six. She wants her independence. It's my mom who's petrified of her living on her own."

"Well, it's a big step for both of them. Your dad, too, don't forget."

"I know. I didn't mean to leave him out. He's the voice of reason. It's a good thing he was able to talk her into it, because I wasn't getting anywhere. But I get it. She's nervous, we all are."

No, you don't get it, Josephine, he thinks, even as he nods in agreement. *You don't have a child with special needs. You don't even know what it is to be a mother yet.*

A mosquito lands on his arm, and he flicks it away. "Gracie tells me that Amanda's moving to a smaller apartment in the same building."

"Yeah. One just opened up last month. Same floor plan, just one less bedroom. So she's already familiar with the layout, and she knows how to get to and from work, which is key. It took a long time for her to learn how to use the buses."

Tim takes his eyes off of Luke for a moment and looks at Josephine. Strange, that he thinks of her as a peer now. When they first met she was still in middle school, and he was already a married man with a young daughter. An authority figure. Yet he's tempted to confide in her now, his hope buoyed by her lapsed connection to their church. Ellen and Chuck attend about once a month. But it's been years since Josephine has come.

What is that saying—a secret is something you tell one other person? And if he tells her, then that other person will be Wes, of course. Then

Wes tells another, and so on, until he's discovered as a coward as well as a heathen. *Once I say it out loud, I can never take it back.*

He sees her glance at him out of the corner of her eye and busy herself by brushing sand off her towel again. She straightens it next, unearthing the sunscreen that had been swallowed in a fold, and applies more to her cheeks. She pulls the elastic out of her hair and then ties it up again into another variation of a messy ponytail. Out of tasks, she clears her throat, and breaks the silence. "Something on your mind?"

"No, not at all," he says, ashamed of how good he's become at lying. He no longer worries if his face or voice will expose him. "Just got side-tracked thinking about tomorrow's sermon." He pulls his buried toes out of the sand, and refocuses his attention on the lake.

Amanda is passing a floating pail to a little girl, but where is Luke? Hasn't she noticed that he's missing? Tim's eyes dart to the shoreline, but Luke isn't resting there. He can feel the panic shoot up within him, and he runs towards the water's edge. "Luke!" he screams, as he runs into the water, t-shirt still on. "Luke!" He looks up at the lifeguard, who he sees in profile, and waves both hands. *Why doesn't she notice me?* He runs a few steps towards her, but then he's blocked by something pushing against his shin under the water. Luke bursts from underneath, holding up a red ring.

Tim clutches his chest, can feel his heartbeat pounding in his ears and pulsing in his neck. He spins around and bumps into Josephine, who's a step behind him.

"That was scary," she says. "Are you okay?"

He nods and stumbles back towards his towel. "I've never seen him put his whole body under the water before."

Luke turns to face Amanda, his back to Tim and Josephine. His bathing suit has fallen too low, exposing most of him from behind. The children surrounding him begin to point and whisper, but he either doesn't notice or doesn't care. He's singing some sort of gibberish—"kow-da-pay," it sounds like—on a loud and repetitive loop, drawing further stares and snickering.

"I'll take care of it," says Josephine, and she bounds over to the edge of the lake once more.

Tim wonders, as he does every time he sees Luke, what Shayla would think of her enigma of a grandson. She'd be able to reach him better. He's sure of that. The question he can't answer, that can never be answered, is whether there would even be a Luke had Shayla lived to see Gracie's teenage years.

It's the wedding, he supposes, that's responsible for this constant dredging up of the past. He does the math in his head. More than three times as long, it comes out to, but that can't be right, can it? It's hard to believe that his marriage to Jane has been that many years.

It's not fair to compare them. He and Shayla never had to deal with any of the troubles that worm their way into a long-term marriage. And time, which colors the past, has made his memories rosy. *It's human nature to want what you can't have. It's normal, even after all these years.*

But deep within him, underneath the rationalizations, lies the truth. That despite the passage of time, despite the hundreds of people he's met before her and after her, despite the life he's created with Jane, only one opinion has ever mattered to him: Shayla's.

* * *

Tim first noticed her in Old Testament Survey, a mandatory course for Gladen University freshmen. He was one of the first to arrive every Tuesday and Thursday, since he came straight from another class three doors down the hall. His roommate, Andrew, entered class from the doors at the top of the stairs, so Tim would take a seat in the back row and save a seat for him. No point in saving one up front. That would guarantee him ten minutes of staring at an empty podium. Much more interesting to people-watch as the class filled.

Most days, she arrived just before the start of class, trailing a couple of steps behind two other girls, both with long ponytails and an excess of cheeriness. He could hear the forced laughter of the Phony Girls echo in the corridor long before they made their way into the classroom, and he wondered if they thought they were fooling anyone with their act. *No one's that happy every day. Especially at OTS at nine-thirty in the morning.*

This third girl, though—the one with the pale blonde hair often held back by a headband—was harder to figure out. Her smile was fixed, just like the Phony Girls, but it wasn't accompanied by cartoonish facial expressions or exaggerated gestures. Was she embarrassed by her friends, distancing herself on purpose? Or was she shy, uncomfortable with being the third wheel?

She had a refined look about her, with wide-set, downward-sloping eyes, and a long nose that seemed to dip too low when it was paired with her frozen smile, as if it might graze her upper lip. But when her face was at rest, its length lent her a certain elegance.

It was her body, though, that drew his attention first. As required by university dress code, she wore skirts or dresses with hemlines no higher than the top of the knee, and blouses with no low necklines or thin straps. But he could still see the slender lines of her body through the light cotton sundresses she wore, could see where the fabric strained over her breasts and hips. Once, when she turned around to pass handouts to the student behind her, he was able to see the strap of her bra as the shoulder of her dress shifted too far to the left. It was a muted pink, with delicate scalloped edges. He'd been surprised, hadn't known that bras came in any colors other than white or black.

Forcing female students to cover up didn't stop him, or any of his friends, from looking. It made them look harder. How was it, he wondered, that a Bible college could have such a poor understanding of forbidden fruit? It seemed unfair that he should be held to a higher standard than Adam, who'd only had to resist an apple, and was lucky enough to be commanded to be fruitful and multiply.

He found himself looking forward to the fall. *Life will get easier once the weather changes. Once girls start wearing jackets and sweaters.* But when would that happen in South Reyling, Texas? He was too far south now to expect the cool autumn mornings of Oregon.

He wondered what her name was, and tried out every one that he knew. She didn't look like a Jennifer, or an Amy, or a Beth. Maybe Mary? Christine? Kim? He couldn't find a match that satisfied him.

He was hoping that he'd bump into her on campus. Every week during Sunday worship services he'd scan the crowd for her, but wasn't able to find her. Maybe she was teaching Sunday school at a local church? He'd heard that students could be excused from campus services by volunteering. Word was that the sermons were so repetitive that by the third year, most students had been driven off-campus out of boredom.

Her dorm didn't seem to be near his, either. Only one road led to Abbott Hall, the largest freshmen dorm, as well as its sister dorm, Hunter Hall, yet he'd never seen her on it. And there was no way to strike up conversation after class. She was always gone by the time he made it down the steps, trapped behind a stream of slow-moving students.

It came as a complete surprise to him when their paths crossed a month and a half later. It was late afternoon, the day before their midterm exam, and he'd made the unpopular choice to study on the library's third floor. Since it wasn't air-conditioned, students avoided the stifling upper level. The trade-off for sweltering was silence, though, and it was well known that the top floor was the place to go if serious studying needed to be done.

He'd been studying for a couple of hours, and was considering heading back to his dorm, when he heard her voice.

"Is this seat taken?"

He looked up, startled to see her up close. Something about her looked different, but he couldn't pinpoint what it was. "What? No, no one's... you can sit here." He stood up and began collecting the piles of paper that he'd spread out over the entire table.

"Thanks. Sorry to squish you in like this. The library's packed tonight."

"It's not a problem, really."

"Wait," she said, and he saw that she was noticing their matching textbooks. "Are you in Old Testament Survey?"

"Yeah."

"No way! I am, too."

"I know." He could feel heat creeping from the back of his neck up to his ears. *I sound like a stalker.* "I, uh... I sit in the back, and I'm always early, so I see you run in with your friends right before class starts."

"Oh." She paused, and he wasn't sure if she was surprised that he recognized her or embarrassed that she didn't recognize him. "They're not exactly my *friends*. They're just people I know from my dorm." She shifted her books to her other hip. "Anyway, I'm Shayla."

"Sheila?" It was hard to tell if her slight southern accent was distorting her name.

"No, *Shayla*. With an *a-y.*"

So he'd been right. None of the names he knew *had* suited her. But Shayla did; it was soft, subtly distinctive. He felt his mind go blank, and all of the polished conversation starters he'd imagined vanished. He put a hand to his chest. "Tim."

She nodded, then sat down, the powdery scent of her perfume wafting towards him as she pulled her chair in toward the table. "Ready for the test tomorrow?" she asked.

"I think so. You?"

"I don't know. I'm okay with essays. My guess is there'll be at least one that'll ask you to take themes from Scripture and apply them to your life.

So that part's no problem. What gets me is the memorization. I mean, the order of the thirty-nine books? There's no way I'll remember that."

"See, I'm the opposite. Essays are the hardest part for me. I never finish in time. But memorization is no big deal. I can help you, if you want."

"Really? Because I don't want to bother you if you have another class to study for."

"I have time now," he said, thinking of how unprepared he was for his Fundamental Theological Issues exam. But this was his opportunity.

She eyed his hefty pile of books. "Are you sure?"

"I'm all set for that class."

"Positive?" She glanced back and forth between him and the books in question.

"Yeah." He pushed them aside. He could feel heat again, this time on his cheeks. *I must be bright red by now.*

She studied his face for a moment, then leaned back in her chair. "So tell me… what's the secret?"

"No secret. I just pick a song that sticks out in my mind, and I replace the lyrics with the answers. The trick is to pick a song that you can't get out of your head. You know that song that came out a couple of years ago—'You Light Up My Life?'"

She smirked. "You listen to Debby Boone?"

"No, but my mom does. All the time. She played that tape pretty much nonstop for a year. I heard that song *every day.*" He peeked at the students at the table across from them, shaded his mouth with his right hand, and lowered his voice to a whisper. "Ready?"

"Uh-huh."

"Okay. You've got to start from the chorus. I forgot to tell you that." He cleared his throat, and then began to sing. "*Gen*-e-sis… Ex-o-dus Le-*vit*-icus… Numbers Deu-te-*ron*-omy… Joshua Judges Ruth… two Samuel, two Kings, two *Chron*-icles."

She shifted in her seat and turned her back to the students at the other table. "People are looking at us."

He'd blown it. *What was I thinking? Debby Boone? I'm such an idiot.*

"You do realize that you're singing on the *third floor*, right?" She looked horrified. "People come here to study, not to fool around."

He opened his mouth, although he had no idea what to say. *Sorry? Please don't tell anyone, or I'll never live it down?*

She stared at him, a pinched expression on her face. Then her features began to shuffle, until her wide set eyes no longer squinted and the corners of her mouth crept upward. "Got you!"

He breathed a sigh of relief. "Cruel. Very cruel."

"You should've defended yourself! You *were* studying, just in an unusual way."

He grinned. "Right! With Christian music, too. I should get extra credit for developing a new third floor standard."

"I think that song might've started out as a regular love song. Because the movie wasn't about God. I think that was just Debby Boone's interpretation."

"Didn't you just make fun of me for picking that song? Because you seem to know an awful lot about it."

She ignored him, ran her fingers down the list of books instead, humming. "This could work. The 'Joshua Judges Ruth' part fits in really well."

"Ha! You know exactly how the song goes!"

"Of course I do. Everyone does. But that's only fourteen books," she said, counting down the list. "What about the other twenty-five?"

"I start over with the chorus again, since that's the catchy part. *Ez-*ra… Nehemiah *Es-*ther, Job, Psalms, *Pro-*verbs… Ecclesiastes, Song of Solomon… Isaiah, Jere-*mi-*ah… Lam, E-*ze-ke-*ial, Daniel."

" 'Lam?' "

"I had to cut Lamentations down to fit. The second set didn't flow as well."

"Okay, let me try the last one." She looked over her shoulder to see if the other students were still watching them.

"You're stalling. Come on, you can't have a worse voice than me."

She took a deep breath, and then began to sing in a voice that was just above a whisper. "Ho-*se*-a... Joel, Amos, Oba-*di*-ah... Jonah, Mica, Nahum... Habakkuk, Zephan-*i*-ah... Haggai, Zechar-*i*-ah, Malachi."

He pretended to clap. "You've got it."

"It's really hard to sing that softly," she said, laughing. "I admit it. You're a better library singer than I am." She paused, frowned. "But what happens if I can't remember the start of each of the three sections?

"God Established Heaven."

"What?"

"The start of each chorus is G, E, H—Genesis, Ezra, Hosea—so I just remember God Established Heaven. Knowing the first book is enough to get me through the whole chorus."

"I hope it is for me, too. My dad's a pastor—he's going to expect me to get an A in an intro course." She glanced downward at the list again, tucked her hair behind both ears.

That's what was different! She wasn't wearing her headband. He'd never seen her with her hair all the way down. It was then that he noticed that her left ear was smaller than her right. *She could cover it up with her hair. Most girls would.* But Shayla wore headbands. Shayla tucked her hair behind her ears.

She looked up. "But however it goes... thanks." She looked up at the clock behind him. "Any chance you have time for a couple more?"

"Yeah," he said, without glancing at his watch. "I have time."

The next morning, as he waited for class to start, it occurred to him that Shayla now knew where to find him. *What if she looks over here when she comes in? Should I wave? Nod? Pretend I'm studying?* As he weighed his options, the Phony Girls entered class with their typical theatrics. But where was Shayla? Class was going to start any minute.

He felt a tap on his shoulder and turned around. "Is this seat taken?" Shayla asked with a smile, as she looked at the empty one to his right.

"I think I can make space."

The professor entered the classroom, and began giving instructions for the exam.

"God Established Heaven," Tim whispered.

The tests were distributed, and fifteen minutes later, he could hear her humming, just above a whisper.

CHAPTER 4

It's Sunday morning, and Josephine is up far too early, jarred awake by a sharp pain in her right breast as she turns in her sleep from her back to her side. She's used to sleeping on her stomach, but for the past couple of months she's only been able to get comfortable on her back. Her breasts are too swollen to bear any body weight.

She's eleven weeks along, but has yet to tell Wes. It seems odd that this monumental shift in her body has gone unnoticed by him, but to be fair, she hasn't had any morning sickness. She doubts he even knows of any of the other signs of early pregnancy. *Do I honestly expect him to be counting the number of times I pee? Charting increases in frequency of mood swings or fatigue?*

Still, she can't help but be disappointed by his lack of intuition. Isn't he curious as to why she takes her bra off and changes into sweats the moment she gets home from work? Why she flinches when he hugs her? Why there's no monthly filling of the bathroom wastebasket?

She turns her head towards him, touched by how boyish he looks in his sleep, jaw lax, his sandy hair falling over his brow instead of moussed back as it is during the day. His breathing is rhythmic, shallow inhalations followed by sour exhalations.

Maybe he'll be happy. He's always said that he wants kids. She considers this possibility, allows herself to think past the pregnancy and daydream about the child that she's wanted for close to a year. Or ten, depending on how you count it. She indulges herself with the thought of Wes pulling her close, kissing her, and wiping tears of joy from his eyes. Of him rubbing her belly as the months pass, setting up the crib, running to the grocery store to buy pickles and ice cream. But this fantasy collapses the instant she admits to herself that she's ignored the critical word that he includes every time they talk about children: *someday.*

Wes flips over and slings his arm around her waist. He nestles his face close to hers, trapping her hair between the pillow and his cheek and pulling it taut. She nudges him until he shifts onto his back and releases it. He mumbles something she can't make out, then rolls back towards her, filling the space between them again.

She rests her arm on his, smiles as she watches the specks of dust swirl and glitter in the sunlight that has burst through the slim column of space between the shade and the windowsill. She loves that she's the only one who knows this side of him, the affectionate side so different from the composed face that he projects to world. It makes him hers.

There's no need for him to know how *it happened.* Birth control isn't one hundred percent effective, she'll point out to him. Far less effective when you don't take the pills, of course, but it's better not to disclose that information right away. She won't be able to see his true reaction to impending fatherhood if the news is tainted by her deception. The two issues should be examined independently, methodically. Conflating them will just complicate the situation further.

Almost half of the pregnancies in the U.S. are unintended, she'll add. She first learned this statistic from Mommy By Mistake, an anonymous blogger, but a CDC study had backed it up. Mommy By Mistake's husband had told her flat out that he didn't want kids. He had three grown ones from his first wife, and no interest in starting over. But when she told him she was pregnant, he dropped to his knees, overcome with emotion. It was fear, he said, that had kept him from making the leap. He'd just needed a little push. The baby was a blessing, not a mistake.

Josephine scrolled down through the comments from the initial posting, afraid of what she might find yet compelled to look. The first was from a woman calling herself Mommy Maybe By Mistake, whose boyfriend had responded to the news by calling her a "slutty whore who'll fuck anyone who buys her a beer." Next, a woman who'd been raped by her boss; a woman who'd gotten pregnant while having an affair, leaving her unsure of who the father was; a woman whose boyfriend had told her pulling out would work; a woman who was a victim of incest. A myriad of variations of the same problem.

It was uncomfortable, knowing that she could be lumped into this same group of women. She'd assumed her life would unfold in the traditional order of love, marriage, children. But Wes had said that a piece of paper didn't prove their love for each other. Affording a wedding would be a stress on her parents and them, and what was the point? Why should they throw a party for a bunch of relatives they barely knew when they could save up for a down payment instead? It was practical argument, and she'd agreed. She didn't want the white dress and the gift registry. But as time went by, she found that she did want that piece of paper.

She knows the real reason why he won't make a trip to the courthouse. It's not philosophical, as he claims. It's fear, a result of his parents' bitter divorce when he was three. She's picked up scraps of information over the years, knows that his father remarried soon afterwards, started a new family, and had little interest in his old one. That Wes has only seen his father a handful of times since then. But that's all she has. Tidbits tossed to her from time to time to keep her questions at bay.

She shifts position so she can look at him. She imagines him as that boy—erases his stubble, rounds his jaw, smoothes the imperfections in his skin. That piece of paper hadn't protected his parents, or him. *So why is it that I still want it?*

It occurs to her that Gracie's wedding may be the closest her parents will ever come to celebrating a daughter's wedding, and she feels a sudden pang of guilt for depriving them of that joy. But then again, Gracie—the pastor's daughter, of all people—has made more of a mess of traditional order than she has.

It's sweet of Gracie to ask her to be a bridesmaid, although she feels far too old to be one. She's been a bridesmaid before, once for a childhood friend and twice for college roommates, but never before for... well, how to define Gracie? Family friend? Amanda's roommate? Pseudo little sister?

She adjusts her pajama top, which has twisted and is now bunched under her. She closes her eyes, and has begun to drift off to sleep when she's jolted awake once again, this time by thought. The dress!

Her first fitting was over two months ago, before she knew she was pregnant. What if it doesn't fit anymore? There's no time to order a new one, and the old one might not be alterable. She already had it taken in across the bust and waist.

She inches her way out of bed, careful not to wake Wes, even though she doesn't need to be. It's next to impossible to wake him. She opens the lower drawer of her night table, and searches through its contents for her strapless bra. She pulls it out, then tiptoes down the hallway and into the guest bedroom, closing the door behind her. She opens the closet, and yanks the plastic cover off of the dress.

I can't believe I have to wear this. It's a daffodil-colored chiffon, with a sweetheart neckline and spaghetti straps. She'd known at the bridal shop what a poor match it would be for her even before she tried it on. The color, well suited for Gracie's golden undertones, sallows her. The lower neckline and A-line skirt, perfect for Gracie's voluptuous figure, hangs on her narrow hips and flat chest, making her appear girlish. *At least Gracie didn't try to feed me the it's-so-classic-you'll-wear-it-again-and-again line.*

She strips down, puts on her bra, and then steps into the dress. She pulls it up backwards so that she can zip it, turns it around into its correct position, and then slips each arm under a strap to pull the bodice up. She can feel the fabric straining and knows the answer before she even looks at herself in the mirror.

She turns to face it, and gasps. The lower halves of her breasts are mashed against her, and the upper halves overwhelm the fabric, spilling over the top. What was once a demure neckline is now far too revealing for a wedding, Gracie's in particular.

She's about to change back into her pajamas when Wes knocks on the door. "What are you doing in there?" he asks, yawning.

She panics. *As soon as I open the door, he'll know. The only explanations are pregnancy or a boob job.* She struggles with the zipper, tugs at it even though she knows she might tear the strained fabric.

"Jo, seriously. What's going on?"

"Nothing. Just trying on the bridesmaid's dress." She gives up on the zipper, tries to extricate her arms first in the hopes of giving the zipper some slack.

"Let me see. I want to get a look at this hideous dress that you've been complaining about."

"I never said hideous."

"Yes, you did. You said—"

"I said it looked hideous *on me*. It'd look great on Gracie."

"But that doesn't make any sense. She's the only woman in the wedding party who *won't* be wearing it. Why would she pick it?"

Damn it, I can't get my arm out, either. "I don't know, maybe it'll be good on Keith's sister or his brother's wife. Amanda looks pretty in it. She's excited for Jack to see her all dressed up. It's really sweet."

She can hear him jiggle the doorknob. "You locked it?"

"I don't want you to see me in it."

"You're going to have to wear it in front of a lot more people than just me in a couple of weeks."

"I'll have it fixed by then."

"Jo, I see you naked all the time. What's the big deal?"

One arm freed! "You're not supposed to see me until the wedding."

"Nice try. That's for brides, not bridesmaids. Open up."

"What's wrong with me asking for a little privacy?"

"What's wrong with it is that you never have before. So something's up. I'm getting the pin."

Damn it. She hears his footsteps down the hall, the squeak of his armoire door. She shoves her arm back in the dress just as he pops the lock open.

"Wow," he says. "*Gracie* picked this dress out?"

"Yeah, but she didn't mean for it to look this way. I can't go to the wedding dressed like this!"

"Why not? You look hot."

"Are you kidding? What am I going to do?"

"Guess you're going to have to go back to the store. Did they order the wrong size?"

She hesitates. "No, it's the right size."

"Not everywhere, it's not. Are you wearing one of those push-up bras?"

She touches the spaghetti straps. "I can't wear one under these. I have to wear a strapless."

"Oh. So you have on some kind of combo?"

"A strapless push-up? How are my boobs supposed to stay pushed up if there are no straps to pull them?"

"Don't they make ones that look like bathing suits?"

"What?"

"The kind that covers your stomach and back. You know, the old-fashioned kind. Like in westerns."

"A bustier?"

"How the hell am I supposed to know what it's called?"

"You're talking about a bustier. And the women wearing them in those movies are usually prostitutes."

"Just the ones who don't wear anything over them."

She rolls her eyes. "Listen, this conversation about lingerie has been fascinating, but you're drifting way off-topic." She points to her chest. "Do I look like I need help pushing my boobs up? They're already falling out of the dress. Think!"

"Okay, okay," he says, gesturing for her to calm down. "Don't take it out on me. I'm trying to help."

She sighs. "You're right. I'm sorry, I'm just frustrated because—"

"It's a pain in the ass to go back to the store. I know."

No, Wes. I'm frustrated because you can't seem to put two and two together. And I need you to figure it out, because I don't know if I'll ever be able to tell you, and every day I'm silent is another day that you'll hold against me.

She takes a deep breath. "It's already been altered once. *Correctly.* It needed to be taken in." She stares at him, waits for realization to dawn.

"Huh." Wes scratches his head. "Look, I'm way out of my league here. But you should go back if you're unhappy with it, whether they say they did it right or not." He rifles his hands through his hair and yawns. "Want some coffee?"

CHAPTER 5

"I won't wear it," Gracie says.

She's staring at the diamond and sapphire bracelet resting in the center of the kitchen table, arms folded in defiance. Jane turns to Tim, who's seated at the head of the table. Her eyes plead with him, beg him to intervene, and then she drops her gaze to the plate in front of her, still half full.

He sighs, readies himself for the conflict that will soon ruin the rest of their Monday night dinner. It's his favorite time of the week, his time of respite from the constant demands of ministering to his flock. There's no sermon to write, no counseling to be done, no home visit to be made. It's a tradition carried over from Shayla's childhood, one that they continued with her parents even before Gracie was born. Monday night is Family Night.

He glances down the hall, and then looks at Gracie. "Did Keith take Luke to the bathroom? Or to play with the chess set?"

"Chess set." She looks at Jane, disgusted. "I assume that's why you waited until now to bring the bracelet out."

Luke has been mesmerized by the set since he was a toddler, must play with it every time he visits. It's not the game itself that draws him in, as he has no understanding of the rules or interest in taking turns. He's fascinated by the magnetic board. Every time, without fail, he starts by matching up black and white pairs and placing them to the side of the board, leaving it clear for the only ones of interest: the kings and queens. Next he tests the magnetic pull of each of the four pieces, one by one, in every square, attempting to snatch them upwards just before the force drags them downwards. He ends by placing all pieces back on the board, white pieces on white spaces and black pieces on black ones. The entire process takes close to half an hour.

Jane pushes food around on her plate, separates the pot roast from the green beans and the potatoes. "I thought we'd need some uninterrupted time to talk. So yes, I waited, because I thought it'd be best for Luke to be occupied."

"Please," Gracie says with a snort. "You waited so Keith wouldn't be here to take my side."

Tim looks at Jane, surprised. Was it a calculated move on her part? Although he knows her intentions are good, he can't help but feel protective of his daughter. He feels a rare flash of anger towards Jane for putting Gracie in a vulnerable position, and for bringing up the bracelet at all.

She broached the subject with him several weeks ago, after her closest friend, Carol, had come to visit. He did his best to talk her out of it. "Gracie's not going to wear it, and I—" he'd started, and she interrupted with a flurry of counter-arguments. It was so unlike her to talk over him that he stopped, speechless. He waited for her to wind down, then kissed her on the top of head to soften the blow. "I know how important Carol is to you. But Gracie's not going to want to wear it, and I don't think we should pressure her."

She hadn't brought it up again, so he assumed that she'd either begun to see things his way or had forgotten about it. But instead, he realizes now, she'd devised a plan of her own.

Jane clears her throat and forces a smile. "There's no need to decide today, Gracie. Carol doesn't need it back right away. Why don't we just leave it that you'll think about it?" She begins clearing the table, pulls his plate away from him even though he's not finished. She places glasses and silverware upon the dishes, and passes the first pile to Gracie. But Gracie doesn't bring it to the kitchen as usual. Instead, she leans back further into her chair, stretches and rests the back of her head on her hands, which are clasped behind her. Jane's smile flickers, then disappears.

Jane points to the pot roast. "How about I wrap some of this up for you? I know how much Luke loves my pot roast. It'll save you a day of cooking." She picks up the serving platter before Gracie answers, and walks past her toward the kitchen.

Gracie ignores Jane's question about leftovers, returns to the more important one. "I don't need to think about it." Her words are measured, her voice crisp, and he recognizes this tone, unchanged from childhood. He and Shayla used to call it her lawyer voice, and they'd try not to laugh at her controlled, serious manner while she made the case for a later bedtime, or no broccoli with dinner.

Jane turns back and places the platter down on the table again. "Gracie, I understand your… hesitation. But it's such a beautiful bracelet. Your father and I don't have anything as beautiful as this to give to you. Did you know that Carol lent it to us for our wedding? So in some ways it *is* a gift from us." She waits for Gracie to respond, then fills the silence. "Plus, it's something old, something borrowed, and something blue, all in one."

48

Gracie turns her back to Jane, and flashes Tim a look that says *do I have to listen to any more of this?*

Against his will, a smile flits across his face. He loves that they still communicate in this private way, so unlike any other father-daughter relationship that he knows. He has been hoping for time alone with her tonight, wanting to gauge her reaction should he somehow summon the courage to come clean. He even planned how to start the conversation. All he would have had to do was bring up Keith's final year of grad school, starting in the fall. It would have been an easy segue to Greg Stonewalt, an old Gladen classmate who left in the middle of their senior year after a loss of faith. *Can you imagine what it must have been like for him to give everything up when he was so close to graduating?* he would have asked. It would have been the perfect test. But now, thanks to Jane, he could throw this plan in the trash.

They're both facing him, waiting for him to end the standoff. He stalls for time, wipes his mouth with his napkin, folds it and places it down as if it's still clean. He looks at Gracie's steely eyes, Jane's apprehensive ones. He has no choice but to enter the fray. "Gracie. I know how hard this is for you."

"No, you don't."

He stops, their moment of solidarity gone. "Okay. Point taken. I have more insight than most into this situation, though. Agreed?"

She gives him a grudging nod.

"The way you feel about Carol—about her family, really—is completely understandable. But remember, she and Jane have been friends for longer than you've been alive. Not inviting Carol to your wedding was extremely difficult for Jane, but she did it out of respect for you."

"Respect? You want to talk about respect? How about the past eight Christmases? All of those ridiculous clothes Carol sends. No boy over the age of two wears baby blue sweat suits with puppies and hearts. But did I send them back, unopened, like I wanted to? No. I did what you both asked. I dressed him up in them, made him stand out even more than he already does, and sent her pictures of him wearing them in my thank you notes. *Out of respect.* But this is too much."

She's right. But it's his job to broker the peace. "Think about it from Carol's perspective, Gracie. She knows what you think. To not invite her or Ed, even after all these years? That's a strong message. But she still drove two hours to get the bracelet to Jane."

"It was her grandmother's," Jane adds. "An heirloom. You'll get to wear it before her own daughter."

"Since when are Carol's feelings more important than mine? And Lisa! I can't believe you'd even say her name to me."

He shifts in his seat, unsure of how he's ended up on the side of an argument that he doesn't support. Of course Gracie's feelings should be paramount on her wedding day.

"She's always been sorry, Gracie, always," Jane says. "But what was she supposed to do? She had to choose her family."

"Then why aren't you choosing yours?"

Jane's cornered, and he struggles to think of a way to defend her before Gracie pounces. "Why don't we all just take a step back, and—"

"Lisa betrayed me! And your *wonderful* friend Carol let her get away with it. Do you honestly think she didn't know the truth? The fact that you still talk to her makes me sick to my stomach."

He looks at Jane, who's picking up the chunks of food that are strewn on the tablecloth around Luke's plate. "No one's denying what happened. Look, let's forget about respect, let's even forget about forgiveness for Carol or Lisa's sake. But we can never forget God." He turns to Gracie, tries to make her meet his eyes. "You know what I'm about to say. 'For if you forgive other people when they sin against you, your heavenly Father will also forgive you.' "

He's filled with self-loathing as he says these words. Quoting Scripture that he no longer believes in order to coerce Gracie into doing something that he doesn't think is fair? It makes no sense, but he hasn't been able to stop himself.

"But it's my wedding, Daddy."

He watches as one wayward tear rolls down her delicate, angular nose, the only feature that she has inherited from him.

Daddy. Not *Dad.* He wants to scoop her up in his arms, lift her up in the air like he did when she was a little girl. He wants to tell her that she shouldn't listen to her father. That she should rip the bracelet apart, stomp on it until it breaks into pieces. But he must finish what he's started. "The Lord has brought you and Keith together, Gracie. He's blessed you, made your family whole. What greater thanks can you give to Him than to follow His teachings?"

She covers her face, tries to muffle the choking sounds that are escaping her. She turns sideways in her chair, hugs her knees to her chest, and rests her forehead on top of them as she rocks back and forth.

Where was the comeback? There was no way to trump his argument, but still, he'd expected more of a fight. He looks at Jane in bewilderment, catches her as she closes her eyes and takes a deep breath, studies her as her clenched jaw releases and her creased forehead relaxes.

Tim feels a sudden and vast distance between them. For a moment he envies Jane her steadfast, absolute belief. Not so long ago, he would've been confident in his decision to take her side. Scripture guides man to love God first, then his spouse, then his children. A husband and wife are one flesh, Ephesians teaches, and a husband must love his wife just as Christ loved the church. *But Ephesians also commands a wife to submit to her husband as she does to the Lord. Jane doesn't seem to mind bending that rule.*

It bothers him that she sees nothing wrong in picking and choosing from Scripture as it benefits her, and it bothers him more that her questionable behavior is still more ethical than his. At least she's acted in accordance with her convictions.

He expected to solve a problem tonight, to make some headway at the very least, but instead, a new one has been added. He watches Gracie as she wipes her eyes and uncurls herself from the chair. She picks up the pile of dishes that are still in front of her, and turns to the kitchen without a word.

I have to make this right. He tries to think of excuses he could make to see Gracie during the week, but comes up blank. Between church, jobs, classes, therapies, and wedding planning, there's no time. *It will have to be next Monday. My last chance.*

CHAPTER 6

Tim feels the familiar symptoms in the shower Wednesday morning: the dull band of pain across his forehead, the faint blurring of his vision. He presses his head against the shower stall, grateful for the pressure. He throws on shorts and an old t-shirt, and makes his way to the kitchen, careful to walk around the creaky floorboard just outside of his room. Jane is still sleeping, and there's no need to wake her until he's done with his morning prayers.

Maybe it will clear if I eat. He skips his usual coffee and pours himself a bowl of cereal instead. He prefers to study before eating, but today he needs to take his medication right away, and he can't do that on an empty stomach.

He yawns and scratches the side of his neck. Guilt has kept him awake the past two nights, Monday night replaying in his mind. How had he managed to get so off track?

It's probably just a run-of-the-mill headache. Couple stress and exhaustion and you get a headache, pure and simple. But as he places his half-eaten bowl of cereal in the sink, an ominous thought burrows its way through his logic: *it always happens in the morning.*

He shivers, feels sweat poke through on his upper lip. What if it's not just a headache? What if it's what he suspects it is—the onset of a well-known constellation of symptoms that have appeared sporadically since childhood? It can't be. He doesn't have time to be sidelined today. He concentrates on breathing as he walks down the hallway to his office, fills his lungs until they can no longer expand, then lets the air out in a controlled stream. *Time will tell.*

Wednesday mornings are reserved for sermon preparation—the first draft, at any rate. After all these years it's still a daunting task. Conveying God's truth with his meager words, providing a message that offers comfort and insight to his fellow brothers and sisters is no small undertaking. It's an agonizing, deliciously painful process. But when he's able to connect with his flock—when the church swells with shared love for the Lord—he feels joy, peace, *purpose.* He looks forward to that moment every week, still feels the warm bond of community, even though he no longer believes that the presence of the Holy Spirit is responsible for it.

For years, he tried to write sermons during office hours, just as his former father-in-law did. He had no idea how John was able to block out the everyday goings-on of their church. How was it that he could concentrate when there were phone calls to be returned to colleagues and members, elder board meetings and Bible study to plan for, newsletter articles to be written? It was only after John heeded the call to serve a different ministry that he felt comfortable insisting that he work from the quiet of his home at least one morning per week.

He opens the shades and examines the shelves of texts. Out of habit, he reaches first for the New International Version of the Bible, his preferred translation. It aligns well with the King James' version—the classic, four hundred-year-old translation that the older members of his flock have grown up with—but is less flowery and more relatable to younger members. It's drawn from older manuscripts, ones that hadn't been discovered when the King James' version was authorized, making it, in his opinion, a more precise translation of the Word.

He doesn't pull it from the stack, though. Instead, he finds himself reaching for the New American Standard Bible. Over the past several months he's surprised himself by selecting it more and more often. *Maybe because it's the one we used at Gladen.* The New International Version was adopted as Gladen's official translation during his sophomore year, two years after it was first published, once faculty had been given enough time to review it. But it was the orange-covered, New American Standard Bible that he'd been studying the day he met Shayla.

He feels a slight fluttering in his stomach. Or does he? It disappears so quickly that he wonders if he imagined it. He settles into his chair, and flips to 1 Kings 19:11–13, in which the Lord reveals himself to Elijah:

> So He said, "Go forth and stand on the mountain before the Lord." And behold, the Lord was passing by! And a great and strong wind was rending the mountains and breaking in pieces the rocks before the Lord; but the Lord was not in the wind. And after the wind an earthquake, but the Lord was not in the earthquake. After the earthquake a fire, but the Lord was not in the fire; and after the fire a sound of a gentle blowing.

Interesting the change that one word can make. He dislikes "gentle blowing," prefers the New International Version's "gentle whisper," or even the King James Version's "still, small voice." But whatever the wording, the message speaks to him. How easy, how *human* it is to search for powerful signs from the Lord when we'd be wiser to listen to His soft murmurings of guidance.

This passage has provided him with strength over the years. Listen closer, look harder, be patient, and you'll find Him. It's a reasonable, achievable task. All that's required is diligence and faith.

Out of habit, he pulls open the lower drawer of his filing cabinet, where he keeps hard copies of his sermons, dated and organized by book. As a general rule, he tries not to reuse a passage for at least a year. But there's no need to pull the "1 Kings" file. He remembers when he last quoted these verses. It was in September, just days after meeting the Muslim man in the hospital.

* * *

He had gone to visit Marion Dixon, a choir member, who'd been recovering from heart surgery. She'd been placed in a shared room, and when he entered, he could hear voices praying in Arabic on the other side of the curtain that partitioned it.

"Been keeping me up all day and night with that nonsense," she said to him by way of hello. She motioned for him to sit in the seat next to her bed, then turned her head to the side and yelled through the curtain. "Hush up, already! Praying to that terrorist god of yours ain't gonna do you no good, anyway."

He felt himself blush. Clearly these people needed to be guided, not mocked, especially in a time of need. After rushing through prayers with her, he mumbled an excuse and tried to slip out unnoticed.

As he waited by the elevator, the door to her room had opened, and out walked a man wearing a white, knit hat. *A Muslim prayer cap.* They stood side by side in uncomfortable silence, Tim wondering if the man had identified him as Marion's visitor.

He pressed the down button several times in a row, desperate for the elevator to rise to the fourth floor. He glanced over and offered an awkward smile, but the man either didn't notice him or didn't want to talk to him. *Maybe he doesn't speak English.* After another uncomfortable minute, Tim pointed to the door. "Family?"

The man nodded. "My mother."

"I'm so sorry. I'll pray for her."

"I thank you," the man said, but the smirk he'd been too slow to hide belied his words. And his tone. How to describe it? Not condescending, not rude, but... *indulgent.* As if Tim was a child who needed humoring. The man dismissed Christ the Lord, in whose name millions of lives have been slaughtered and saved, in the blink of an eye.

As Tim prepared his sermon the next morning, he realized that the Lord had placed the man in his life in order to remind him, and his flock, of the importance of evangelism. "If too few are hearing God," he preached that Sunday, "then it's our duty to bring Him to them."

* * *

Tim closes the filing cabinet, and tilts his head from side to side to loosen a kink in his neck. What worries him now isn't that too few can hear the voice. It's that too *many* can.

If there's only one God, as both Christianity and Islam claim, then no matter which is right, over two billion people are praying to a god that doesn't exist. Yet throughout time, Christians have claimed to hear Jesus and Muslims have claimed to hear Allah; Jews have heard Adonai and Hindus have heard Vishnu. But how can that be?

This is where logic batters his faith, because the conclusion that he's spent close to a year trying to discount is inescapable. That hearing a god doesn't prove that one exists; it proves that people *want* one to exist. That what he was taught as a child and has spent his life teaching is backwards. That God didn't make us in His image. We made Him in ours.

He could rework this passage, discuss why it's important to heed one's inner voice. He wouldn't even need to mention God. The congregation would assume the inner voice was the voice of the Lord within each of us. Deceitful, yes; but not a lie.

He doesn't have to play it that close, though. It's been surprising, how easy it's been. All he has to do is stick to the moral aspects of Christ's teachings that are universally accepted. Give to the poor. Help the sick. Love one another.

He looks at his laptop, tempted. Writing longhand is such a waste of time. His hand can never keep up with his thoughts. But today, the glare from the computer screen is a risk.

He resists, pushes the laptop away, and flips the pages of the Bible forward until he reaches Matthew. He feels the jerk then, the abrupt contraction and release of his intestines. The words begin to jumble on the page, and then he's aware of a fizzing inside his head, like the bubbles in a can of soda. He places the well-worn Bible face down and rubs his eyes. The day is over before it's begun.

If he's to remain safe, he'll need to take lorazepam and go to sleep. There is no option. Experience has taught him that he can't will away a seizure, and that medication or sleep alone doesn't work. Only the two in combination will prevent it. Once he considered this warning period, this aura, as his doctor refers to it, to be a blessing from God, a far more comforting explanation than what he believes it to be now: neurological luck.

He doesn't take his own advice, though. Instead, he heads back to the bedroom, strips down to his boxers, and climbs back in to bed.

Jane rouses as he pulls at the covers. "Why aren't you writing?" she asks, eyes still unfocused.

"I needed a break. Go back to s-sleep."

She sits upright. "I heard that. Did you take your meds?"

"I'm fine."

"You didn't answer my question."

"Yeah, I did. The lamotrigine."

"Not the extra?"

He shakes his head. "I was going to, but I... uh... " Confusion takes over. He can't remember what he was about to say, or what her question was.

"I'm going to get it."

The medicine. That's right. "But I have so much to do today." The fizzing in his head again, this time followed by shivers.

She ignores him. He can hear her pushing bottles aside in their medicine cabinet. She returns with a circular white pill, hands it to him without a word.

"But it's Wednesday."

She shakes her head in impatience. "This is why you have your file. Why you exhaust yourself trying to write two extra sermons per month. For this exact situation. Right?" She waits for his answer, and when there isn't one, she climbs back into bed with him and strokes his cheek. "Don't do this to yourself, sweetie."

He hesitates, and then places the pill under his tongue, tasting the mild bitterness. "You need to call Craig—"

"I know, I know." She reaches over him and picks his cell phone up from his nightstand. "He has your calendar. Anything he can't take care of as associate pastor will have to be rescheduled."

"But—"

"There's no 'but.' Go to sleep." She kisses him near the ear, turns off the ringer on the phone, and then closes the door behind her.

At least it only happens every couple of months. He repositions himself, concentrates on slowing his breathing. The jerks in his stomach haven't subsided yet, won't for another twenty minutes or so. Now for the balancing act. He has to remain alert when the jerks hit; he can't allow them to drag him into unconsciousness. But in between, he tries to let his mind go blank, wills his body to slide into it on its own terms.

It dawns on him that there's a bright side. It's doubtful that he'll have to worry about this happening on the day of the wedding now. He considers canceling Friday's visit with John, now that it's less likely that he'll need his help. Even now, Shayla's father makes him nervous. But he knows that canceling wouldn't be wise. Illness isn't the only reason that he might have to rely on John to officiate. Yet it had been John's suggestion that they meet, not his. A rarity, to say the least.

They're coming farther and farther apart, the jerks, the fizzing, and the shivers. His last thought before drifting off is of Shayla, when she discovered his secret on a Sunday afternoon in the spring of their sophomore year.

* * *

The phone rang at eight in the morning. Tim licked his lips, dry from sleep, and fumbled for the handset, his face still buried in his pillow. "Hello?"

"Tim. I need to see you. Can you—wait, did I wake you?" Shayla asked.

He opened his eyes and tried to focus on his alarm clock. "Campus Worship's at nine instead of eight thirty this week, remember?"

"Oh. Sorry. But listen, I *really* need to talk to you. Can you meet me at the RUC after services? Around eleven thirty?"

"Yeah, sure. Everything okay?"

"I'll explain later. Eleven thirty, at the outside tables."

"Shay, what's going on?"

"Just meet me there," she said, and hung up before he could get in another word.

He didn't call back to press for more. He knew her schedule—eight thirty services followed by ten o'clock Sunday school at South Reyling Church of Christ. She'd have to hustle if she was going to make it on time. Whatever the problem was, he'd know about it soon enough.

He sat up, eyes still bleary, and looked over at his roommate Andrew's bed, perpendicular to his. Still asleep. He considered going back to sleep, but decided it wouldn't be worth it. Better to shower and eat, now that there was time.

He undressed, wrapped a towel around his waist, and walked down the hall to the community bathroom. He could hear the hiss of two or three showers, far fewer than usual. *I guess everyone's decided to roll out of bed.* He hung his towel on the hook to the side of the shower stall, stowed his Dopp kit in the cubby, and closed the yellowed plastic curtain behind him. Mold surrounded the curtain's edges, as well as the drain and the rim of the shower lip. He grimaced as he stepped into the closest mildew-free spot.

He squeezed the bridge of his nose to relieve the pressure in his forehead as the water hit his back. He could've really used that extra half hour of sleep. *This better be good, Shay. My head is killing me.*

It was when he had toweled off and stood in front of the sink to shave that he noticed that his face was out of focus. He wiped the fog off of the mirror, opened his eyes wide and then squinted, trying to sharpen his reflection. *Probably the steam.*

He walked back to his room, shivering in just his towel. "Breakfast?" mumbled Andrew, when Tim opened the door.

"Yeah. You coming?" He put on his khakis, looked in his closet for a button-down.

Andrew groaned, fished dirty clothes out of his hamper, and dressed without a word. He shuffled cross-campus with Tim, offering no more to conversation than the occasional mumble or grunt until they reached the cafeteria.

"Only two doughnuts left," Andrew said, perking up as he eyed the buffet options. "You want one? Otherwise they're mine."

"No, you ta-ke them."

Andrew raised an eyebrow. "You okay, man?"

"Fine." Tim could feel a flash of heat and the prickling of sweat under his arms.

Andrew put his tray on a table, and dropped his backpack underneath it. "Wait, where's all your stuff?"

"What stuff?"

"For baseball. Intramurals. We're all meeting right after Worship for team selection. Mike, Chris K., and lots of second- and third-floor guys. I thought you knew about it."

"Oh man, I completely forgot. Can you sign me up? I told Shayla I'd meet her at eleven thirty."

"I'll try. Don't know if they'll let me, but it's worth a shot." Andrew took a huge bite out of his doughnut, and then wiped powdered sugar from the corner of his mouth. "Not sure what day we can use the field. I think they said Tuesday or Thursday after varsity practice. Is that okay for you?"

His mind was blank all of a sudden. "Tuesdays and Thursdays?" he asked, stalling for time. What classes *did* he take on Tuesdays and Thursdays? He couldn't think of the names of any of them, let alone which days they took place. Small talk was still manageable, but comparing schedu—

He felt his lower left lip twitch, and, for a fraction of a second, was absent.

"Dude, are you sure you're okay?" Andrew was looking at him, concern and skepticism on his face. " 'Cause for a second your eyes blinked kind of funny, and it seemed like you were going to pass out or something."

Confusion swirled around him, and he felt the familiar unease of knowing that time was unaccounted for in his memory. A shiver of hot, followed by cold, ran down his back as he swallowed and tried to rejoin the conversation.

"No, I'm good. Sometimes I get migraines, that's all." This was his token explanation. It explained his symptoms, gave him an acceptable reason to leave, and didn't trigger panic.

"Oh, my mom gets those real bad. Has to go to bed, turn off all the lights, unplug the phone. This one time, she… "

He weighed his options as Andrew rambled on, even though thinking hurt. Very little would be expected of him at Worship—just some responsive reading and singing, both of which could be avoided. But it was disturbing that he'd progressed to this phase in such a short period of time. It usually took a couple of hours to get this bad. Not a good sign. He'd be up to eight warnings if he skipped, but he wouldn't have to meet with his Resident Advisor until he got twenty-five. He could afford it.

But what to do about Shayla? He had no way of getting in touch with her, since the church office was closed on Sundays. He'd have to find a way to make it work.

He looked at his watch. 8:41. If he went back to the dorm right now, he might be able to take his medication and sleep it off in time. Fifteen-minute walk back, a half an hour to fall asleep, two hours to sleep, walk to the RUC in ten—two hours and fifty-five minutes total. He'd just make it.

He stood up. "You know what, man, my headache is getting bad. Sorry to do this to you, but I've got to go back."

Maybe I should take two pills instead of one, he thought, once he got back to his dorm room. *The faster I fall asleep, the better.* He swallowed the first pill, took out a second, then thought better of it and placed it back inside the bottle. It would knock him out for longer than he had time. He kicked off his shoes, crawled into bed, and pulled the pillow over his head to block out the sunlight spilling in through the room's curtainless windows.

Indistinct music entered the darkness of his sleep. A man was singing, but the words were muffled. Did he know the song? There was talking next, and laughter. Was he dreaming? There was a fuzziness to the sound, a static, like when a radio station doesn't quite come in—

His alarm clock! The volume must have been set too low. He turned it off as he checked the time. 11:27.

"Shit!" he said, too groggy to substitute its approved its Gladen stand-in, *shoot*. How much sleep had he gotten? The last time he remembered looking at the clock it was 9:54. Just over an hour and a half. It could be enough, had been before.

Shayla was sitting outside the RUC we he got there, her expression unreadable. *I'll just tell her I can't stay and go back to bed. Give her a quick sorry-I'll-call-you-later, and get out of here.*

"Where were you?" she asked. Her tone was light, not accusatory as he'd feared, but Tim could see by her expression that she was struggling to give him the benefit of the doubt.

He hesitated, then sat down across from her. "Sorry. I fell back asleep."

"You slept through services?"

He couldn't think of an excuse that didn't make him seem lazy, but couldn't bring himself to tell her the truth, either. He'd never told anyone. There had been no need to as a child. His seizures had been milder, then—a mere rolling back of the eyes, no shaking or falling. He hadn't had a convulsive seizure until junior high.

"This is a big deal for me." She picked up her bag and stood up to leave. "Maybe it's not important to you, but—"

"Shayla." He could only operate in slow motion, and his mind and mouth couldn't keep pace with her. He needed to slow her down if he was to help her. "You haven't even told me what this is all about."

She paused for a moment, deciding whether to stay. "My parents found out that I declared psychology as my major." She sat back down. "They're going to pull me unless I switch to PWS."

He grinned. "You mean Family Studies?"

"Don't laugh. Do you think I haven't heard *Pastor's Wife Studies* before?"

"Is that so terrible?"

"Yes!" She hit the table with a fist, knocking over her half-filled water glass. She pushed her chair back to move out of the water's path, and then sopped it up with their napkins. "Sorry. I don't mean to take it out on you. And I do like some of the courses I've taken, like Child Development and Early Education. But Nurturing a Christian Family? Marriage and the Christian Wife? Are those classes you'd want to take?"

"No, but Gladen doesn't offer Marriage and the Christian Husband."

"Exactly! Why do I have to take courses that don't teach me anything except how to support other people? Why can't I take a class just because it interests me? Why do my parents even bother sending me to college if all they care about is marrying me off?"

He could feel his left lip twitching as he tried to respond. *An hour and a half wasn't enough*. He needed an excuse to leave. Right away.

She stopped, mid-tirade. "What's wrong?"

"Nothing."

"It's not 'nothing.' Why are your eyes half closed?"

"I just didn't get a lot of sleep last night. "Listen, I'm not feeling gr—" His voice caught, just as it had earlier with Andrew. "Great. I'm not feeling great, so... " He felt himself lose a split-second.

"Tim, are you okay?"

"I'm going to head back. I'll call you later." He stood and pushed his chair back in. "I just didn't want you to wait here and not know where I w-was."

"I'm coming with you."

"No, I'm fine."

"I'm not stupid."

"You can't. You know that."

"I don't care about their ridiculous warnings."

"Twenty, Shay. Plus a seventy-five dollar fine and community service."

She shrugged. "I'm going with you. Didn't I just tell you my parents were thinking about pulling me, anyway?"

He was too tired to argue. It was so hard to think, and he couldn't get the words out, anyway, the warm shivers would burst from within while he was speaking and then he couldn't remember what he was saying, but if he stopped thinking and opened his eyes wide and just concentrated on getting back—one foot in front of the other, one foot in front of the other, one foot in front of the other—then the shivers and the twitches and the jerks in his stomach would go away and he would stay on his guard and then he would be safe and it wasn't that far away he could make it all he needed to do was open his eyes wide and just concentrate on getting back where he would be safe because it wasn't that far and—

"Lie back down."

Tim wasn't sure who'd spoken these words, or what they even meant. He should know. They sounded like words he should know. He felt hands pushing him back down on a bed, although he couldn't figure out where he was or why he was trying to sit up. He wanted to, *needed* to—it would make things better, he was sure, because how could it not? He hurt. He hurt everywhere.

It was the frantic look in Shayla's eyes that began to free him from confusion, the first loosening of the knot. *I know her.* But this room—it wasn't his room from home. Why were there two beds in it? He could see the sun through the blinds, so it must have been day, but what day? And what month?

He had no idea what had happened. But deep within his core, he felt a familiar layering of shame, embarrassment, and disappointment. He'd felt it before, this peculiar combination of confusion and humiliation, but only when—

And then he knew. He was at Gladen. It was Shayla, whose eyes looked so terrified.

He hadn't been able to stop it. "No," he moaned, turning onto his side to face the wall. He was determined not to cry.

"Tim, can you hear me? Are you okay?" Shayla was pulling his shoulder now, trying to get him to face her. "Do you want me to call someone? I think you had a seizure. Tim? Tim?" She was shaking him now, worsening his headache and nausea.

"No, don't." There was a dull pain in his mouth when he spoke. He rubbed his tongue against the inside of his lower teeth, and could feel the cut in the flesh, taste the salty blood. "I'm sorry, I'm so sorry," he said, choking on his words.

"I don't understand. I think we should call someone. You need to go to the hospital." She leaned over him and picked up the phone.

"Shayla, I'll be fine."

"That's what you said at lunch! And looked what happened!"

"There's nothing a doctor can tell me that I don't already know."

He heard her place the phone back in its cradle, felt his mattress shift as she sat down on the edge of the bed. When she spoke, her voice was soft. "You have epilepsy?"

He'd planned on telling her, but not now, not this way. He should've known that setting an alarm clock was a mistake. He should've missed meeting her and apologized later with some stupid excuse. It would've been easy. But no, he'd had to push it. And now here he was, nodding yes to a wall, because there was no way he could look her in the eyes. "What happened... you know, *before?* I remember, we were walking back, right? But then... "

"You got in bed, said you needed to sleep. Said something about a plan that you didn't follow, I think? You weren't making a lot of sense. You said that you'd been nervous about meeting me, and that you were glad that you'd made it back before it happened. I was about to leave, but then—" She started to cry, and he turned to face her then, hugged her and stroked her hair even though his arms were sore. He'd never been this close to her before.

She quieted, brushed away her tears, and then looked up and studied his face. Was she going to kiss him? Should he try to kiss her? He'd imagined how her lips would feel, whether her lip gloss had a taste. *Now* he got a chance? Now, of all times?

But then her eyes hardened. She placed both hands on his chest, and shoved him backwards, knocking him off balance. "You jerk!"

So he would lose her, after all. He swallowed, noticed that his throat was raw, as if he'd been panting. Had he been? "Shayla, I get it. I'll understand if you don't want to be... you know... "

"No! I'm not mad because you had a seizure! I'm mad because you didn't tell me!"

"I'm sorry. I should have. I wanted to, I just didn't know how."

She locked eyes with his, then looked down at her nails and picked at her bubblegum-pink nail polish. When she spoke again her voice was hushed. "I was really scared." She glanced at him out of the corner of her eye. "I don't get it. Why'd you meet me at the RUC if you knew this might happen? Why'd you risk it?"

"I wouldn't," he said, "for anyone but you."

She leaned in, and he braced himself for another shove. But this time, she tilted her head, and brushed her lips against his.

The sound of the front door of the dorm opening interrupted them. "You need to go," he mouthed, as they pulled away from each other. If caught, they might be able to justify her presence in his room by telling the truth, or at the very least lessen their punishment. But kissing? On his bed? Grounds for expulsion.

He could hear footsteps in the hallway outside of his room, the opening and closing of another door further down, and then silence again. He sighed in relief. "Now," he whispered.

She nodded, and then walked to the door in exaggerated, silent steps. She peered outside, turned back with a quick wave, and was gone.

CHAPTER 7

The bells hanging from the doorknob of Annabelle's Bridal Boutique clang as Josephine enters, dress in hand. Five forty-five. She'll just make it before closing.

It was a light day at work, a rarity for a Wednesday, and she was able to leave right on time. She didn't have any intra-op consults, which left her with time to prepare for next week's grossing conference and to catch up on a backlog of slides, reports, and emails. She'd been grateful for the extra time at the beginning of the day, but found, as the hours passed, that she missed the excitement of analysis under pressure.

There's no denying that it's stressful, knowing that the entire OR team is waiting for her diagnosis. There's no room for error. Her evaluation of the frozen tissue is what the surgeon relies upon when determining whether to close up or continue to cut. But it's immensely gratifying, too. If she concludes that the surgical margins of the tissue are clear of residual cancer, then the surgeon will close, sparing the patient more extensive surgery. If they're not, the surgeon will resect more, saving the patient from an incomplete procedure and the need for a second one. Either way, it's her decision that drives the direction of the surgery. The buck stops with her.

"Hello, welcome to Annabelle's," says the sales lady, as she comes around the corner. "I'm Ginny. How can I help you today, darlin'?"

So it's 'darling' this time. An improvement over last time's 'sugar' at least. Josephine rests the dress on the counter. "I had this dress altered a couple of months ago, but I need to have it fixed again."

Ginny's eyebrows furrow in confusion. "But we have all of our customers try their dresses on again after they've been altered. Didn't you try it on when you picked it up?"

"I did, but, well, it doesn't fit now." She can see from Ginny's face that her explanation is inadequate. "It's too tight across the bust."

"Is it tight anywhere else?"

"No, the rest is fine."

"I see." Ginny opens her mouth to speak, then closes it, concentrates instead on the computer resting in front of her on the glass countertop. She adjusts her tortoise-shell glasses and offers Josephine a fresh smile as she squints at the screen. "What's your last name, darlin'?"

"Wallis."

Ginny types on the keyboard, fingers splayed to protect her long ruby fingernails. The clacking is painstakingly slow, and Josephine drums her fingers on the countertop in frustration. *I could have dictated a full report in this amount of time.*

"Let's see… I have an Amanda, and a Josephine."

"Josephine. Amanda's my sister."

"All right, then, just give me a second to access your account, Josephine." The labored typing continues, Ginny hunting and pecking for each letter. Josephine catches the irritated expression on her face in the mirror behind the counter and replaces it with a more pleasant one.

"Here it is. Our records indicate that you had the bust taken in one and a three quarters of an inch on both sides, correct?"

"I don't know. That sounds about right," says Josephine, surprised by her imprecision. *I spend my days examining biopsies down to the millimeter. Accuracy is what I do for a living.*

"May I see the dress?"

Ginny handles the dress as if it's fine china, peels the plastic protective sheath from it in a steady, gentle motion, places it flat on the countertop, and then smoothes out the rumpled fabric. She turns the bodice inside out and examines the seams. "Our tailors try to sew extra material into the seams instead of cutting, just in case. But they can't do that with a sweetheart neckline like this. It has to be cut real close so that the material rests nice and flat against your curves."

"There's nothing you can do?"

Ginny looks at Josephine's distraught face and squeezes her shoulder. "My goodness, dear, don't look so nervous. Lynn's here today, and if anyone can fix it, it's our Lynn. Why don't you slip it on while I go and get her?"

She's guided to the same dressing room that she and Amanda shared at their first fitting. She throws her bag on the bench to the side of the full-length mirror, wriggles out of her clothes, and leaves them in a heap on the floor. The zipper in the back needs coaxing, and she struggles with it as it catches on material halfway up. *Damn it. How many things can go wrong with this dress?*

Rather than risk tearing it, she cracks the door and looks for Ginny, who isn't in sight. She ventures out into the center of the store, holding the front up with one hand and the hem up with the other, but Ginny is nowhere to be seen. *Where are you when I need you, darlin'?*

Voices carry from down the hall, and she follows them until she reaches the tailors' room. She peers in, can see Ginny from behind, talking to a stout woman with a tape measure around her neck. *Must be the famous Lynn.* "Excuse me? I was wondering if—"

"Be with you in a minute, sugar," Ginny says, without turning.

"But my zipper is—"

"We'll take a look at everything as soon as Lynn's available. Just take a seat in your dressing room. You can grab a magazine from the front if you'd like."

Josephine doesn't bother with a magazine. What could possibly be of interest in *Brides* or *Town and Country Weddings*? Instead, she hobbles back to the bench in her room, and reaches in her bag for her phone. Might as well catch up on email. But the battery is down to four percent, so she gives her inbox a cursory look and then puts it back in her bag, saving the remaining charge for the ride home.

She looks at herself in the mirror, pulls her elastic out of her hair and runs her hands through it. She notices the dark circles under her eyes, present whether she's tired or not, and then takes a couple of steps back. *No one looks good that close up without airbrushing.* She examines her face from different angles, tests whether the lighting is to blame, then makes a mental note to buy some concealer. She hates buying make up, because it always ends up a waste of time and money. How is she supposed to know if she should buy liquid, cream or stick? Which of the dizzying number of shades is the best match for her skin color? Should she apply it with her finger, a brush, or a sponge? There are too many options, and she usually throws most of her purchases out within a day or two, Wes teasing her that she should save time and just throw their money directly into the trash.

She looks at the worn, five-inch pumps in the corner, left for customers to try on with their dresses, and thinks of Amanda. *Got to give her credit for trying.*

* * *

The shoes had been far too tight on Amanda, but she'd forced her feet in regardless and teetered around the dressing room with the concentration of a tightrope walker.

"Amanda, what are you doing?" Josephine said, sure that she'd sprain an ankle. "Those look like five-inch heels! You're going to kill yourself."

Amanda brushed her fingers along the wall for balance. "Mom says I can get high heels."

"Come on."

"She did! I s-swear."

"How many times did you ask her?"

"Uh… I don't know."

"Ballpark." Then, as she noticed Amanda's confused expression: "Take a guess."

Amanda shrugged. "A lot."

I'll bet it was. Good for you. "Your first pair, right?"

Amanda nodded, and then grabbed Josephine's arm as she swayed too far to the left. "I have to practice."

"Are you sure you want heels? The dress is so long—people won't even see them. Your feet are going to hurt all night for no reason."

"Everyone else is going to."

"I'm not."

Amanda wobbled, then regained her balance. "Well, *I* want to."

Josephine was careful not to smile at this, knew that Amanda would misinterpret her admiration as ridicule. *She's not going to give in. She must have really worn Mom down.* "Okay. Have Mom take you to get them soon, then, so you can practice in ones that fit. She's not going to let you get ones that high, though. Even she doesn't wear heels that high."

"I know. They're un*lady*like," she said, drawing out the second syllable in their mother's voice. She took a few more steps towards the mirror, and then toppled over as she tried to pivot. "Ow, ow, ow!" She rubbed her ankle, and then flung the shoes against the wall. "I can't do it."

"Amanda! I know it's frustrating, but you can't—"

There was a knock, and Ginny's voice. "I've got your dresses right here, ladies," she said, as she passed them over the top of the door. "Try them on, and come on out when you're ready."

Josephine changed, then stood behind Amanda to zip her up. She looked over her sister's shoulder, and her breath caught at the mirror's reflection.

It was transformative, the dress. Not in the tired Hollywood tradition of the ugly girl with glasses putting on a gown and becoming the belle of the ball. Amanda was still *Amanda*. Her figure was still fleshy; her movements uncoordinated; her mouth ajar. But never before had Josephine seen her sister look so… *womanly*.

A shy smile spread across Amanda's face as she looked at herself in the mirror. "I like this dress," she said, blushing. "I feel pretty."

Tears sprung to Josephine's eyes. "You look beautiful, Amanda."

Amanda's smile broadened. "I think Jack will l-like it, too." She opened the door and lumbered into the middle of the open fitting area, admired herself in the three-way mirror.

Until that moment, Josephine had never noticed how unisex Amanda's wardrobe was. Her clothes consisted of cotton shirts, pants, and shorts. Nothing low-cut, nothing fitted, no skirts or dresses. Not even jeans.

Maybe Mom just got into the habit of buying the same clothes year after year. She considered the explanation, then discarded it as the image of her impeccably manicured, accessorized mother formed in her mind. Had her mother made a deliberate attempt to downplay Amanda's sexuality?

Amanda fished out a pair of smaller heels from behind the three-way mirror, and held them up for Josephine to see. "Better?"

She nodded, smiled as she watched Amanda take tentative steps. For the first time, she wondered if her sister was a virgin. She and Jack had been dating for close to two years. Josephine had always thought of it as a chaste, junior high type of relationship. But Amanda was a twenty-six-year-old woman, Jack a twenty-seven-year-old man. A man who she'd never seen without a baseball cap and gum, but a man nonetheless. *How much does Amanda even know about sex? There's no way Mom's talked about it with her. The only sex ed I ever got from Mom was a box of pads left in the bathroom the day I got my period.*

Privacy. Their mother had depended on it, or the lack of it, to avoid tackling the issue head on. Jack and Amanda were always supervised. The monthly dances at the Harrington Center were monitored, as were the community outings they went on over the weekends. They were never at the apartment without her or Gracie and Luke. But that would only be true for another two months. *Mom can't gloss over it much longer. Looks like I'm going to have to talk her into having The Talk.*

* * *

It feels like an eternity, but Josephine's iPhone shows that she's only been waiting for seven minutes. *Five more. I'll give them five more, and then… well, and then what?* She has no card to play. *Don't they want to go home? It's past closing.*

She returns to her thoughts. As far as she knows, The Talk has yet to happen. What's frustrating is that this time she's to blame as much as her mother. She never found the right time to bring the subject up. Company would be over at her parent's house when she'd call, or she'd be on her way to or from work when her mother called. Saturdays were out—she couldn't talk about Amanda right in front of her. And the truth is, after she found out she was pregnant, she forgot about Amanda altogether.

It occurs to her, now, that her mother may be thinking along the same lines. She'd asked her to come by after dropping Amanda off this Saturday. But why not include her? The only reason Josephine can come up with is that her mother wants to talk about Amanda, too.

There's a gentle knock on the door. Ginny has returned, Lynn a step behind. She barges in past Ginny as soon as the door is opened, pulls the bodice down and examines the seams without a "hello" or a "may I?"

"Like Ginny said, there isn't much material in the side seams. It's a sweetheart. All right, let's see it done up." She spins Josephine around, instructs her to hold her hair up, and in one, powerful tug, releases the stuck zipper. She pulls Josephine's right shoulder towards her, making her spin until they're face to face again.

Lynn shakes her head. "Oh, my. Looks like releasing the seams won't do much good, anyhow. It'll release some of the flattening on the sides, but it won't cover the center. The only thing I can do is make a modesty panel."

"Which is?"

"It's extra material sewn across the bust to cover the cleavage. It'll change the shape of the neckline some, but if the bride doesn't mind, I can call the company and get a matching swatch sent here."

"I'm sure she'll be fine with it. Let's do it."

Lynn turns and gives a look to Ginny, who clears her throat and joins them inside the room. "Honey, do you mind reminding me when the wedding is?"

"A week and a half from now."

"Wonderful." She looks relieved. "So there shouldn't be any need to alter again."

Josephine blushes. So she's that transparent? How is it that Ginny and Lynn have figured things out, and Wes is still clueless? Maybe she shouldn't have been coy, but it hadn't seemed right to have two strangers be the first to know.

Lynn measures and pins, then hands Ginny a ticket. "Give me until next Monday," she says, and then leaves.

Ginny pins the top portion of the ticket to a dress strap, and then hands the bottom portion to Josephine. "Just leave your dress on the counter out front after you change." She smiles and pats her on the shoulder. "See? I told you. Our Lynn can fix anything." She exits the dressing room, then turns back before the door swings closed. "And sweetheart? Congratulations."

CHAPTER 8

Tim watches Gracie's life unfold in photos as they flash across his computer screen. Gracie on her first day of life, eyes squeezed shut and body swaddled; taking her first bite of birthday cake; learning to ride a bike; posing before her first school dance; performing in a high school play. The cycle begins anew with Luke, with picture after picture of him as a beaming toddler.

But Luke's smiles dwindle between ages two and three, along with his interest in posing. Tim can't find a single photo of him looking at the camera. Even in shots with Gracie holding him and coaxing him to face it, Luke looks everywhere but straight on. His expression is confused, irritated, sometimes vacant. In the rare photos that capture a smile, he's looking at something outside of the frame.

"Please tell me you're going for a candid shot," Jane had said, when Tim told her that he planned on getting a picture of him at the lake. "He's not going to say 'cheese' for the camera, no matter how hard you try."

He'd taken her advice, had allowed Luke to venture beyond the path on the way back from the lake two weeks ago, followed him as he meandered around rocks and brush. The buzzy call of warbler caught Luke's attention, and he turned towards a juniper tree behind an outcropping. It was then that Tim managed to snag one of him in profile, face upturned towards the sun, a serene smile on his face.

Tim smiles at the image, now on his computer screen, and then turns towards Jane, who stops tidying to come and look. Her eyes fill with tears. "It's beautiful. She's going to love it. Everyone will."

"I thought it'd be nice to show it during my toast, right before the father-daughter dance. What do you think?"

"Sounds perfect." She rubs his arm, waits for him to take his eyes off the screen and look at her. "It's missing one thing, though."

"I didn't forget about the groom, if that's what you're implying. Kelly and Bill just emailed Keith's baby pictures. What do you think makes sense: showing all of Gracie's and then all of Keith's, or going back and forth between the two?"

"Back and forth. But that's not what I was talking about."

"What, then?"

"Shayla. You need more pictures of Shayla."

He feels his throat constrict, and he leans over to kiss her. She's parented Gracie for far more years than Shayla, a thankless task at times, yet not once has she tried to take Shayla's place. *It must have been so hard for her. Especially after we found out that she couldn't have a child of her own.*

He points to the photo of Gracie on her first birthday, blowing the candle out with Shayla. "I only have this one."

"You have more. You have those two albums."

"But I thought you threw them out years ago."

Jane looks surprised, and then wounded. "Why would you think that?"

He gestures towards their bedroom. "They were on the top shelf in our closet for years. We had an argument about Shayla one night, and the next day they were gone. So I just assumed that... "

"That I'd get rid of them?"

"Don't be mad, Jane. I wasn't. I was sad that you felt the need to, but I figured that after so many years you had the right to... I don't know, get rid of ghosts."

She cocks her head, appraises him with serious eyes. Then she turns and walks out of the room without a word.

"Jane," he calls, but he doesn't follow her. Silence is her signal for space, and he's learned that forcing her to talk before she's ready is pointless. *She'll cool down after fifteen minutes or so.*

He doesn't hear the bedroom door slam, as he expected. Instead, he hears her steps going down the basement stairs, and she reappears after a few minutes with the albums. She drops them on his desk with a thud. "I don't remember the fight you're talking about. I moved them because we were running out of space. I put them in the same box with all of my old photos. I told you about it."

"You did? I don't remember you telling me." He notices a slight quivering of her chin, realizes then that her anger is masking hurt. *This is ancient history. Let it go.* "Maybe I was distracted when you mentioned it. Don't know if you've noticed, but occasionally I get sidetracked."

Jane teeters between resentment and forgiveness. "No... you? I *always* have your full attention on Sundays." She studies him for a moment, and then the caustic tone in her voice fades. She offers the beginnings of a smile. "And Saturdays, too, sometimes Fridays... definitely Wednesdays... "

The fight is over. He's willing to take the blame, but doubt nags at him, the memory of her deception on Monday night still fresh. Does she expect him to believe that there's no connection between their fight and the photos' sudden disappearance? But once again, he finds himself guilty of the greater moral lapse. He's the one who made the ugly assumption that she'd destroyed something of value to him on purpose.

He pulls her close, lifts her chin with his fingers. "I didn't mean to hurt your feelings, sweetie. I love you."

"I know you do." Her words are distorted, muffled by his shirt. She eases out of his embrace, and pats his chest. "I need to get dinner together." She turns towards the kitchen, but he doesn't let go of her wrist.

She smiles, a full one this time, and then looks over her shoulder at the time on the microwave. "Pork chops tonight." She disentangles herself and heads to the kitchen. "Dinner will be ready in half an hour. In the meantime, why don't you flip through the albums and see what you can find?"

He pulls the worn albums towards him, and wipes the dust off of the covers. They don't lay flat, since some of the picture pockets are overburdened with duplicate photos. He chuckles, remembers Shayla's insistence on getting doubles of every roll.

"Who wants to go back with the negatives?" she'd say, when he complained that it was a waste of money. "If we got a good shot, then we have an extra, and if not, we'll toss them."

But the book is evidence that Shayla didn't thrown out any of the blurry, off-centered ones. At first he wonders why there are more doubles of bad ones than good, but after he thinks about it for a moment, he realizes that they're the leftovers, the ones she said she'd throw out.

As he flips the first page, the photos in one of the pockets begin to slide out, and he notices that the colors of the bottom photo are different than the one above. He pulls the hidden one out of the pocket. It's of Shayla, very pregnant and wearing his Gladen t-shirt, the word *university* stretched tight over her belly. On the back of the photo is scribbled, "Ask if I'm having twins at your own risk," the words Shayla said she thought should be on the only shirt that she could fit into.

He'd forgotten, and he laughs out loud. She'd been wearing that same shirt the day they decided what to name Gracie, he recalls now, and the memory comes flooding back.

* * *

Shayla had been sitting on their couch sideways, her legs crisscrossed and her large belly resting on top of them. "What about Faith?" she asked Tim, her nose buried deep in a book of baby names.

He was watching baseball, his mouth filled with potato chips. "Ummm… what about faith?" He dug into the bowl for another handful without taking his eyes off of the TV.

The Rangers made a double play, and he jumped to his feet. "Yes. *Yes.* That's how you turn two." He pumped his fist in the air, then walked to the kitchen to grab a Coke as the commercial began. He gulped down half a can, followed it with an extended burp, and then pointed to the chips. "Those are *salty*. Want some?"

She shook her head. "I'm reading." She held up the pastel pink and blue book so he could see the title: *Baby Names from A to Z.*

"Oh. Okay. Can we later? It's the bottom of the ninth." His eyes wandered back to the TV before she could answer. "No, no, no, no, no, no, NO," he yelled at the TV, as three easy outs were made. "It's over." He slammed his Coke down, spraying brown, bubbly droplets over the table, then looked sideways at her to see if she'd noticed him rubbing them into the table.

She didn't glance his way, underlined a section and dog-eared the page instead. "A napkin would be more effective."

He wiped his hands on his pants. "No need. Clean up complete." He threw his Coke bottle into the empty bowl, brought them to the kitchen and loaded the dishwasher. "Shay? I think I'm going to go to bed. You coming?"

"Sure you're not forgetting something?"

"What?"

She raised the book again, and waited for him to reappear. "I was wondering what you thought of the name Faith, remember?"

"Faith? Really?"

"You don't like it?"

He leaned against the doorframe. "Honestly, it makes me nervous. All those kinds of names do."

"All *what* kind of names?"

"The ones that mean something."

"They all mean something."

"You know what I'm talking about."

She smiled. "I'm just giving you a hard time. They're called virtue names."

"Exactly. Virtues. It's a risk. Because what if she—if it *is* a she—turns out to be the opposite? What if Faith turns out to be faithless?"

"So no Joy, no Hope, no Patience or Prudence?"

He smirked. "Do you really want Patience or Prudence?"

"No." She glanced at him, her eyes cautious. "But I really like Grace. Gracie, when she's little." She paused. "You know how sometimes a name that's great for an adult is too serious for a kid? Or one that's perfect for a kid is too cute for an adult? Grace works for both."

"My point still stands. What if she turns out to be really awkward?"

She rolled her eyes at him. "*God's grace*, Pastor Tim. Our baby is a blessing." She rubbed her distended belly. "But you're right, I hope she'll be graceful in the way you're talking about, too, that she'll be poised, elegant, kind—"

"Are you reading a list of synonyms?"

She laughed. "You got me. Also benevolent, dignified—"

Grace. That was the quality he'd sensed when he first saw Shayla freshman year. The subtle difference that he hadn't been able to define.

"—and even if the name *itself* isn't a virtue, its root usually is. So you're getting a virtue no matter what. You'd be surprised. Give me any name. I'll look it up."

"All right. Let's test your theory." He snatched the book out of her hands. "Hmmm… what name should we start with? Maybe… Shayla?"

She tried to grab the book back. "Wait, I haven't looked it up yet. I want to do it."

"How could you not have looked up your own name?"

"I don't want my choice for the baby to be swayed by what *my* name means."

"Sounds like you've decided on one already, so I think it's safe to check it out now." He scrolled down the page with his finger. "Let's see… Sharlene, Sharon, Shauna, *Shayla.*"

"Give it." She tried to swipe the book as he held it over her head, just out of reach.

"No way. You're the one who started this."

She sat down in defeat. "Fine, just tell me. I'm too huge to jump this much."

He scanned the book, then laughed and hid it behind his back. "I bet your parents didn't read a baby names book."

"Why? What does it mean?" She wrested the book away from him. "'From the fairy palace?'" She looked up at him, mouth open. "That can't be right. Most of the girl names mean beautiful, or loving, or even wise. How did I end up with 'from the fairy palace?'"

Tim stroked his chin as if in deep thought. "What were you saying before? Something about every name having a root with a virtue?"

"It's still true! Mine just happens to be one of the few exceptions to the rule."

"Seems to be."

She shook her head. "Just my luck. If it meant wise, or intelligent, I'd have a leg to stand on. But it's not that hard to dismiss the opinion of someone 'from a fairy palace,' is it?"

He mussed her hair, then hugged her as closely as he could, her protruding belly pushing them apart. "You don't have to sell it anymore. You're right. It's perfect."

She looked up, searched his face. "You're serious? What convinced you?"

An unexpected shyness came over him, and he was surprised to find that he couldn't share his memory of freshman year, that he couldn't share his innermost thoughts *about* her *with* her. "You made a very persuasive case." He rested his chin on her head. But I do have one question."

She stepped back, a wary expression on her face. "What's that?"

"What if it's a boy?"

She cupped her smaller left ear. "What did you say?"

"Funny."

"Huh? Speak up."

"Your mutant ear works fine. You heard what I said."

" 'Mutant' ear? Before we were married it was my 'special' ear."

"Shayla. Be realistic."

"It's going to be a girl. I'm sure of it."

"We need to pick boy names, too, just in case. Your maternal instinct still has a fifty percent chance of being wrong."

"*Fine.* My turn, then. How about we start with Timothy?" She grabbed the book and flipped to the boy's section. "Here it is: 'Timothy. Also from Greek, Timotheos. Meaning: Honoring God.' " She looked up, eyes wide. "Your calling is right there in your name. Just like our mailman!"

He rolled his eyes. "I'm pretty sure Roy *Letterman* has me beat." He held his hand out for the book again, leafed through pages. "It looks like lots of names relate to God in some way or another." He flipped back to the table of contents, and then held the book up for her to see. "Look. There's a whole chapter devoted to them."

"But *Timothy*... come on."

"You think Titus would have been a better choice? I can't see that going over well on the playground. My parents named me after my Grandpa."

"Your dad's dad? Or your mom's?"

"My dad's."

"But wasn't his name Lester?"

"Yeah. Lester Timothy Lundstrom," he said, with a triumphant raise of his eyebrows. "Wouldn't you go by Tim if your name was Lester Lundstrom? Look, we can pick a biblical name if you want, Shay. But not a common one like mine. I say if we go biblical, we go all out."

"As in?"

"What do you think about Job? No, wait—Judas. Judas Lundstrom. It's got a certain ring to it."

"Funny."

He grinned, then stood up and stretched. "I'm exhausted. I've got to go to bed. How about we work on boy names tomorrow?"

"Sure. No rush, anyway."

He waved her assurances away as he walked down the hall. "I know, I know. Your all-knowing maternal instinct."

* * *

Tim closes the albums and gives his cheek an absentminded scratch. Fourteen. There are only fourteen photos of Shayla altogether.

He sighs, thinks of how he used to tell her to put the camera down, to enjoy the moment instead of wasting time documenting it. It made sense then, back when he thought he had the luxury of time.

It's been a long time since he's let himself think about that day. *The* day. For years afterwards, every detail was seared into his memory. But over time, order eroded, as did words. The sounds have endured, though, have refused to degrade. The composed voice on the phone; the guttural screams of his mother-in-law, Lillian; the hushed questions of a bewildered five-year-old.

He closes his eyes, and allows the memory of the day that changed the trajectory of his life to come back. The day that he lost Shayla.

* * *

The other driver hadn't been drunk or on drugs, Tim was told. He hadn't fallen asleep at the wheel. He'd been driving with his wife and son when a white-tailed deer darted into the middle of the highway. He swerved to the left to avoid hitting it, veered onto the sandy inner shoulder, and then over-corrected to the right in panic. The car skidded and swung out from behind, and, for a split-second, was positioned perpendicular to the road. As the front tires dipped into the sunken, grassy median separating the eastbound and westbound lanes, it began to roll, and slammed into Shayla's car as she approached from the opposite direction. The man lost his son in the accident, leaving Tim with no one to blame and no one to hate.

He said goodbye in the hospital to a gray, waxen imitation of Shayla, stroked her hair and held her hand in his. Already it wasn't hers. How was it possible that this hand, this pallid, rigid hand, was the same one that had clasped his the night before as they slept? The same one that had tickled Gracie before school that morning?

He studied her features, tried to commit to memory the details that hadn't needed to be catalogued until now. Would he remember the freckles across the bridge of her nose? The chicken pox scar on her chin? The mole on her collarbone? All of the imperfections that made her *Shayla*, would they be lost to time?

He didn't want to stay. He didn't want to remember the overpowering smell of antiseptic and the sickening stillness of a body that no longer breathes. But he was unable to leave, rooted by the finality of death, by the knowledge that once he closed the door behind him, he would never see her again.

Eventually he forced himself to stand. He walked around to the other side of the table, leaned over, and kissed her left ear. Then he turned, and willed his feet to alternate, one foot in front of the other, one foot in front of the other, one foot in front of the other, until he passed through the doorway that separated his old life from his new.

John made the funeral decisions alone. As senior pastor, he handled the church's bereavement services rather than Tim. Decades of pastoring had made him familiar with the burial process, and he handled Shayla's in an orderly, efficient manner. Not once did he ask for an opinion.

Tim's parents flew in and stayed for a week, his mother occupying her time cooking, cleaning, and caring for Gracie; his father doing not much of anything at all, as far as Tim could see, except reading the paper and calling the office every couple of days.

"You have the right to have your voice be heard, son," his father said, after two days of watching John make choice after choice without asking for Tim's opinion. It hadn't occurred to him, until then, that he should be angry with John. The truth was that he was grateful. The selection of the casket and cemetery, the details of the visitation, funeral, and gathering—none of it mattered.

Escape. He could do it, when he concentrated hard enough. The first step was to pick a focal point, whether it be the crease on a shirt, the crumbs on a plate, the design on a doormat. The only rule was that it be inanimate. He'd examine the object from every angle; classify its planes, textures, and hues. Light was next—how did the sun alter its colors? What about lamps? Shadows? He'd chant its name in his head as he studied it, combine rhythm and pitch, until all the voices in the room melded into white noise, and all the hushed whispers, sobs, and questions were indistinguishable.

She's in a better place now, he was told, over and over, at the visitation and the gathering. It was meant to bring him comfort, but it didn't. It made him feel guilty. He wanted Shayla here, in Loring Point, with him and with Gracie. Where she belonged. Had he been able to, he would have ripped her down from heaven without a second thought. And what kind of pastor, what kind of husband, would wish to deny his wife a place in the Kingdom of God?

He found himself tallying platitudes in his head to pass the time until he could stop smiling and thanking people for coming. God must have needed a special angel, friends and relatives offered, but he couldn't fathom why a benevolent God, *his* God, would have taken Shayla. *He is omnipotent, He created the earth and the heavens. What could He need her for that He couldn't do Himself?*

Towards the end of the gathering, he noticed Janice Cullum, a Sunday school teacher, walking towards him. He braced himself. Janice had lost her daughter, Amber, to cancer close to a year ago. She'd been seven.

It was terrible of him, he knew, but he didn't want to bond over tragedy. He didn't want to hear her say, "I know just how you feel." There was no space within him to consider anyone else's pain. *Be polite. She's only trying to help.*

There was a faint tremble in her lips as she spoke. "I'm so very sorry, Pastor Tim. I can't imagine what you're feeling right now."

He looked at her, confused.

"With Amber," she said, and her voice broke. She dabbed at the corners of her eyes with a tissue, before clearing her throat and trying again. "With Amber, there was time to say goodbye." She took a breath in and reached for his hand. "On bad days I try to remember that God has a plan for all of us, one more intricate than we can understand. And that when I see her again, the reason will be made clear to me, and I will finally understand why it had to be this way."

CHAPTER 9

*T*aylor, *Eleanor K.*

The name, listed just above the accession number on the upper left-hand corner of the pathology report, doesn't catch Josephine's attention at first. She's more interested in the name of the resident who has prepared it: Allison Jacobs, a timid first year. *Motion. When I think of Allison, I think of constant, excess motion.*

She wonders if Allison is aware of how pronounced her behaviors are, or if she's aware of them at all. But how can she not be? During morning conference last Wednesday she drummed the lid of her coffee cup so hard that she knocked it out of her own hand. Whenever she's at the microscope, her leg jiggles up and down the entire time. How can she concentrate that way? How can she maintain any sort of visual focus when she's moving nonstop? Her nails are bitten to the quick, and Josephine can hear her picking at her cuticles under the desk when they meet to sign out cases.

Josephine looks forward to July every year, when a fresh batch of interns begins their residencies, and training in the grossing room begins. It's rare that she has the chance to gross in anymore, and there's something satisfying about starting at square one and seeing a case through from beginning to end.

She'd taught the third week, demonstrating how to examine a kidney with the naked eye, cut proper specimens from it, then prep the tissue in cassettes and formalin for the histotechs to process into slides. Preparing tissue requires precision, and she was concerned that Allison's first experience cutting in would end with her harming the specimens, herself, or both.

Because of Allison's constant jitters, Josephine had to be more vigilant than usual about safety precautions in the grossing room. Disposable gowns and double gloves were already standard practice. But most staff chose not to use cut-resistant gloves, layering the latex ones instead, because the chain mail mesh made it difficult to manipulate the tissue. Since she didn't want to single Allison out, she decided to require all interns reporting to her to wear a cut-resistant glove on their stabilizing hand.

Safety glasses were her next concern. Nobody wore them, unless the specimen had the potential to spray. The room was well ventilated, so there wasn't a need to worry about irritation from fumes. But if anyone was to splash an eye with formalin or fluid from a punctured cyst, it was Allison. So she made glasses mandatory as well.

To her great relief, Allison proved herself to be competent when cutting. Not efficient, perhaps, but *steady*, a far more important skill. Efficiency would come with time. At first Josephine wondered how her initial assessment could have been so far off, but Allison's modest smile afterwards had shown that even she'd been surprised by her performance.

This past week, Allison had started asking questions when they reviewed slides together, rather than nodding, wordless, as they sat across from each other at the double-headed microscope. Her shaky voice began to even out, her jitters began to subside, and her eyes no longer darted around the room. Josephine had even heard her humming as she studied at the scope, and knew, then, that she was hooked.

Josephine knows that feeling well, is still awed and inspired by how much there is to learn. She remembers her first year of residency, how exhausted and miserable she was in general surgery. The only bright spots in her week were the few times that she was able to make it down to path to check in on patients' results.

"Why do you want to give up surgery to go sit in a lab all day?" her boyfriend had asked when she confided in him. Evan's implication was clear: pathology is dull, low-status work for doctors who aren't tough enough to handle *real* medicine. But she found it to be far more intriguing than surgery. How could it be considered boring when there were so many patterns to hunt for, so many clues that had to be synthesized in order to come to the correct diagnosis?

She'd dropped the subject for another month, too daunted by the prospect of orchestrating a switch in residency to even discuss it. Risking a repeat of her intern year was hard to even entertain as a possibility, but the idea of a career in surgery made her feel desperate. When she did bring the subject up again, Evan looked confused. "I don't get it. You have good social skills. It's not like you don't know how to interact with patients."

She smiles as she remembers his words, grateful that she'd trusted herself. Over the years she's learned that his perception of pathology couldn't have been farther from the truth. She discusses interesting cases every day with colleagues, interacts with physicians across all specialties, advises surgeons during intraoperative consults, and teaches residents. Truth be told, she doesn't miss patient care at all. No more demands for antibiotics for viral infections or for immediate cures to vague symptoms. No more noncompliant patients refusing to take medications as prescribed.

She doesn't mind being invisible to patients, because even though she's behind the scenes, she's critical to their care. Without her, the oncologist can't determine the course of treatment and the surgeon doesn't know if there's more cancer to be removed. True, she doesn't receive the glory that either of them does, but on the flip side, she never has to tell a patient that he's going to die.

She looks at the slides that Allison has left on her desk. It's standard for path assistants to take care of specimens as small as this, but in the beginning there's learning at every level. It's a straightforward case, a ruling out of esophagitis. She slips the first slide of biopsied tissue under the microscope, and then reads Allison's analysis: "Mildly inflamed squamo-glandular junction mucosa with changes most consistent with GERD (up to 6 eosinophils/high power field). Negative for intestinal metaplasia."

This is good news. Allison's diagnosis is correct, and now she has the chance to bolster the girl's confidence when they review the slides together at sign out. But the news is even better for the patient—a treatable diagnosis of reflux and no precancerous lesions. Excellent news for—who is it, again? She checks the report. Eleanor Taylor.

This time the name stops her. There's a vague familiarity to it. She knows three Taylors—Ron Taylor, a med school professor; Tracy Taylor, a friend from junior high; and Andrea Taylor, a friend of Amanda's. But not one Eleanor.

She turns to her computer, enters her name and password on the hospital's home page, and then the medical record number. She feels guilty, trolling for more information this way, since Allison has already opened the woman's records to check for previous biopsies. There's no reason to access information at this point other than to satisfy her curiosity. *But I'm only looking at public info. Nothing wrong with that.* She presses enter, and reads the identifying information that pops up on the screen.

Name:	**Taylor, Eleanor K.**
DOB:	**02/24/1951**
Street address:	**37 Plainview Street**
City/State:	**Hinchfield, TX**

Hinchfield. For some reason that rings a bell. Maybe she knows of this mystery patient through her mother? They're only a couple years apart in age.

She leans back in her chair, and looks up at the ceiling, thinking. Hinchfield is about twenty minutes away from Loring Point. Who might her mom know from Hinchfield? She tries to think of a way that she could ask her mom without divulging patient confidentiality, and then memory bursts through the fog and she knows. She doesn't know an Eleanor Taylor.

But she does know a Nell.

* * *

Josephine slumped down in the passenger's seat of her mother's car. *Only one more year until I get my license. Then I'll get to do the pizza runs by myself.* She glanced over at her mother, who was reapplying her lipstick in the rearview mirror.

"Why do I have to go?"

"Josephine. *What* is the problem? We'll be done eating before your show even comes on."

"What show?"

Her mother blotted her lipstick with a tissue, then placed it in the ashtray and backed out of the driveway. "Isn't *Growing Up* on tonight?"

"It's *Growing Pains*, Mom. And I don't even watch that show anymore."

"I wanna s-see it," said Amanda, from the back seat.

Ellen looked in the rearview mirror. "It's on too late for you, sweetie."

Josephine slid down in her seat further, until the seatbelt tugged at her neck. "Why can't I stay home? I'll even watch Amanda."

"You know why." Ellen pointed her thumb towards the backseat.

"Because I want gumballs!" Amanda chimed in. "Can I get three, Mommy? Please?"

Ellen gave Josephine a look that said *I told you so*. "Two, Amanda. But you have to promise not to swallow them this time."

Josephine crossed her arms. *A million places to get pizza, and we have to go to Carmine's, where all the seniors hang out, just because of a stupid gumball machine. It's so embarrassing.* "Fine, take Amanda. But I can stay home by myself."

"You said you need a new backpack for camp. Target's right next door. We'll grab one on the way out."

"It's not *camp*, Mom. I'm not a kid anymore. I'm going to be a CIT."

Ellen glanced at her, an irritated expression on her face. "Last time I checked, counselors-in-training work at camps. Now stop being such a pain."

Josephine turned as much as her seatbelt would allow and looked out the window. "Can I at least go to Target *while* you get the pizza?" *That way no one will see me.*

"Look!" said Ellen, pointing to Tim's open garage door rather than answering. "They must be home. This'll just take a minute," she said, as she pulled into the driveway.

"But Mom, I—"

"Oh, for heaven's sake, Josephine. The man lost his wife last month! Save whatever excuse is about to come out of your mouth, because we *are* stopping." She ran up the steps, then called over her shoulder, "Roll the window down for Amanda, too."

Josephine watched her mother pat her hair into place as she rang the bell, then take a step backwards as the door opened. "Tim! I'm so glad I caught you at home. Is this a bad time?"

"No, not at all. Just finished dinner." He looked out at the car and waved. "Want to come in?"

"Oh, no, no, no. We're on our way out." She paused for a moment. "I wanted to stop by because of the park play dates. Josephine tells me that Gracie hasn't been home to join."

"Park play dates?"

"Yes. Didn't Shayla tell you... ?" Ellen searched his face for recognition, then gestured towards Josephine. "Josephine watches Amanda for a couple of hours after school, until I get home. She takes Amanda to the park, and Shayla and Gracie used to join them most days." She turns to the car. "Josephine, what time have you been stopping by?"

"Three, three-fifteen. Same as always."

Ellen pivots back towards to Tim. "I don't know what Gracie's schedule is now, but I was hoping I could help out in some way. That Josephine could, I suppose. She'd be happy to take Gracie with her."

Josephine sat straight up. *What? It's bad enough that I have to watch Amanda. Now I have to watch Gracie, too?*

Shayla had made the time go faster, had helped her try to figure out her problems, like why Hillary Jenkins started sitting next to Jamie Wyatt in study hall instead of her, and why Mike Sullivan would be really nice to her one day and then ignore her the next. Shayla took care of runny noses, and even let her go home to watch TV sometimes.

"That's a really nice offer, Ellen, thank you. It does ring a bell now, the park play dates, but with everything, I... " He looked down, and swallowed hard before continuing. "Anyway. I signed Gracie up to stay later at school, but I still need to pick her up. And once she sees me, she gets clingy. Lillian's been meeting me back at church, but once Gracie sees me, it's all over."

"Lillian can't pick Gracie up?"

He shrugged. "She's afraid of driving on the highway. She was scared even... *before*. She offered, but I know how nervous it makes her."

"I see."

Josephine slumped further down in her seat. Why was her mother still standing on the doorstep? *He said no, didn't he?*

Ellen tilted her head to the side. "Gracie goes to Little Learners, doesn't she?"

"Yeah."

"Who's her teacher?"

"Miss Taylor."

"Miss Taylor! She's *wonderful*. She had Josephine in her class, and then Amanda for one year, before we decided to switch preschools. Amanda needs a little extra help, so she goes to Palmer now. Miss Taylor was so supportive."

Josephine rolled her eyes. *A little extra help.*

"I'm sure Miss Taylor wouldn't mind driving Gracie home. She could drop her off at my house, and then Josephine could take her to the park with Amanda. That will give you close to a full day's work, and you won't even have to pay for extended day."

He smiled. "Again, I appreciate the offer, but I don't feel comfortable asking her. I don't want to put her on the spot."

"Then I will, if it's okay with you." She jumped in as he hesitated, cutting off any more objections. "Perfect! It's settled, then. Say hi to Gracie for us," she said, as she turned to leave.

"Ellen? Where does Miss Taylor live?"

"Hmmm?" She stopped, but didn't turn to face him.

"Where does she live? I don't want her driving too far out of her way. Assuming she says yes."

Josephine watched as a polished smile appeared on her mother's face—the just-for-company smile—before she turned and looked back over her shoulder. "Don't worry. She's close by. Right in Loring Point."

"Really? What street?"

"You know, I can't remember. I'll confirm when I call her tonight." She waved, and as she turned back towards the car again, Josephine saw her smile disappear.

I love how Mom's way of helping out is making me babysit, thought Josephine, as she flipped through the pages of *The Great Gatsby* at the playground two weeks later. She glanced up, and located Gracie and Amanda at the swings. Gracie was trying to coordinate pushing Amanda from behind without getting knocked over on the swing's return. *If they keep each other busy, I can probably get through a chapter or two.*

"Josephine! *Josephine!*"

She turned her head to see Tim walking towards the playground from the parking lot. He gave an abbreviated wave as he struggled to keep the stuffed grocery bag he was carrying from tipping.

She placed her book page side down on the bench. "You're early. It's only three forty-five."

"I know. Where is she?" He walked past her until he reached the chain link fence, shaded his eyes from the glare while scanning the playground for Gracie.

"They're over there." He turned to face her, and she pointed to the swings.

She watched him follow her point until he located Gracie, and then take a deep breath, as if coming up for air from underwater. He stepped backwards towards the bench, eyes still trained on Gracie, and then sat down next to Josephine, a peculiar expression on his face.

What's he so nervous about? Or mad, maybe? Is he mad at me? She jumped up from the bench. The last thing she needed was for him to tell her mother that she wasn't paying attention. "I'll go help them. I'm sorry, I just have a lot of homework today, and I was trying to—"

"Don't worry, sit back down. I just—I needed to see Gracie." He placed the grocery bag in between them, and chuckled as he watched Gracie narrowly escape being hit by the swing. He glanced at the book. "What do you think of *Gatsby*, old sport?"

"You've read it?"

"Of course. I went to high school, too, you know."

"Oh. I didn't know they were teaching it back then."

"*Back then?* How old do you think I am?"

"I don't know… thirty-five?"

"Ouch. Twenty-eight. Although I guess that seems pretty old to you, too, right?"

"No," she lied. She shifted, felt the metal ridges in the bench digging into the back of her thighs. Was it because he was the pastor that she'd assumed he was older than Shayla?

He dug through the bag. "I've got some great stuff in here. Brownies, chocolate chip cookies, you name it, it's in here. Bake sale leftovers. Want something?"

"No thanks."

"Come on! Look how much is in here." He lifted the bag and pretended to fall under its weight.

"Any of Mrs. Hill's brownies in there?" she asked, with a cautious smile.

"You're in luck today. She made a special batch for Gracie."

"Oh, forget it then. I'll have something else if they're for Gracie." But Tim was already rifling through the bag, tin foil crunching as he searched.

"A-ha!" He passed her one, then chose a larger one for himself. He took a huge bite, and then a second before swallowing the first. "This is why I'm here early."

She looked at him, confused. "To give Gracie a brownie?

He shook his head and pointed to the bag. I wanted to give the rest of the goodies to Nell. Just to say thanks for carting Gracie around these past couple of weeks."

"Nell?"

"Doesn't she go by that? I know it's her nickname, but I can't remember what it's short for. It's not Ellen, I would remember that, obviously. Elena, maybe? Helen?" He looked at her with an expectant expression.

Who is he talking about? "Uh… I don't think I know—"

"Miss Taylor," he interrupted, smiling. "Teachers have first names, you know."

She felt her cheeks warm. She'd never heard Miss Taylor's first name before, had never been curious as to what it was. "But she drops Gracie off at my house. She doesn't come here with us."

"Right. I went to your house around three o'clock. I was going to leave them with you before Nell—Miss Taylor, I mean—dropped Gracie off. I had an open slot in my day, so I thought I'd run them over to you and then and head back to church. But no one was there."

"So why did you come here if you knew that Miss Taylor *wouldn't* be here?"

"I came to find Gracie. And to talk to you."

"Me?"

He nodded. "Since no one was at your house, I figured that Miss Taylor had dropped Gracie off earlier than usual, and that you'd already left for the park. So I drove to her house on the way back to church to drop off the treats. But the house I went to wasn't her house."

"What do you mean?"

"Your mom told me that Miss Taylor lives on Pemberton Road. In Loring Point. Does that sound right?"

"Loring Point? Mom told me that Miss Taylor lives all the way out in Hinchfield, and that if there was ever a problem I should call *her* at work, not Miss Taylor, because she could get back quicker." She thought for a moment. "But you know what's weird? I thought I heard her say Loring Point at your house, but she told me later I must've heard her wrong."

He pulled a scrap of paper from his pocket. "So she doesn't live at Forty-Three Pemberton Road?"

"Uh-uh. But that sounds familiar."

"It said 'Henderson' on the mailbox."

Josephine frowned. "That's Natalie's house."

"Natalie?"

"She's a junior. She pretends she doesn't know me in the hallway," she said, rolling her eyes. "Her mom Paula and my mom are friends. I guess my mom got mixed up."

"Huh," he said, mulling something over that Josephine couldn't discern. "Are they close friends?"

"Really close."

A smile crept across his face. "Huh," he repeated.

What? Why is he suddenly acting like everything makes sense? She was still confused, and it irritated her that he'd figured things out before she had. She felt a pang of empathy for her sister. *This must be how Amanda feels all the time.*

"Can I borrow a pen?" he asked, holding his hand out. He flipped the paper over and laid it flat on his leg instead of the ridged bench seat. He scribbled a note and handed it to her, folded. "Can you give this to your mom for me?"

She nodded, too embarrassed to ask for an explanation.

"Thanks." He stood and picked up the bag. "I'm going to head back. Want a ride?"

She shook her head. "Amanda won't want to go yet."

He stood, cupped his hands over his mouth as he called to Gracie in a singsong voice. "Gra-cie. Time to go-o."

"Daddy!" Gracie squealed, just noticing him. She and Amanda had switched positions, and she was now on the swing. She jumped off as it hit its peak, pitched forward as she landed, but managed to catch her balance. She jumped into his arms. "Daddy, guess what Miss Taylor brought to school today?"

"What?"

"A hamster! We have to come up with names tonight and tomorrow we'll decide what to name her. I want to name her Silky, because her fur is really soft, but Ryan M. says we can't because that's not really a name, not like Gracie or Ryan, and I said that it doesn't matter, because she's a hamster not a person, and he said how do you know it's a she? Silky's a girl's name and what if it's a boy? And I said Silky could be a boy's name, boy hamsters are soft, too, and then Miss Taylor said—"

"Gracie," he interrupted, kissing her on the cheek, "you can tell me all about it in the car. But now it's time to say goodbye to Amanda and Josephine." He picked up her backpack, which had been propped up against the chain link fence, and slung it over his shoulder, holding the bag in his left hand and Gracie's hand in his right.

"Bye, Josephine," Gracie said, as he lead her away. She let go of her father's hand after several steps, and ran back towards the playground. "Bye, Amanda!" She turned again and ran to catch up with Tim.

Josephine used Tim's note as a bookmark, then shoved the book inside her backpack. She straightened her shorts, which had ridden up while she was sitting, and walked towards Amanda.

"I'm tired," Amanda said, when Josephine reached her. She was sitting on the ground, in the shade next to the swing. "Can we go home now?"

"Now? Because I just told Gracie's dad that—"

Amanda held her hand out, waited for Josephine to pull her to her feet, and then brushed mulch off of the back of her shorts. "I'm thirsty. I want apple juice."

"I've got some water. Is that good enough?" She pulled a water bottle from the side pocket of her backpack, unscrewed the top, and handed it to Amanda. She chose to wait rather than walk towards the gate, knew that her sister wouldn't be able to walk and drink at the same time. Amanda spilled onto her shirt after the first gulp, and started to cough. Josephine hit her on the back and then held the water bottle for her, controlling the speed and the angle of the flow. "All set?" she asked, when Amanda pushed it away.

Amanda nodded, wiped her mouth with the back of her hand. "Wait! I have to go on the twisty slide one last time."

Josephine sighed. "Go. *Hurry.*" She took her book back out, knowing that what would take Gracie one minute would take Amanda five. Everything with Amanda was so *slow.* It was too frustrating to watch sometimes.

She fingered the scrap of paper as she opened the book, considered reading it. What had he figured out that she hadn't? *He never said it was private. He would have told me if he didn't want me to look at it.* She pulled at the perforation on the edge of the paper, debating. Then she opened the note, and read:

Ellen,

I tried to drop some bake sale leftovers at Nell's today. Just wanted to give her a very small thank you for all of her help. What a coincidence that she lives with your friend Paula! Small world.

THANK YOU.

Tim

CHAPTER 10

Tim is sitting uncomfortably on John and Lillian's couch, and the crocheted sofa shawl is to blame.

It's positioned as a diamond, with the top half hanging behind the couch and the bottom half draped over most of the center cushion in a v-shape. When John led him into the living room, Tim hesitated before sitting. Should he move it out of the way? It didn't look like a blanket that could be tossed aside. Lillian had made several blankets for Gracie when she was little, but those were woven out of a soft, heavy yarn. He doesn't know the name of the material used to make the shawl, but it's glossy and fragile. Assuming Lillian made it, it would be disrespectful to sit on it, wouldn't it? And so he finds himself perched on the forward corner of the cushion, fighting the backwards slope of the couch in order to avoid touching the shawl with his back.

Lillian joins them in the living room with a pitcher of sweet tea. She takes the glasses off the tray and sets them on coasters. "Tim?" she asks, as the pitcher hovers over his glass.

"Please." He forgot how much he loves Lillian's tea, he realizes, as he takes a drink. Hers is always flavored, sometimes lemon, sometimes mint. Today it's a berry of some sort. Raspberry, maybe?

"Delicious, Lillian, thank you. Shayla and I could never get it quite right. Even with your recipe."

She looks offended. "Shayla was an excellent cook."

No, she wasn't. Shayla didn't like cooking or crocheting. The only time she cooked fancy meals was on the rare occasion that they hosted Monday dinner. "That's not what I meant. I—"

"We know," John says, as he pats Lillian on the knee. "Gracie's wedding is… stirring up memories for us."

"For me, too." Tim hands them a manila envelope that he's brought with him. "I've been putting together a slideshow for the wedding, and I found some photos that I thought had been lost. I thought you might like them. The top one's my favorite."

Gracie is a toddler in the photo. Her arms are outstretched for balance, and Shayla is crouching behind her, supporting her waist.

There's an audible, sharp intake of breath from Lillian. "I remember this day. This was the day Gracie learned to walk."

"Really?" Tim asks, surprised. "You were there?"

She nods. "This was at the old house. The backyard."

"So you took the picture? I assumed that I did, that Shayla and I took Gracie to a park."

She points to the bottom right corner of the photo. There's a row of alternating pink, orange, and white flowers, all scorched. Behind them is a fence, painted in the exact shade of green as the leaves. "That's my garden. I planted impatiens that year. I don't know what I was thinking, planting them in full sun like that. The saleswoman told me not to when I bought them, said they needed shade, but I thought they'd be fine if I gave them enough love and attention. I got overconfident, since my zinnia and lantana had always turned out so well."

She passes the photo to John. "Remember the green fence? I wanted to paint it orange to match, but you talked me out of it."

"One of the very few times my decorating advice has had any value." He traces the lock of hair that the wind is blowing across Shayla's cheek with his finger as if to smooth it into place.

John places the photo on the coffee table, and the three of them stare at it, wordless. It's Tim who finally breaks the silence. "This one will be in the slideshow. I didn't think surprising you at the wedding would be fair."

John looks at him with approval. "Appreciate it, Tim." He pauses. "And I'm glad you'll be recognizing Shayla at the wedding. That's why we wanted you to come by. Lillian and I were … concerned that Shayla wouldn't be mentioned." He clears his throat, and then coughs into his closed fist. "I know it would have been a wonderful day for her."

"Of course she'll be included," Tim says, taken aback. How can they think so little of him? "I loved Shayla. Her death was my loss, too."

"Yes," John says. "But a child can never be replaced."

Resentment pulses through Tim's body, replaces his surprise. Why? Why have they always discounted his grief?

What did you expect? he wants to yell. *That I wouldn't crave love or companionship ever again? That I'd be celibate for the rest of my life?*

John places the photo in his lap and guards it with one hand while he pushes his iced tea to the other side of the table. He cradles the photo, strokes its edges, and despite himself, Tim sees his point of view. What if Gracie were to meet the same senseless fate as Shayla? He'd like to think that he'd still consider Keith family. But how would he feel if Keith remarried soon afterwards, just as he did? Who is Keith to him, after all?

"Are you done?" asks Lillian, holding her hand out for Tim's glass. She doesn't ask him if he'd like a refill, doesn't ask if he'd like a bite to eat. Instead, she loads the tray and returns to the kitchen. He hears the clinking of glasses being loaded into the dishwasher, the refrigerator open and close. She'd like him to leave, now that her fears have been put to rest. But he can't forget the reason he's come.

He looks at John, who's still holding the photo. "I'd like to ask you a favor. I wanted to know if … if for some reason, I couldn't lead the ceremony, would you be able to?"

John looks confused. "What reason could there possibly be?"

"I just want to make sure all bases are covered. Always good to be prepared."

"There's nothing that would've kept me from Shayla's wedding, or will from Gracie's."

Tim can feel his jaw clenching. *You conceited, self-righteous old man. Don't you dare imply that your love for Gracie is stronger than mine.* "God leads us down unexpected paths sometimes, John. I don't need to tell you that. Forget I asked." He nods his head in goodbye, and turns to leave.

"Tim, wait." John reaches out for a handshake. "It would be an honor."

* * *

Shayla had been gone for two months, and despite the stress and sleeplessness, Tim was stable. Not one aura. But the question wasn't *whether* they'd come back; it was *when*. And what would he do then, without Shayla's help? He wouldn't be able to drive Gracie to her summer session at preschool, and he wouldn't be able to care for her at home. He'd need to sleep. But how would he be able to, knowing she was downstairs, unattended?

He tried not to think about Sundays, either. What if it were to happen then, when a whole congregation was depending on him? God had blessed him so far, but he couldn't continue to be so reckless. *I can't put it off any longer. Risking a seizure in front of the entire church? In front of Gracie, when she needs to see me at my strongest?*

John was the answer, of course. With his father-in-law's help, he'd be covered in case he wasn't able to deliver the sermon, and Gracie would be safe with Lillian. He bet that she'd help out on weekday, too, if he needed it, once John was on board. *Today, after services. I'll tell him today.*

He shifted his weight on the pew, already uncomfortable. He'd taken a seat in the back this week. Sticking to the front row meant that he'd be seated next to the same observant members every week, and it was his job to look after all of his brothers and sisters, not just a select few.

"A shepherd must be among his flock," John had told him time and time again, and while he agreed, it bothered him that John never took his own advice. It had taken a couple years' worth of pressure from Shayla and the board to get him to share the pulpit. *And even on my one Sunday a month, he doesn't leave the chancel. Apparently his advice only applies to associate pastors.*

He scanned the front row until he found Gracie. Lillian was braiding her hair, pushing the roots down with one hand while combing with the other, so as not to hurt her. He smiled as she secured the braid with a violet polka-dotted elastic bow, and then pulled Gracie onto her lap. *Staying here was the right decision.*

He'd wanted to move back home. It would have been easier to rely on his parents' help than his in-laws'. But he had to think of Gracie, and the truth was that she didn't know his parents very well. They came to visit every January, but the cost of plane tickets was too high for them to come more than once a year. Gracie had only been to Oregon twice. As tempting as it was, he couldn't take John and Lillian away from her after she'd lost her mother. She needed stability, not change.

The commotion began halfway through the service, while the choir was singing his favorite hymn, "Rejoice, the Lord is King." He didn't notice until the choir quieted for the instrumental, and then he heard the scurrying of feet a row behind him. Turning, he saw the hunched backs of several people kneeling in a circle, and within it, a boy of eight or nine, convulsing.

The boy had been lain down and turned onto his side. The boy's father, who Tim could only see from behind, was repositioning him so his head didn't hit the base of the pew. The boy's mother had taken off her sweater, folded it, and placed it under his head as a pillow. His arms and legs were extending and retracting in a mechanical rhythm, and drool was running down his left cheek.

"You're okay, honey, you're okay," his mother whispered, and then, as he stilled, he began to breathe deeply, ragged snores in, gusts of air out. "It's almost over."

He couldn't gauge how long it took until the boy began to try to sit up, his eyes blank and unfocused. The choir had just begun to start up again, but that couldn't be, could it? Only a minute or two had passed?

The boy's father wiped the spit from his face, and then picked him up and carried him out of the sanctuary. As he glanced back at his wife, Tim caught a glimpse of him in profile. It was Jeff Hannaford, from Bible study group. The boy must be Josh, then.

Several people rushed to open the doors for them, relieved to have found some way to help, but besides those few, no one seemed to have noticed. Josh's collapse had been blocked by the rows of people standing in front of him, and his tortured breathing had been drowned out by the choir.

So this is what it looks like. He'd never seen someone have a seizure before, and he was surprised by the panic that had shot up within him. The drumming of his heart filled his ears, blocked out all other sounds, and the acrid stench of his sweat wafted out from under his arms.

He motioned for people to return to their seats, and rushed after Jeff and his wife. They'd turned to the right, and had found their way into the conference room, the farthest one from the sanctuary.

"He's coming out of it," explained Jeff, when Tim caught up to them. Josh was marching from one end of the room to the other, frantic and purposeless. He was crying, and his mother—Alicia, Tim now remembered—was shadowing him, guarding against another fall. "He's going to walk around like that for a couple of minutes, and then he's going to get real sleepy. We'll get him in the car then."

"Of course. So you don't want me to call 9-1-1?" he asked, even though he knew there was no emergency. Josh's breathing had regulated, and Jeff and Alicia's rehearsed actions proved that this seizure wasn't their son's first.

"There's no need. Josh has epilepsy. We're trying a new medication, so he's at higher risk right now. Night time's been the problem, though, so we thought he'd be okay to come." He stopped, then smoothed his tie and offered an awkward smile. "I know that it looks scary. Sorry for putting you through this."

"Please, don't apologize." *I understand, more than you can imagine. I know exactly what Josh is feeling right now.* The forced surrender to blackness; the flashes of consciousness that burst through the darkness and then disappear; the confusion, the swirling emotions; the exhaustion; the unbearable headache afterwards. But he can't say this, because he must tell John and Lillian first.

Josh circled the table, his steps slowing. "No, nooo …" he said, and then he slumped against Alicia, his weight knocking her to the ground.

She positioned his head in her lap, and rubbed his forehead. "It's okay, Josh. You're safe." She turned towards Jeff and nodded her head. Sleep would come soon.

"Can I pull your car around? What can I do?" asked Tim.

"We're fine now. But thanks," Jeff said. He knelt next to Josh, assessed how to best pick him up.

"Come get me if you need me for any reason," Tim said, as he reached for the door. "I'll be in the last row." He began to pull the door closed behind him, and then poked his head back in. "I'll have Pastor Harlow check in with you later in the day."

Jeff glanced at Alicia, whose eyes had hardened. "Not necessary. Please tell him not to bother."

"It's no bother. Pastor Harlow will always make himself available to families in times of need."

Alicia jumped in before Jeff could reply. "Thank you for the offer, Pastor Tim, but we're not concerned about inconveniencing him. We don't *want* him to contact us."

Josh turned to his side, moaned as he swiped at his forehead. "Mom?" he said, his voice thick with sleep.

Tears began to flow down her face. He was back. "I'm here, honey. Just rest."

Tim tried to push Alicia's unsettling words out of his mind as he knocked on the half-open door to John's office after the service. The church had emptied over the course of the past half hour, with the exception of a few stragglers chatting outside. Lillian had taken Gracie back to her house for lunch, to give John and Tim time to discuss how the day's message had been received and to prepare for the upcoming week.

John glanced up from a large stack of papers and waved Tim in with one hand while scribbling notes with his other. There was just one other chair in his office, placed opposite his desk, giving Tim no choice but to stare at the framed photos of Shayla resting on top of it while he sat and waited. Two of the photos were of her as a young girl, recognizable only because of her blond hair and wide-set eyes. These were the safe ones. He'd never known that girl. But the one to the right of them was dangerous. He had to be vigilant; if he let his eyes wander he'd see the one in the silver frame that stuck out among the wooden ones. The one engraved with the caption "my first birthday" and the date.

"It's comforting, isn't it? Having her close by?" John put his pen down and repositioned the base of the silver frame so that it was angled more towards Tim.

No. It's agonizing. His fingers itched to put the frame face down on the desk, to cover the image of Shayla feeding Gracie her first bite of cake. "Actually, it's hard for me," he said, as he pinched the flesh of his left palm with his right fingers. The physical pain was merciful, a salve.

"I see. Well, we all grieve differently, don't we? Both of our reactions, while quite different, are very common and to be expected as we move through—"

He tuned John out, focused instead on fine-tuning the pressure of the pinch. Too hard, and he wouldn't be able to sustain it long enough to feel numbness radiate through his fingers and forearm; too soft, and John's words would break the barrier, demand consideration and response.

"—don't you think?" John asked, an expectant look on his face.

"Yes, absolutely." He snapped to attention, felt warmth return to his hand as he released the pinch. *Focus. You can't let yourself be sidelined by a photo. Remember why you're here.* "Did you hear about Josh Hannaford?"

John paused, and Tim couldn't tell if it was out of surprise or concern. "Yes," he said, the lines in his forehead deepening. "I'll call Jeff and Alicia later today to see how we can be of help, but I doubt they'll be receptive." He sighed. "So. Let's get started." He took his weekly planner out of his desk drawer. "On Tuesday I'll be—"

"I didn't know that Josh has epilepsy." Tim could tell by John's expression that he was annoyed by the interruption, but there was no other choice. He couldn't let this opportunity slip away. Josh's seizure couldn't be a coincidence. To be offered the perfect segue on this day, of all days? It didn't make sense, that God would choose to help one of His children by hurting another, but his job was to follow the Lord's plan, not to question it. God's words to Isaiah flashed through his mind: "For my thoughts are not your thoughts, neither are your ways my ways. As the heavens are higher than the earth, so are my ways higher than your ways and my thoughts than your thoughts."

John nodded. "They've known for several years now."

"Jeff never told me."

"They're a very private family. And Josh had been doing well until recently."

"How did you find out?"

John folded his hands on top of his planner and looked Tim squarely in the eye. "Haven't you noticed that Jeff hasn't been to Bible study since the end of February? He'd been coming regularly for years."

"Yeah, I did, but you said that he'd started coming to your prayer group. I figured he didn't have time for both."

"Didn't you wonder why he switched?"

Enough with the teaching moment. Just tell me already. "I assumed he wanted to support a friend who was in crisis, or that he wanted to serve the church."

John frowned. "As pastors, we must avoid assumptions. Often they lead us to incorrect conclusions, as you've discovered." He paused to let his lesson sink in. "I called Jeff right after Easter, because I was surprised that he hadn't come to any of the services. Not like him at all. He confided in me, and so I invited him to prayer group."

Tim struggled for words. "I don't know what to say. I should've noticed. Especially since this happened before Shayla … "

Died. Died was the word, and he still couldn't bring himself to say it. The problem was that there was no better one. "Passed away," "moved on," "departed"—he'd heard these substitutes countless times, had even used them with Gracie, but she was still a child. He hated them, the removed niceties that glossed over his pain.

John bowed his head for a moment, and when he looked up again, his chin was trembling. "I know. We're both still grieving, and only the Lord knows how long it will take for us to heal. But we must rise above our grief, and remember that we've been called to care for our fellow broth-ers and sisters in Christ. Their sorrows don't disappear because we feel burdened with our own."

Tim looked down at a large pull in the rug, and flattened it with his foot. He nodded, not yet able to return John's gaze. "I understand."

"Good." John picked up his planner again. "How does next week's visitation schedule look for you?"

Easter. He called Jeff right after Easter. That was four months ago. "John, before we start, I have to ask: why didn't you tell me?"

John sighed. "I suppose I should have."

You 'suppose?' The board said that if you wanted to run prayer group on your own, you had to at least let me know if a family was struggling.

"But I was hopeful that the Lord would intercede and heal the child. The group prayed for several weeks, but Josh's seizures became more fre-quent, and more severe. So I asked Jeff if he'd bring Josh to our meetings. He was hesitant, said that Alicia didn't want him to. But she must have changed her mind, because Josh began coming a week or so later."

"Why wouldn't she want Josh to go?"

"His seizures were only happening at night, and she was concerned that having him out late would tire him out and put him at risk for another one."

Tim shook his head. "I'm still confused. If Jeff and Alicia took Josh to prayer group, then why do you think they won't want to hear from you? Do you think they're angry with you because he's still having seizures?" It was ridiculous to blame John—he was a pastor, not a doctor—but what other reason could there be?

"Alicia's angry with me, much more so than Jeff. But I don't think prayer group is the reason." John took off his glasses and rubbed his eyes. "Obviously, our prayers weren't received. It wasn't the Lord's will that Josh be cured."

"They must have asked why. What did you say?" Tim fiddled with the wristband of his watch. *Please tell me that you didn't blame them. Please tell me that you didn't accuse them of having too little faith.*

"I told them the same thing that I tell anyone who's struggling with illness: that God is merciful. Perhaps He's protecting Josh from something that we haven't considered. That by curing him, events would be set in motion for a situation that would be far more harmful. Sometimes we must accept that healing doesn't occur, even when we don't understand why. Even when faith is strong."

Tim breathed a sigh of relief. John had counseled Jeff and Alicia well. God didn't heal Paul's "thorn in the flesh," or Job's leprosy. He let His only Son suffer and die on the cross. Until His kingdom is established, illness will continue to be part of human existence.

John hunched over his desk and leaned in as if sharing a secret. "Tim. Don't you find the timing of Josh's seizures to be rather … suspicious?"

He felt his breath catch. "I'm not sure what you mean by that."

John spoke in a slow and even manner, as if he was teaching at Sunday school. "Think about it. His seizures used to be rare. Then, out of nowhere, they started happening frequently, at night, *keeping Jeff away from Bible study.* And today, a seizure prevented his entire family from worshipping the Lord. Who could cause that to happen?"

Who? No, he can't possibly mean—

"Don't you see? It'd be one thing if his seizures had increased but occurred at random times during the week. Then we'd have known that we were dealing with a physical ailment, pure and simple. But the fact that they were interfering with Jeff's attempts to communicate with the Holy Spirit led me to an entirely different conclusion: it must be the work of a demon. That was when I realized that Josh needed a healing, not a prayer group."

So this is why he didn't tell me. Aligning himself with Pentecostalism could get him fired. Faith healing, speaking in tongues, prophecy—these were gifts of the Holy Spirit that Southern Baptists believed came to end with the death of the last Apostle.

John crossed and uncrossed his legs, offered him a fleeting smile. It was the first time Tim had seen him less than completely self-assured. "I don't have experience with healing, or in the discernment of spirits. But I knew that Terry Binterman was going to be in town, so I offered to set up a meeting."

"Terrence Binterman? From last summer's conference?"

"We've kept in touch." He paused, and when he spoke again, it was in the dramatic, formal tone he used when he preached. "We evangelicals are strong in the study of the Word, but sometimes neglect the Spirit. We know the Bible, but in our quest for understanding we overlook our personal connection to God. Pentecostals and mainline charismatics approach worship in the opposite way. They understand how essential it is that Christians rejoice in the Spirit, but on occasion they overlook the necessity of scholarly investigation." He paused again, his prepared words exhausted. "I'm hoping Terry's movement is right. That there's a way to get the best of both worlds."

Tim was silent, stunned. He'd been to a Pentecostal service with a high school friend once, and had expected it to be similar to the ones that he'd grown up with. But instead of sermons and hymns, he saw people with their arms in the air, speaking in tongues. Preachers laying hands on the sick, causing them to fall backwards into the arms of a catcher. People praising God and then dropping to the ground, writhing, being "slain in the Spirit."

He'd left uncomfortable and skeptical. Everyone the preacher touched had claimed a complete recovery, but all the illnesses that had been cured—headaches, stomach pains, arthritis—had vague symptoms that couldn't be measured objectively. No one had stood up from a wheelchair and started walking. No one who was blind suddenly regained sight, as the beggar cured by Jesus, in John, did. Where was the miracle?

Tim looked at John, who was flipping through the Bible. "Had Jeff and Alicia even heard of Terrence Binterman?"

"No. I told them that Terry was experienced in healing, and pointed them to a passage that I thought would be helpful to read prior to meeting with him." John passed the Bible to him. "Mark nine, verses—"

Seventeen to twenty-seven. Tim didn't need to read the passage; he knew it well. But John was standing over his shoulder, waiting for him, giving him no choice but to read it again.

> A man in the crowd answered, "Teacher, I brought you my son, who is possessed by a spirit that has robbed him of speech. Whenever it seizes him, it throws him to the ground. He foams at the mouth, gnashes his teeth and becomes rigid. I asked your disciples to drive out the spirit, but they could not."

> "You unbelieving generation," Jesus replied, "how long shall I stay with you? How long shall I put up with you? Bring the boy to me."

> So they brought him. When the spirit saw Jesus, it immediately threw the boy into a convulsion. He fell to the ground and rolled around, foaming at the mouth.

> Jesus asked the boy's father, "How long has he been like this?"

> "From childhood," he answered. "It has often thrown him into fire or water to kill him. But if you can do anything, take pity on us and help us."

> "If you can?" said Jesus. "Everything is possible for one who believes."

Immediately the boy's father exclaimed, "I do believe; help me overcome my unbelief!"

When Jesus saw that a crowd was running to the scene, he rebuked the impure spirit. "You deaf and mute spirit," he said, "I command you, come out of him and never enter him again."

The spirit shrieked, convulsed him violently and came out. The boy looked so much like a corpse that many said, "He's dead." But Jesus took him by the hand and lifted him to his feet, and he stood up.

So this is why Alicia's so angry. He turned and looked up at John. "How did they respond?"

"Alicia had some … less than flattering words for me when I called them a couple of days later. Jeff didn't let her on the phone, but I could hear her in the background."

"So he didn't feel the same way?"

"He seemed more open to discussion. But Alicia put her foot down. So I never scheduled the meeting. And now, I fear, the Devil's work continues."

"You know, John, I've always interpreted this passage another way. Jesus knew the truth, but he needed to communicate with people on a level that they'd understand. A neurological explanation would've been out of the question."

"Perhaps. That's what I believed, too. But Terry believes that we shouldn't be *interpreting* the Word of God at all."

"But what about when Jesus heals the sick in Matthew?" Tim said, flipping through the pages as desperation rose within him. "Here it is. Chapter four, verse twenty-four: 'News about him spread all over Syria, and people brought to him all who were ill with various diseases, those suffering severe pain, the demon-possessed, those having seizures, and the paralyzed, and he healed them.'"

He looked up, searched John's face. Didn't he notice the distinction? "See? 'Demon-possessed' and 'those having seizures' are categorized separately."

John shook his head. "You're missing my point. Here we are again, poring over every word, investigating the nuances of every phrase. But that's not what matters. The only way Josh can be healed—the only way *I* can be healed—is through connection with His Spirit." John collapsed back into his chair. He looked up at the ceiling, and then closed his eyes. "I was afraid, Tim. Afraid that I would turn away from God."

He could feel tightness at the back of his throat. He'd felt that disconnect, that fear. He'd pledged his life to God, yet where was He when he needed Him?

John opened his eyes. "Terry prayed with me several times after Shayla passed, and he noticed something about my prayers that had never been pointed out to me. He asked me if I realized how often I used the phrase, 'Lord, if it be thy will.'"

Tim shrugged. "All the time. So do I."

A grin spread across John's face. "Exactly!"

"I don't get it. Why shouldn't we? They were good enough for Jesus when he feared execution."

"True. But here's where we go wrong: if we pepper every thought with those words, then we begin to disengage from Him. It makes us feel passive, as if we have no ability to interact with Him, when we should instead be trying to discover His purposes and carry them out as best we can."

"So what does Terrence suggest?"

"He recommended that when we pray, we should assume that God *wants* to help us, not that he'll be bothered by our requests. Don't forget, Jesus also said, 'whatever you ask for in prayer, believe that you have received it, and it will be yours.' Since I've begun following Terry's advice, I've felt

God come back into my life. I wanted to share that joy with Alicia and Jeff, but things didn't turned out as I would've liked."

For me, either. He'd been wrong about the workings of the Lord. Josh's seizure hadn't been divine intervention on his behalf. John wasn't to be the confidante he'd hoped for.

Josh, Alicia, Terrence, John—it was too much to process. Would John ask him to keep his secret? Would he tell the board himself? What if he were to leave? As Tim tried to sort through his harried thoughts, he noticed a flurry of motion through the rectangular glass panel in the door.

"Did you see that?" he asked John, who shook his head. "I'm going to see who that was. I'll be right back."

As he stepped outside of John's office, he saw Josephine, who'd turned around and was trying to slip away unnoticed. Her skirt was still swinging from the abrupt movement.

Had she heard? He caught up to her with loud, brisk steps. "Josephine. I didn't think you'd still be here."

She stopped and turned, did an exaggerated double take. "Oh! Hi. I didn't hear you."

"Do you need something?"

"Mom sent me in here to see if you were busy. I wasn't trying to…"

She looked down and then tucked her hair behind her ears. "Is Josh okay?"

Tim nodded. "He's fine now. Do you know him?"

"I've only met him once. I know his stepsister, Michelle. She's in my English class. But I didn't see her today. She must be at her mom's."

"So you saw what happened?"

"No, I just saw Mr. Hannaford carrying him out." Her voice lowered to a whisper. "He had a seizure?"

"How did you find out? You were sitting all the way up front." And then, when she reddened: "Josephine, how much of my conversation with Pastor Harlow did you hear?"

Tears sprung to her eyes. "I wasn't trying to listen in, I promise! Mom told me she needed to talk to you about pick-ups for Gracie next week, but then you weren't in your office, so I kept looking … " She turned towards the window and looked out into the parking lot. "I'll go tell her you're busy."

He followed her down the hallway. "Josephine, wait. I'm not mad at you. I just want to know what you heard. Did you hear what Pastor Harlow said about a demon causing this?"

"I heard all of it," she said, wiping away her tears. "Is it true?"

He shook his head. "God is inerrant. Of that I'm sure. But man is not. Do you understand?"

She nodded, but he could see uncertainty in her eyes. Josephine was wise beyond her years, so much so that he sometimes he forgot how young she really was. *Young enough to have* inerrant *as a vocab word.*

"Let me put it another way. If you had the flu during services one Sunday, and then, maybe a headache the next one, would that mean that a demon caused them to keep you away from church?"

She shook her head.

"Of course not. It seems silly, because those are such familiar illnesses, right? But just because something looks scary and isn't understood well doesn't mean that the Devil's to blame. Josh has an illness that's not that uncommon. There are lots of different types of medication he can take to help him."

He looked at Josephine, her face filled with conflicting emotions. Suddenly he was furious with John. The pillar of the community, spouting nonsense. "What Pastor Harlow said to the Hannafords was said out of a desire to help." He paused for a second, tried to bite his tongue, but outrage prevailed. "Pastor Harlow is a godly man, a learned man. But let me be perfectly clear: he's wrong."

CHAPTER 11

Josephine's keys, which always hang from the rack mounted to the wall in her foyer, are missing.

The key rack is designed to look like a key itself. Attached to the left of the horizontal rod that holds the hooks is the ornate, bronzed bow of the key, and to the right is its intricately cut blade. It looks like the type of key a wizard might use, or a king from medieval times. *It has Ellen Wallis written all over it,* she'd thought, when her mother gave it to her as a housewarming gift three years ago.

It would never have crossed her mind to buy this type of knick-knack. She'd always thrown her keys on the side table in the entryway; that was the whole point of having it there. But the key rack, her mother told her, was not only *charming*, but also a clever way to keep the foyer tidy.

She couldn't exchange it as she'd done with most of her mother's gifts over the years. Make-up, body wash, creams—her mother had no way of knowing whether she'd used them or not. But she couldn't win with the key rack. If it had been artwork, she'd have been able to hang it somewhere out of the way, maybe next to the linen closet or in the extra bedroom. The problem with the key rack was that it served a function, demanded to be the focal point of the entryway.

"Who cares?" Wes said, when she'd complained that it was cutesy. "Is it worth making your mom feel bad every time she comes over?" She'd known that would be his response, and even worse, knew that it was the right one. After stalling for several weeks, guilt triumphed over taste, and the key rack was hung.

It's not just the keys that are missing, though, she notices now. It's the entire rack, which was there when she came back from her run a half an hour ago. She turns and scans the walls that extend from the foyer to the guest bedroom. All bare. What had happened while she was in the shower?

"Wes?" She travels from room to room, calling his name. As she nears the garage, she hears his familiar off-key whistling. "Wes?" she repeats, as she peers into the garage. He's backed her car out, and taken all of their lawn and sports equipment and moved them away from the perimeter of the garage and into her parking spot. She can hear him scuffling outside, the trunk opening and closing, and walks over to him. "Wes! Where are all of our pictures?"

"In here." He leans his head towards the car, and she can see that he's stacked their framed photos and artwork inside. "Trying to be careful. Remember what happened last time Rob helped out? Talk about a disaster. But this time there's not that much to move."

"What are you talking about?"

"Seriously? You don't remember?"

"No. And I need my keys. I've got to pick up Amanda."

"Rob's coming over to help me get all of the gym equipment into the downstairs bedroom. We talked about this. Every time I want to work out I have to go to the basement for the treadmill, and it smells down there—we need to do something about that, by the way—and then I've got to come to the garage and pull your car out to do weights. It's ridiculous."

"Oh, that's right," she says, remembering. It made sense at the time. *But that was before.* "So you're going to put all the guest bedroom furniture into the office?"

"Yeah. There isn't that much stuff up there. I can squeeze it all in."

But the downstairs room is for the baby. "Maybe we should rethink this. What do you think about moving the gym equipment into the office instead? That way when we have people over they won't be crowded into a half-bedroom, half-office situation. I'd be embarrassed to have our friends sleep in between a filing cabinet and a shredder."

He throws his hands up in the air. "Do you know how heavy all of that is? Why would I bring it upstairs? Besides, how often do we have guests?"

"That's not the point. If friends make the effort to come visit, then it's our responsibility to put them up comfortably."

"Okay, Ellen."

"Not funny."

"You sound just like her, and you know it. Seriously, Jo, I don't get it. We didn't even *have* an extra bedroom in our old apartment. We just pulled out an air mattress and had our friends crash in the living room. You weren't embarrassed then."

"That was different."

"Because?"

"Because we were younger. We're way too old to act like college kids now. We were too old then, too, we just didn't know any better."

"Nice try. What's *really* bugging you? Is it that you don't like how it looks?"

"No, I don't care about that. I'm not my mom, despite your hilarious joke."

"Then what? What's the point of having a room reserved for a couple of visits a year? It's not like we live in a mansion. It's such a waste. I'd use it all the time if it was set up as a gym. I can't even run in the basement anymore—I feel like I'm sucking in mold the whole time."

"It's that bad?"

He nods. "It'll be done before you even get back from the lake," he says, with a lopsided smile.

"Are you using my keys?" She pats the left pocket of his cargo shorts. "I need them back."

He pulls them from his right pocket and dangles them in front of her. "You're not answering me. You can have them when I get a yes."

"Can you reschedule? He's your brother, he'll understand. That way we can talk about it more. I can't now, I have to go. I told you about that time with Luke on the dock. You can blame it on me. It *is* my fault for forgetting. Okay?" She gives him a quick peck on the cheek, and brushes past him as she gets into her car.

He knocks on the window until she rolls it all the way down. "It's not okay. I'm not canceling out of nowhere. It's taken us months to find a day that works for both of us. And there's no soccer this week, so it's perfect."

"I'm asking you, Wes. Please." She puts the car in reverse, and begins to back out.

He holds onto the base of the open window, and walks with it. "Call me from the road."

"Can't. My phone's almost dead."

"The hell it is. I charged it this morning. You'd better call me."

"Wes, let go! I don't want to hurt you."

"Josephine, what is going on with you? You've been acting really weird lately. If you don't stop the car right now, I'm going to get in mine and follow you there."

She slams the car into park. "Well, that would be the first time you'd come then, wouldn't it?"

"What's that supposed to mean?"

"I mean *Amanda*. Every time she comes up … it was the same with the Norden Street house." She stops, knows that she isn't making sense.

He looks at her as if she's crazy. "What does Amanda have to do with any of this? And the Norden Street house? I get it, it was bigger, you wanted it, we wouldn't be fighting over space now—but my God, that was years ago. Let it go already."

"It's not that it was bigger. It's that it had an in-law suite. Remember? I said that we should have it for Amanda, for after my parents are gone, and you said no, and then you never come to the lake with us, and some-times I wonder—"

"You wonder what?" His voice is cold.

She can feel her lip quivering, and she concentrates on trying to steady it. She hadn't meant to drag Amanda into their argument. The words had tumbled out before she could stop them. "I'm sorry, forget I brought it up." She buries her face in her hands, wishes she could erase what she's just said. She looks up after a moment, covers his hand with hers.

He pulls it away. "Brought *what* up? You haven't told me what it is that you wonder about."

"You're trying to make me say it now. And I don't want to, because it's not true. I shouldn't have implied that … " She waits for him to jump in and rescue her, but he's silent. "I know you're not ashamed of her, Wes. I was just frustrated that you weren't listening to me, and you weren't letting me go, and I was nervous because I was starting to run late—"

"That's your excuse? You were mad about furniture so it's okay that you made up some horrible shit about me? Not wanting to buy the same house as you and liking to play soccer doesn't make me an asshole who's embarrassed by your sister."

Then what does it make you, Wes? Selfish? Or just immature? She rubs her forehead, lets these words die instead of giving voice to them. Who is she to hurl these insults at him? Don't these same labels apply to her? "You're right. I'm sorry, I've just been so hormonal lately … I know that's not a good excuse, either, but it's true." She waits for him to tell her that blaming hormones is a cop-out, and she braces herself. She deserves his anger. She'd be livid if the situation was reversed. But instead he's nodding, and she's shocked to see that he's buying her rationalization.

"So this is all PMS? I mean, you get cranky sometimes when you're getting your period, but not this bad."

She takes a deep breath. The time has finally come. "I'm not getting my period, Wes. I haven't for close to three months."

CHAPTER 12

Tim is in the sanctuary, placing Bibles on the interlocking seats that have already been assembled by the Sunday morning set-up team. He centers a book on each chair cushion, letting his fingers trail on the ridges in the fabric as he does. They were Craig's idea, the chairs. "Who wants to sit on those hard, uncomfortable pews?" he said, when the time came to replace them. "You spend the whole service counting the minutes until you can leave, instead of participating."

Third times a charm. After John, after Ed, finally Craig. To be fair, the thirteen years he'd spent pastoring with Ed had been wonderful; it was the abrupt ending of them that sours his memories of those years. But without that loss, he thinks now, he would never have become senior pastor. He would never have met Craig, whose sunny nature balanced his serious one, and brought joy back into a wounded church.

He's made his way to the back of the sanctuary, and after positioning his last Bible, he looks up and marvels at the changes he's seen at his church over the years. Gone are the hymnals, replaced by PowerPoint presentations; the pews by chairs; the lone piano by guitars, drums, and keyboards; the choir by several lead singers. But he doesn't long for the past. The church has grown with the flock, changed with the times, as it should. The one vestige of the past, near and distant, the one *constant,* he holds in his hands. For his entire adult life, he's considered sharing the good news with his flock the greatest gift he could give.

"Sean's on his way," says Craig, as he enters the sanctuary and props the door open with the doorstop. "He just called. Probably another—"

"Ten minutes?" Tim finishes.

Craig smiles the endearing, dimpled smile that makes him seem boyish even though his dark hair is now peppered with gray. "As always. But what he lacks in punctuality he makes up for in talent, right?" he says, as he walks backwards towards the stage.

Replacing the choir with a worship band had been Craig's idea, too. "High school kids don't want to sing hymns anymore," he said, after several years of dwindling youth group attendance. It had been a hard sell to the board, but Tim went to bat for him, persuaded them that the future of the church was dependent on its ability to stay in touch with the needs of the younger generation. And the years since have proven Craig right.

Tim can't hear the words with Craig all the way down the aisle, but can see by his gestures between the band, the screen above them, and the pulpit, that he's coordinating the flow of the service.

"So here's where we stand," Craig says, as he walks back towards him. "Audio is all set, but visual needs another fifteen—some sort of computer glitch. Once Sean gets here the band can do a quick run-through. You're ready?"

"Yep."

"Great. So let me run down the order you laid out for today to make sure I heard you right. After opening prayer, you said that—"

"Craig?"

"Yeah?" he says, rolling his pen between his fingers as he reads his notes.

"Thanks for all of your help."

Craig looks up, his eyebrows knit in confusion. "Uh, sure."

"No, not for today. I mean yes—today, too, like every Sunday—but I was thinking about *next* Sunday. I want to thank you in advance for running the service. I just couldn't bring myself to cancel. We've only canceled once before."

"For Shayla?"

He nods. *A lifetime ago.* Only bits and pieces of that day remain. "Any chance you'll change your mind about coming to the reception?"

"I'd love to, Tim, but you know better than anyone … "

He does, of course. Saturday night is for prayer and preparation. Coming home late and exhausted isn't an option. Still, it feels unsettling for Craig to not be part of the celebration.

"I'll be there for the ceremony," Craig reminds him. "That's the most important part."

"I've stuck you with a raw deal."

"Stop. Four people have volunteered for set-up and clean-up. I'll be fine."

"I just wish I could help out in some way. Maybe Jane could take Luke…" He trails off, knows that his offer isn't possible. Luke's too strong and unpredictable for Jane to handle alone.

Craig gives him a knowing look. "The only way Gracie will be able to relax is if she knows that *you're* taking care of Luke. The church will survive. Tuesday will come around before you know it."

"Monday, actually. Gracie'll be home in the evening."

"That's quick. Are they taking a longer honeymoon some other time?"

He shook his head. "They're saving up for a car. Keith doesn't live near public transportation, so once Gracie moves out of her apartment, she's going to need one. But the bigger reason is Luke."

Craig nods. "Then all the more reason to make it a stress-free couple of days for her."

They both turn to the sound of Sean's guitar case banging against the door. Somehow the doorstopper has been dislodged, and Craig springs towards him to help. "You made it!"

Tim catches up and reaches out to shake Sean's hand. "Good to see you. Looks like there's still plenty of time for rehearsal."

Craig motions for Sean to follow him to the stage, and as they walk away, Tim looks at the winged pulpit, adorned with a simple oak cross on the front. There's no angled bookrest atop it, as the one before it had. Ed chose one without, said that they made pastors look too professorial and removed, that they got in the way of natural gesturing. But Tim misses having edges to hold on to, a place to put his hands.

He thinks of the shabby, discolored pulpit, now long gone, and of how tightly he'd held onto it the first time he preached after Shayla died.

* * *

It was the sensation of falling that woke him that morning.

Gracie had been inconsolable in the middle of the night, moaning for Mommy, and the only way he'd been able to stop the torrent of tears and snot was to sit on the floor beside her bed, rubbing her back until he could feel the spasms of hiccups turn into the rise and fall of sleep.

Once she'd calmed, and the promise of his own bed awaited him, he could feel his love for her surge within him. As he stood up, he kissed his fingertips and placed them on the red splotches that hadn't yet faded from her cheek; a tender but critical error. "Daddy, Daddy ... " she mumbled, as she clutched his hand.

"Good night, sweet girl," he whispered, trying to free his fingers. She whimpered and grabbed his arm this time, pulled it in closer and rolled on top of it. "Shh ... sleep," he said, as he eased his arm out from underneath. Her eyelids began to flutter, and she grimaced as she tried to snatch it back. Fearing she'd wake, he crawled over her, and squeezed himself into the narrow, empty strip of space between the mattress and the wall.

He had no idea what time it was when he woke. *Seven? Eight? Please, not nine.* Sunlight was streaming in through the seams between the window frame and the shade. He rolled back onto the mattress, which had shifted away from the wall during the night. *So it wasn't a dream. I was actually falling.* He pushed the twisted covers off and inched towards the foot of the bed, careful not to rouse Gracie.

He tiptoed to his bedroom, and checked his alarm clock. 7:12. Plenty of time. They'd be able to make it to church by nine easily, giving him a whole hour of prep time before services began.

As he waited for the shower to warm up, he rubbed his eyes, then opened and shut them in repeated, exaggerated movements. Was the tic in his left eye from exhaustion? Or could it be something worse? He looked in the mirror, and found, to his relief, that his reflection was sharp. His stomach wasn't fluttering, either—a good sign—but it felt as if it *could*. As if this was a precursor to an aura: a warning of a warning.

He stepped into the shower. *How am I supposed to do this by myself, Shayla? You left me alone, and you know what? I hate you for it.* He turned the dial higher and higher until the water scalded him, left enraged swaths of pink across his chest and arms. Higher still, until it forced him to jump back and adjust the temperature. Once it was tolerable, he turned and stood under the showerhead, let the water mingle with his tears. *Please Lord; please grant me health today, so that I may serve You and my brothers and sisters. I've withheld the truth from John, and by doing so I've failed Gracie. Let me redeem myself by spreading Your Word.*

He dressed, and then rehearsed his sermon over breakfast. Next he filled Gracie's backpack with a change of clothes, a snack for the car ride afterwards, and a coloring book and crayons should the service run long. He checked his watch. 8:07. Gracie never slept this late.

The poor girl was so tired. He wanted to let her sleep in, but time was getting tight. He emptied the dishwasher, hoping the clattering would wake her. He picked up the laundry basket filled with clean clothes and dropped it outside of her bedroom. Still, silence.

Peering in through the crack in the doorway, he could see the outline of her body curled up under her comforter. He'd given her as much time as he could. He opened the door and pulled up the shade. "Gracie," he said, shaking her shoulder, "Time to get up."

She rolled over and wriggled away from him.

"Gracie, time for church. This is a big day for me. I'm giving the sermon."

"Mmmmhh."

"C'mon, Gracie."

"No," she said, pulling her comforter over her head. "Too tired."

He tugged at it, but she grabbed tight. "Gracie, if you don't get out of this bed in three seconds, I'm going to have no choice. I'm going to have to tickle you." He waited for a giggle. "One ... two ... " he counted, elongating the numbers to give her time.

A slow smile crept over her face, her eyes still closed.

"And ... three! That's it. I warned you."

She squealed and stumbled out of bed before he could reach her. He steadied her, grabbed her in a hug and tickled her until she wriggled away again. "Go run to the bathroom, and I'll get breakfast going. What do you want?"

She yawned. "Cheerios and blueberries."

He pulled her princess dress from her closet and brought it with him to the kitchen. "See?" he said proudly, as she ate her cereal. "It's all ready." He'd almost forgotten to wash it, and had been lucky enough to notice it in her hamper the night before when she was changing into her pajamas.

"But where are my sparkly tights?"

Shoot. The sparkly tights. He hadn't pulled those out with the dress. "How about you wear your pink socks this time? The ones with the flowers. They'll match your dress."

"But I *always* wear my sparkly tights with my princess dress."

"No one will know that they aren't tights. If you pull them up a little, your dress will cover them." He glanced at his watch. 8:37. "I'll go check in your room, just in case. Get dressed while I go look."

He rifled through her drawers, the laundry basket, and then ran to the basement to check the washer and dryer. "Gracie, I'm sorry. I can't find them, and we need to go. I found your special pink socks. Will you be a big girl and wear your pink socks instead? Please?"

"*Mommy* never forgot my sparkly tights."

He felt his jaw tense. *You spoiled little brat. Haven't you noticed that I'm doing the jobs of two people now? One mistake. I make one mistake and you give me a guilt trip?* He looked down at Gracie, who'd sat down on the floor and was struggling with her socks, tears streaming down her face.

He kneeled down to help her. *What's wrong with me? She's only five.* "I'm so proud of you, Gracie. I know you really wanted your sparkly tights. I promise I'll have them ready for next week." He gave her a hug, a kiss on each cheek. "Ready now?"

"Daddy! You forgot to help me brush my teeth. *And* my hair."

Okay, three mistakes. He nudged her from behind, towards the bathroom. "Hurry."

Gracie ran to the bathroom and pushed her stepstool close to the sink. She pushed the toothbrush out of her mouth midway through his brushing, spraying spit on the mirror and dribbling toothpaste onto her chin. "Remember. We have to do the tooth brushing song."

"No time right now." He left the toothbrush next to the sink, still gooey with leftover paste, and then grabbed a hairbrush and an elastic. "Grammy can braid your hair when we get there." 8:51. They could make it by ten past, if they hustled. He'd still have time for last-minute preparations. He strode towards the garage. "Let's go, Gracie."

"Wait ... where's Mr. Cat?"

You've got to be kidding. "I don't know. I haven't seen him today."

"But, Daddy, Mr. Cat told me last night that he wanted to come today."

Mr. Cat. For the past two months, she'd been inseparable from that grungy stuffed animal. "I don't remember seeing Mr. Cat in your room last night. Did you bring him to bed with you?

She shrugged.

"Go look under the bed. I forgot to check there. I'll look around here."

"He's not there," she said, reappearing after several minutes.

Sweat began to bead on his forehead. *Think. You've got to get her in the car.* "You know, Gracie, maybe Mr. Cat is hiding because he's tired and needs to rest this morning."

She gave him a skeptical look.

"It's true. He told me yesterday. I forgot to tell you."

"Mr. Cat isn't a *real* cat, you know," she said, crossing her arms.

Let's test that logic, he wants to say. *If Mr. Cat isn't real, then how could he have told you that he wanted to go to church?*

Then, as if reading his thoughts, she added, "He only talks to me."

He knelt down, and lifted her chin so she was looking into his eyes. "Gracie. We are starting to run *very* late. Think hard. Where did you last see Mr. Cat?"

The shrug again. "I don't know," she said plaintively. "But I *need* him."

His heart twisted. He had to find that worn out cat. He took a deep breath. "Let's see … did he go on errands with us yesterday?"

"I think so."

Where had they gone yesterday? He ran through the schedule in his head. First the bank, then the drugstore, and last, the grocery store. Mr. Cat had made it to the grocery store, he was sure of that. Gracie had put him in the child seat of the cart, since he'd needed a nap. Then home for lunch. Gracie had shared her sandwich with him, because cats like tuna, so Mr. Cat must have made it home as well. "Gracie, did you bring Mr. Cat with you to Amanda's yesterday afternoon?"

"I think so."

But he wasn't in bed last night. "Gracie, I think Mr. Cat's at Amanda's. We'll pick him up after church." He took her hand, and pulled her towards the garage.

"No," she whined, as she flopped to the floor.

Stupid, vile cat! He glanced at his watch again. 9:03. Was it too early to call the Wallises? They didn't go to church every week; he couldn't be sure that they'd be up yet. Maybe he could drive by their house, see if Amanda was out playing in the yard? Knock on the door softly?

"Gracie, let's get in the car and drive to Amanda's. We can do it if you want, but we have to go *right now.*"

"No. I'm not going anywhere until I have Mr. Cat!" She laid on the floor, crying.

He needed Shayla. She'd know how to defuse this situation. She'd always been able to intuit Gracie's needs better than him. *But I wouldn't be in this situation if Shayla were here. I'd be at church by now. And she wouldn't have forgotten the sparkly tights, and Gracie wouldn't be so dependent on that disgusting cat.*

He considered picking her up and letting her scream the whole way to the church. She'd tire herself out, wouldn't she? But she was exhausted, and the thought that she felt deserted by anyone, even a stuffed animal, sent a stab of pain through him. "Okay, Gracie. We can give it one last shot. I need you to go look around the house some more, just in case he's still here. I'm going to drive to Amanda's, and I'll be back to pick you up in a couple of minutes, all right? *Do not leave the house.* Wait for me. I'll be right back."

Gracie sat up, nodding. "Maybe Mr. Cat's behind the couch!"

No he's not—I've already checked. But this'll keep her busy. "Good idea! Go look!"

He scrambled to his car and was at Amanda's house in under a minute. The screen door was closed, but the front door behind it was wide open. He rang the bell, cringing as he heard the loud *ding*.

"Tim!" said Ellen, as she pushed the screen door open. "Looking for the cat?"

"Yes! Do you have him?"

She nodded. "I just sent the girls over with him. I'm so glad you haven't left yet. I didn't notice that Gracie had left him here until I saw Amanda playing with him this morning."

"But I didn't see them when I was driving over," he said, confused.

"They probably cut through the backyards. Nobody seems to mind, except Gail and Ron. They should be there any minute."

He dashed back to his car. "Thank you, you have no idea . . . thank you." He scanned what was visible of his neighbors' backyards as he drove home, but still wasn't able to find Josephine and Amanda. *Must be behind one of the houses.*

He parked his car and closed the garage door out of habit. 9:12. It had taken longer than he'd thought it would. He tripped over the garbage bags piled near the door, causing one to rip open and spew trash behind his left tire.

"Gracie," he shouted into the house from the doorway, while kicking the garbage away from the tire, "I found Mr. Cat! He'll be here in a minute. Quick! Jump in the car." He waited for a moment, but no sound from Gracie. "Gracie, we don't have time for hide-and-seek—I need you here *now*! I'm not kidding."

Silence. The thought of having to deal with John's disapproval was nauseating. He should call him; he must be at church by now. But as he ran into the house and picked up the phone, a deep fear surfaced. Had something happened to Gracie?

Not possible. He'd only been gone five minutes. But he'd known he shouldn't have left her alone, had known it and ignored it. What had he been thinking? *Please, please, please, don't let her be hurt.* Unspeakable thoughts ran through his mind; the countless ways she could have been harmed competed for his attention. "Gracie! Gracie!" he screamed, as he dropped the phone back into its cradle and searched the house. Did she decide to walk over to Amanda's on her own? And where *are* Amanda and Josephine, anyway? *I don't have time to check every backyard in the neighborhood. All I asked her to do was stay in the house. Is that too much to ask?*

He raced back to his car, and put it in reverse without looking in the rearview mirror. He felt his seatbelt tighten around his chest as he heard the sickening crunch of metal on metal. "God *damn* it!" he screamed, shocked to hear the blasphemous words that had just come out of his mouth. He'd backed into the garage door! How was he supposed to get out of a one-car garage with a smashed door?

But more importantly, where was Gracie? He couldn't lose her, not now. His neck, his temples, his chest all throbbed. "God damn it! God fucking damn it! Gracie, where are you? I can't fucking deal with this, where the hell are—"

He ran into the house and out the side door, letting it slam behind him. She was in the driveway, holding Mr. Cat. Standing in the exact spot his car would have backed into had the garage door not stopped it.

She looked up at him, her eyes wide with fear, and held up Mr. Cat for him to see. "Amanda and Josephine found him, so I came outside.

Don't be mad, Daddy, please. I'm sorry, I'm sorry, I know I wasn't supposed to." She started to shake. "Is that why you're yelling and saying all those bad words?"

"You're okay?" he asked, not yet ready to let his guard down.

Her eyebrows furrowed. "Uh-huh. What happened to the door?"

He grabbed her, crushing her in his arms, smothering her face in his chest. *She's safe, she's safe, she's safe. Praise the Lord, she's safe. I've taken Your name in vain, my Lord, and already You've forgiven me, showered me with your abundant mercy.*

She pushed back and turned her head to the side. She reached down to the ground for Mr. Cat, who she'd dropped, and it was then that he noticed Josephine and Amanda, standing at the base of the driveway. Amanda was tugging on Josephine's hand, trying to pull her back towards their house. But Josephine remained rooted, her eyes fixed on Tim.

So they had heard him, too. *What's Josephine supposed to think? First she overhears John's crazy demon talk, and now she catches me cursing like a sailor.* Words from Paul's first letter to his disciple—Timothy, of all people—ran through his head: "He must manage his own family well and see that his children obey him, and he must do so in a manner worthy of full respect. If anyone does not know how to manage his own family, how can he take care of God's church?"

Amanda yanked harder on Josephine, who wobbled, then righted herself. She backed up several steps, still staring at him, and then, wordless, turned and followed her sister.

He didn't call after them with an explanation, a thank you, or a goodbye. Instead, he picked Gracie up, and rocked her side to side, her hands around his neck, as he recited the Sinner's Prayer.

God had saved her, and in doing so, had saved him. Again.

Not until his arms began to shake from exhaustion did he let her down, and it was then that he remembered that they were stranded. He ran through the house and into the garage, Gracie in tow. The bottom two panels of the door were dented, but the tracks hadn't been warped. *Please*, he thought, as he pressed the garage door button, *please let the door open.*

They arrived at church five minutes before the beginning of the service, Tim greeted by John's withering stare and Gracie by Lillian's worried one. It was once Tim finished the sermon, and the stress of the morning subsided, that the thought occurred to him: *What if Josephine or Amanda had told Ellen and Chuck? What if the news makes its way through church, to John?* No explanation would be good enough for him.

He considered biting the bullet. If his behavior had frightened Josephine or Amanda, then it was his responsibility to reach out to Ellen and Chuck and explain. But what if he confessed just to find that neither of the girls had said a word? He would be putting his job—not to mention his frayed relationship with John—at risk for no reason.

Tomorrow, he decided, after an afternoon of deliberation. He would put it off until tomorrow, when he'd be clear-headed again. A better decision would be made if he put the emotion of the day behind him. There was no time to drop by their house by that point, anyway. Sunday evenings had a long-established ritual in the Lundstrom household: pizza at Carmine's followed by popcorn at home with *The Disney Sunday Night Movie.*

It was during the second commercial break that the doorbell rang. "Ellen," he said, as he opened the door. "How are you?" He could feel his stomach fluttering as he peered behind her. "No girls?"

"No, just me." She flattened the collar of her ruffled blouse, smoothed the material that had bunched around her waist. Was she blushing? It was hard to tell under her make-up. Her cheeks were always painted the exact same shade of rose, whether she was doing yard work or dressed for church.

"What's up?" he asked, trying to sound casual, but she said nothing, continued to fuss with her blouse instead.

So one of the girls had told her. And now she was uncertain of how to broach the subject. *Make it easy for her, you coward. You're the one who put her in this situation.* "Ellen. What is it?"

"I'm not interrupting dinner, am I?"

"No, not at all. Come on in. Gracie, we have company," he called. "Come say hello." He cocked his head to the side, listened for footsteps. "Gracie?" He walked into the living room and turned the TV off. "I know you heard me. Come over and say hello."

"But Daddy, it's right in the middle!" She picked up the remote to turn it on again.

He snatched it from her. "Gracie," he said, his voice low, "you're embarrassing me. Go say to hi to Ellen *right now.*"

She brightened. "Amanda's here?" She raced into the kitchen, her face clouding with disappointment when she saw that Ellen was alone. "Oh. Hi, Miss Ellen."

"Gracie!"

But Ellen was laughing, back to her normal self. "No, it's fine, Amanda would do the same." She turned to Gracie. "She's more fun than I am, I'll admit it. It's fine by me if you want to go back to watching TV, as long as it's okay with your dad."

Gracie looked up at him, clasped her hands the same way she did when she recited a prayer before bed. "Fine," he said, relenting. "But not too—"

"Bye, Ms. Ellen!" interrupted Gracie, escaping before he could finish.

"Smart girl," she said to Tim, as she sat down at the kitchen table. "Leaving before you could change your mind. That strategy has been used in my house many times." She paused, and when she spoke again, it was in a voice that let him know that small talk was over. "I don't want to take up too much of your time. I've been putting off asking you, but ... well, did Shayla ever mention anything to you about the bus? For the girls, I mean. When they start kindergarten?"

"No," he said, surprised. *So this isn't about this morning?*

"That's what I thought. It's my fault. I'm making too big a deal out of this." She stood. "I shouldn't have come. Chuck said you wouldn't mind, but you have so much on your plate right now. I'm embarrassed that I even—"

"Ellen, what are you talking about?"

"I'm rambling," she said with an awkward laugh. She glanced in Gracie's direction, and then lowered her voice. "Amanda will be going to a classroom for kids who ... who need some extra help. Have you heard about it?"

He shook his head.

"Amanda will go there for academics, but she'll go to a regular classroom for everything else—art, music, gym, lunch, snack, recess. Chuck and I were allowed to request a classroom, so I asked Shayla if she would mind if I requested Gracie's. And she said yes."

Where is she going with this? What does this have to do with the bus?

"Don't worry, Gracie won't be responsible for Amanda in any way. They can play at recess or snack, but they don't have to. It'd just be nice for Amanda to have a friendly face in the room. Anyway, I found out last month that the school was able to honor our request."

"That's great news," he said, still not understanding why she was so uncomfortable. "It works out for Gracie, too. There's a class list? I don't remember getting it."

"I can get it for you. I know that Jen Davidson and Will Maines will be in her class. They went to Little Learners, too. Do you know them?"

"I know the names, but to be honest, I don't think I could pick them out of a crowd. Shayla took care of all of that."

"Well, maybe I could set up some play dates before school starts. Do you think Gracie would like that?"

He smiled. "That'd be great. Thanks."

"Happy to do it." She paused. "There's one other thing, though."

Finally. "The bus?"

Ellen nodded. "Chuck and I have a choice with Amanda. We can put her on a van for kids who need special help, or the regular school bus. We'd like for her to be on the regular school bus. The more independent she can be, the better, and it sounds like the other kids on the van … I guess the best way to say it is that I don't think it will be as good a fit for her."

"I didn't know there was more than one bus, to be honest. Gracie will be the only kindergartner at the bus stop if Amanda's not there, right?"

"Right. But the issue is this: Amanda *will* need Gracie's help, if we go ahead with the regular school bus. Gracie will need to sit with her, at least at the beginning, make sure she doesn't forget her backpack, and help her get off at the right stop after school. Shayla told me she'd spoken to Gracie about it. But now things have changed, and I'll understand if you don't want to weigh Gracie down with any responsibility. So if this makes you uncomfortable in any way, let me know, I can change it. I just have a deadline to get back to the bus company, so if you could let me know by—"

"You said Shayla spoke to Gracie about it?"

"Yes."

Not to me, though. He sighed. "It's strange, having to analyze what Shayla said, or forgot to say. I still think she's running errands, or at John and Lillian's, and that she'll be back any minute."

Ellen covered his hand with hers.

He could feel tears forming, blinked his eyes to stop them from falling. "Let me talk to Gracie. If she's fine with it, then I am, too. I think it'll be a comfort for her to have a friend on the bus, not an obligation. You saw her face light up when she thought Amanda came here with you."

She smiled. "And I saw it fall when she realized she was wrong."

"Sorry about that. Manners are a work in progress."

"I can't explain how much this means for us. Anything I can do to pay you back—you just let me know. And if it turns out that Gracie has changed her mind, I'll understand." She stood up to leave. "I'll let you get back to Disney, before I blather through all of it."

He walked her to the door. "You know, Tim," she said, as she searched for her keys. I'm not quite sure how to say this, but … everyone loses control sometimes. Everyone curses sometimes. Pastors are human, too."

So she did know! He could feel his cheeks burning. "I don't know if John would agree. Or anyone from church, to tell you the truth."

"Then there's no need for them to know, is there?" she said, as she waved goodbye.

He stood in the doorway, stunned, and watched her as she walked down the steps towards her car. Then, before he could stop them, the words came tumbling out, rushed and hopeful. "Actually, Ellen, I do have a favor to ask you, if you don't mind me cashing in my IOU so quickly. Do you have another minute?

CHAPTER 13

Homemade angel biscuits and peach jam.

Just the thought of her mom's usual Sunday breakfast treat is enough to make Josephine's mouth water. She can feel her stomach rumbling as she tosses her backpack onto the passenger seat and clicks her seatbelt, and the sensation makes her smile. Finally, the nausea is loosening its grip.

Ellen never eats the biscuits—"not good for the waistline," she always says—-but makes them for Chuck, along with allergy-free banana bread for Luke, and freezer-bound lasagnas and casseroles for Amanda and Gracie. *Suggesting they move in together was a smart move on Tim's part. Free babysitting and cooking for Gracie, care of Ellen Wallis. Mom really got the short end of the stick, even if Gracie does help Amanda out at night.*

She canceled on her parents yesterday, and drove home after she'd dropped Amanda off rather than stopping by the house as planned. She had to talk to Wes. The lake was one thing; there had been no way to disentangle herself from that commitment at the last minute. But whatever her Mom had wanted to discuss could wait.

There hadn't been any texts or calls from Wes while she was out. Wes, who could barely be separated from a device long enough to take a shower. She'd braced herself for his reaction during the car ride home, had to wipe the sweat from her clammy hands off the steering wheel at every stoplight. *Juvenile and selfish? Thank God I didn't say it out loud. Talk about the pot calling the kettle black.*

Amanda. Where had that come from? She was almost as surprised as he was when she heard herself say her sister's name. And she took the easy way out afterwards, blamed raging hormones to erase her words rather than stand behind them. She'd always mocked Wes's immediate default to PMS as an excuse every time she snapped or cried, had called him a caveman for implying that women were incomprehensible, illogical creatures bound to the whims of estrogen and progesterone. But she'd erupted, had spewed accusations that she hadn't even realized had been welling up within her. She'd played the stereotypical female role perfectly. Who was right, though? Had she unfairly labeled his absence at the lake as shame? Or was there truth in her words, hidden underneath the hysteria that conveniently let him deflect blame?

As it turned out, there hadn't been any need to steel herself. When she got home there was no Wes. Just three words on a post-it by the phone: "out with Rob."

She adjusts the vent away from her in order to keep from inhaling the moldy smell of the air conditioning, then turns it off and opens the window instead. She breathes in the suffocating air as she drives along the one-lane highway that divides weathered limestone hills, then lets it out in a controlled stream, counting to eight silently. She hadn't expected that he wouldn't come home.

Not since Evan has she felt this vulnerable. How on earth has she managed to get herself into the same position again? *Similar*, actually, not the same, but still, once had been more than enough.

When she woke and found herself alone, she reached for the phone on the end table and dialed Wes's number, then hung up as it rang and dialed her parents instead. Yesterday afternoon visiting her parents had felt like a chore; this morning it was the only place she wanted to be.

They were going to church, her father told her, so how about lunch? She tried to cover the disappointment in her voice, made a joke about not being able to wait until lunchtime for angel biscuits, and he bought the act. Now she'd have to spend the morning wondering about Wes, with no distractions, and wishing her mother had picked up instead. Her mother would have known.

She follows the road as it descends and snakes its way through uncultivated land with scorched vegetation, finally emptying into the manicured suburbs below. After a few minutes, she turns onto Cedar Street, which runs east and west through all of Loring Point. Traffic begins to slow, then comes to a complete stop, a rarity. No matter, though, since the road will soon fork onto Bristol Street, her usual route. She creeps forward in starts and stops, and then realizes the reason for the backup: Bristol Street has been cordoned off for construction by a barrier sign reading "road closed." Yet no detour signs accompany it. She looks ahead to see if any of the cars in front of her are turning to the right to double back through smaller roads, but the straight line of traffic continues. She can't remember the last time she's tried to get back to her parents' house from this direction, and can't form a mental map of which roads lead to where. After two more cycles of lights with little movement forward, she turns right onto—what is it?—Henley House Road.

She inches along the meandering road, searching for another right turn. None materializes, and as the road winds she can feel her internal compass begin to falter. It's an odd street, with pristine houses astride cracked sidewalks and weathered pavement. As she continues, the topography begins to change, and older ranches begin to intersperse with the brand-new, Tuscan-style ones.

She's lost now. She pulls into a driveway to turn around, since she has no choice but to follow the road back to the traffic on Cedar. *My fault for trying to avoid the line.* It's when she turns around, and her eyes are no longer fixed on the right side of the road, that she notices a modest house on the left. It's small but well maintained, renovated rather than razed and rebuilt as most of the neighborhood has been. Nestled in between two larger homes, both out of scale with the plots of land on which they were built, it's the color of the house that stands out: bright turquoise, with hunter green shutters. A complete mismatch with the warm-colored palette of its neighbors. It's been repainted since she's seen it last, but the same vivid color combination remains. Suddenly Josephine knows exactly where she is.

At Bobby Crayton's house.

* * *

The school bus was early.

Josephine could hear the mechanical groan of brakes before she rounded the corner that lead to the bus stop. *Shit.* Gracie and Amanda would be the first to get off the bus, since kindergartners were required to sit up front. She wasn't going to make it in time.

She broke into a jog, could see Gracie in the middle of the street, holding Amanda's hand. *Neither one of them checked for cars before they crossed,* she noticed, with a frown. She ran the rest of the way, the exertion helping the guilt dissipate.

"What's wrong?" she asked, as she caught up to them. Amanda, who tended to lag a step or two behind Gracie even when they held hands, was trailing by more than usual.

"Tired," said Amanda.

"But I thought we'd head over to the park today. It's not as hot as it's been the past couple of days. You'll be able to go on the slide without it burning you."

"Don't want to."

"But maybe Gracie does."

"It's okay," Gracie said. "I brought my sticker collection."

"Good thinking. But your backpack must be really heavy. Let me carry it for you." Josephine slung it over her shoulder and put her other arm around Amanda, nudging her along. "Let's have a snack. That'll help you get your energy back."

Amanda yawned, and nodded her head. But once home, she didn't want to eat a snack or trade stickers. She wanted to watch *Sesame Street*, and whined until Josephine decided she'd rather clean up the remains of Gracie's snack than continue arguing.

The TV was far too loud; she could hear it in the kitchen over the sound of the faucet. "Turn it down," she called, but Elmo's falsetto remained at the same volume. When she walked back into the family room several minutes later, irritated that she'd been ignored, she found Amanda asleep.

"What's going on with her?" she asked Gracie, as she turned down the sound. "I wonder if she's getting sick. Are lots of kids in your class out sick?"

Gracie shook her head.

"Huh," Josephine said, eyeing her sister curiously. She turned, looked up at the clock behind Gracie. She needed Amanda and Gracie to keep each other entertained so she could get her homework done, or there'd be no time for TV tonight. Monday was her mom's night to choose, so she'd have to watch *Murphy Brown* and *Designing Women*, but that was still better than being stuck studying *le subjonctif*.

She nudged Amanda, who'd fallen asleep sitting up. Amanda didn't move; not a turn, a stretch, or a mumble. *She's really out of it. Maybe I should take her temperature.* She lifted Amanda's legs onto the couch and slipped a pillow under her head.

She looked at Gracie, who was rearranging stickers in her album. "I've got to get started on my homework. What do you want to do while we wait for your dad? More stickers?"

Gracie closed the album. "I'm all done with them now."

"Okay, how about TV? Or you could color, maybe? But I can't let you play in the backyard without me."

"Color. *Sesame Street* is boring."

"You're just getting old for it," Josephine said, as she set up one side of the kitchen table with construction paper, crayons, and markers.

"Amanda still likes it."

"Yeah, she does. But Amanda's special." She could hear her mother in her answer, and it bothered her. "Different, I mean. Right?"

"Right." Gracie flipped through the pages of construction paper, and stopped at yellow.

"Need help?"

Gracie nodded. "I always rip them when I pull them out."

"Here's the secret," Josephine said, as she demonstrated. "Hold the seam down with one hand, and pull the paper across real slow with your other one. Make sure you hold the paper near the top. Can you finish by yourself?"

"Yeah."

By the time Josephine returned to the kitchen with her books, Gracie had clambered up onto her knees and was hunched over her drawing. Her left cheek was resting on top of her arm, which she'd stretched across the table so she could support her weight and still leave one arm free to color.

But as Josephine sat down next to her, she could see that Gracie hadn't uncapped the green marker she was holding.

"Are you okay?"

Gracie buried her face into the crook of her left, mumbled something into her arm that Josephine couldn't make out. Did she hear the word *monkey*?

"Gracie, I can't understand you when you're all huddled up like this," she said, tugging at her shoulder. "You can tell me, whatever it is."

"It's because of monkey-in-the-middle! I told her not to play with them, but she wouldn't listen to me!" She was crying now, a rhythm of one sob followed by two quick breaths.

"Who?"

"Bobby! And sometimes Justin and Tommy L."

Josephine turned to grab a napkin from the counter behind her, but Gracie rubbed her tears away with the palm of her hand before she could hand it to her. "You've got to calm down and tell me what happened. It's the only way I can help." She dabbed Gracie's sticky cheeks with the napkin, and guided her back into a normal seated position.

"I told you, it's because of monkey-in-the-middle! That's why she's so tired."

"I don't get it. She's played keep-away before."

"But they always make her go in the middle! *Always*. It's not fair."

Now it makes sense. "Let me guess: they let her run herself ragged while they laughed?"

Gracie nodded, sniffling.

"How long has this been going on?"

"Since last week." She looked up, her lips trembling. "I'm sorry! I shouldn't have played with Kristen. But she knows how to braid and all of the words to songs on the radio and she can do double-dutch and she always saves a seat for me at lunch and I tried to get Amanda to play with us, but she said no, she wanted to play with them, and I told her that she shouldn't, that sometimes they're mean, but she … "

"She didn't get it, did she?"

Gracie shook her head, a second round of tears threatening.

"It's okay, Gracie. You can have other friends, too. But why didn't you tell anyone?"

"I did! I told Mrs. Naylor, and she told them to take turns, but then she started talking to Miss Weschler—the lady who brings Amanda to our class—and Bobby and the other boys didn't listen. So then I told her again and she told me that I shouldn't tattle."

Those little shitheads. Making fun of the kid who can't defend herself. "You did the right thing, Gracie. It's Miss Naylor's fault for not stopping them, not yours. Do you understand?"

She nodded.

"I'm going to have to tell my mom and dad. They'll talk to Miss Naylor and figure everything out."

"No! She already told me not to tattle, and now I'll be tattling on *her*! I can't tattle on my own teacher!"

"Telling a teacher to help a friend isn't tattling. But I'll tell them to tell Miss Naylor that Amanda was the one who told them about everything, okay? And then this whole problem will go away."

Someone seems to have gotten through to Bobby and his buddies, thought Josephine, as she waited for the afternoon bus three days later. She glanced at her watch, and then flipped the mix tape in her Walkman to side B. She had no one to talk to; the other kids at the stop were fourth graders who walked home by themselves. *Shayla. Shayla should be here waiting with me.*

This time it was Amanda who stepped off the bus first. She threw her backpack into the middle of the street, and ran towards the house without waiting for Gracie, still next to the bus.

Josephine crossed the street and yanked Gracie to the other side, then ran back into the road to pick up Amanda's backpack, lunch bag, and homework folder, scattered on the ground. *She didn't even zip it.* She shoved her sister's things back inside the pack and scurried to catch up.

"Tell me what happened, Amanda."

"Bobby Crayton is *mean*. I hate him! I hate him and I don't ever want to play with him again!"

"But I thought Miss Weschler was supposed to play with you and your friends at recess. That's what Mom and Dad said after they had that meeting."

"She *does*."

Josephine was confused. "So what does Miss Weschler say when he's mean?"

"Miss Weschler's not on the *bus*!"

"Bobby's on your bus?" She turned to Gracie. "Why didn't you tell me?"

Gracie shrugged. "He used to sit with Sean and Todd, a couple of rows back."

"But now he wants to sit near you?"

"In the row behind us. They switched with Sarah and Stacey and Jenna."

Josephine sighed. "Did this start happening right after Miss Weschler started coming to recess?"

"I don't know," Gracie answered. "I guess so."

"Amanda, what did he call you?"

"A retard!" She stopped short as she said the word aloud, and then sunk down onto the lawn of the house on the corner.

Josephine could feel her heart pumping, could feel hatred for this little boy she'd never met coursing through her veins. She wondered if Amanda knew what the word meant, but it didn't matter, anyway. Amanda knew that she was being singled out as different and somehow *less than*. An undefined word can still wound. She dropped the backpack and both she and Gracie sat down on the sidewalk in front of Amanda.

"Don't tell Mommy and Daddy, okay, Josephine?" Amanda was looking downwards, concentrating on the blades of grass that she was pulling from the neighbor's lawn.

"But Amanda, I have to."

"Please. Please, Jofee?"

Jofee. What Amanda called her before she could pronounce her full name. She hadn't heard it for a long time, hadn't realized it had disappeared until now. She looked at her sister, slumped over and unwilling to meet her gaze. *How dare he make her feel ashamed.*

"Okay. But just this once."

"Pinky promise?"

She hooked her finger with Amanda's. "Pinky promise," she said, pulling both girls up by an arm. "Listen, Amanda, you're right. Bobby *is* mean, and you don't have to play with him any more. I wouldn't. He's a bully. Do you know what that means?"

"It means he's not nice."

"And that he picks on people," Gracie added.

"Right. But why do you think he does that?"

"Because he l-likes making other people feel sad," said Amanda.

"Maybe. But maybe he does it because he feels sad about himself."

"No, he doesn't. He has friends and he never cries, even when he falls down at recess."

"I don't mean that kind of sad. I mean … embarrassed. So if he's mean to someone else, everyone will pay attention to that kid instead of him, and then—"

"And then no one will pick on *him!*" Gracie finished.

Josephine gave her an appraising look. "Exactly."

They reached the house, and discarded their backpacks and shoes in the mudroom. "Amanda, go change your shorts," Josephine said, without looking at her.

"But I'm not dirty. I was only sitting down for a little."

"Yeah, but the ground was wet from the sprinklers, and you know how Mom is about the couch. And it looks like the bottom of your shirt is damp, too."

"Okay," Amanda grumbled, as she walked to her room.

Perfect. Without help, it would take Amanda a while to find her clothes and change into them. Enough time to talk to Gracie.

"Want a snack, Gracie? We have apples, bananas, pears—"

"Can I have something from there instead?" She pointed to the pantry.

"Sure. What do you want?"

"You know the crackers, the ones with the sprinkles on top?"

"The cinnamon grahams?" Seeing Gracie's nod, she pulled a handful from the box and passed her a plate of them. "So Gracie," she said, pouring her some apple juice, "I need to ask you some questions about Bobby, all right? Like ... is he fat?"

"No."

"Too skinny?"

"Uh-uh."

"Does he look different in any way? Glasses? Is he ugly?"

"No. He looks like everyone else."

"Is he ... " *Hmmm. How to put it?* "Is school hard for him?"

"What do you mean?" asked Gracie, her upper lip mustached with juice.

"I mean, is he smart?"

"Oh. Well, Julie is the best at reading, and Dan is the best at math. Or maybe Becca. Bobby's not in groups with them. He's in the middle, but we're not supposed to know about the groups."

Josephine smiled. *Of course she knows. Kids always figure out that kind of stuff. So if it's not brains and not looks, what is it?* "Does he sound funny? You know, like how it's hard for Amanda to say words sometimes?"

"No. But he makes fun of her behind her back." She lowered her voice to a whisper. "He calls her A-mm-manda sometimes. I don't think she knows."

She can feel the anger mounting again. "What's this kid's last name again?"

"Crayton."

"He must not have any brothers or sisters as old as me. I'd recognize the name."

"Josephine … " Amanda called from down the hall. "I need help. I can't do the snap."

"One second," she yelled back, then turned her attention back to Gracie. "You know what, I've got to get a look at this kid. Is he still on the bus when you get dropped off?"

"No, he gets dropped off way before us. He lives in that really blue house on Haunted House Road. It's *super* blue."

"On *what* street?"

"I forget the real name. It has 'house' at the end of it. But everyone calls it Haunted House Road."

"Why?"

" 'Cause all the houses are really old and they look … you know … not very nice, I guess. I don't know how to explain it."

"Try."

"Like a bunch of them don't have enough paint. And the grass is really high or sometimes it's brown. Bobby's house has a lot of empty bottles on the front lawn."

Josephine's face brightened. "Bingo."

The following afternoon, Josephine was concentrating on feeding twisted ribbon back into a cassette, carefully rotating the wheel hole with a pen, when a flushed Gracie stepped off the bus. "You don't look so good," Josephine said, looking up. "Are you okay?"

Gracie looked at her, contempt in her eyes, then passed her in quick, determined steps. "I'm going home," she said, without looking back, as she crossed to her side of the street.

"She has to throw up," Amanda whispered to Josephine. "That's what she s-said on the bus."

But what's that look for, then? It's not my fault that she doesn't feel well. Josephine motioned for Amanda to hurry up. "Gracie, you know your dad's not home. Are you sick?"

Gracie continued her resolute march until she reached her lawn, and then dropped her backpack and cut through the grass to her porch.

"I don't have the key, Gracie," Josephine said, when she and Amanda reached her. "I can't let you in. Just tell me what's wrong."

Gracie turned away from her, and squeezed herself into the narrow space between the right side of the porch swing and the bannister. "I want my daddy! You need to call him right now."

"But he's at church now. What is it? Do you have a stomach ache?"

She nodded, her forehead pressed against the wall.

"Then let's go to my house. You can lie down inside, in the air-conditioning. You're just going to feel worse sitting out in the sun."

"But the porch is in the shade," Amanda said.

Josephine turned, flustered. "Not the same, Amanda. Inside she doesn't have to breathe in the humid—I mean, the really hot—air. But that's not the point." She walked several steps towards Gracie. "I can't call your dad unless we go to my house. I can't get in your house to use the phone."

"Then go."

"I'll stay," Amanda said. "I can take care of her while you're gone."

"I can't leave you alone for that long, Amanda. Mom and Dad would kill me. And your dad wouldn't be too happy, either, Gracie. Then maybe he wouldn't let you play with us after school anymore." Then, encouraged by Gracie's silence: "Let's go to my house. I can make you some soup, and you can lie down until he comes to pick you up."

Gracie turned away from the wall, but refused to meet Josephine's eyes. "I want to lie down on the swing for a little, first."

Josephine steadied the swing for her as she settled into it. "Okay. You can tell us when you're ready to go."

"I can push you, Gracie," said Amanda. She sucked in her stomach, and tried to force herself between the back of the swing and the front wall of the house.

"It's not that kind of swing, Amanda," Gracie said.

"What about this way?" She grabbed the rusty chains that attached the swing to the porch ceiling and tried to sway them from side to side.

"No, it's a front-to-back swing. But there's no space behind it to push. You're supposed to push off of the ground with your feet a little. But we're too short."

"Oh," said Amanda, deflated. She'd run out of ways to help.

"He has this kind of swing, too, you know," Gracie said, as Josephine pushed it with her foot.

"Who?"

"Bobby."

"Except his is all broken," said Amanda.

"You were right, Josephine," Gracie said, her voice choking. "His clothes are old, and his sneaker has a big hole in the front. His backpack has lots of rips in it."

"Amanda," Josephine said, wary of where Gracie was headed, "why don't you run and get Gracie's backpack for us? Maybe she's hungry and doesn't realize it."

Amanda's face brightened, and she turned and walked down the porch steps.

"What happened today, Gracie?" Josephine asked, her voice low.

"Amanda saw something shiny under the seat in front of us on the bus, so she picked it up to see what it was. It was just that silver stuff that sandwiches go in, but Bobby saw her with it, and said that—" She looked around Josephine's shoulder to see if Amanda was within earshot. "He said only retards play with trash."

"And?"

Gracie took a deep breath. "And then I did what you told me to do! I made fun of him back. I told him that at least Amanda doesn't live in a house that's covered with it, like his." She covered her eyes, tears streaming around them.

"Gracie, sometimes—"

"He *cried!*" she screamed. "Bobby *never* cries. And everybody laughed at him. Because of *me!*"

Josephine was stunned. She'd never considered the impact that being the tormentor would have on Gracie. Maybe it's because Gracie seemed so much older than Amanda—maybe that's why it was hard to remember that she was still such a little kid. "I'm sorry, Gracie. I was just so mad at Bobby for picking on Amanda, and none of the teachers were stopping him, so I thought … I'm sorry, really. I didn't think it'd be so tough on you." Josephine tried to pull Gracie's hands down from her eyes, but she resisted. "Gracie, look at me," Josephine said softly. He'll leave both of you alone now, you can bet on it."

Gracie peeked through her fingers. "How do you know?"

"I just *do*, Gracie. Remember, I went to kindergarten, too. I know it doesn't feel like it, but you did the right thing."

Amanda reappeared with Gracie's lunchbox. "There are s-some Goldfish left. You want them?"

"No. I just want to rest here some more."

Amanda looked disappointed, her attempt to help having failed once again. "Then maybe … maybe I could just sit next to you?"

Gracie nodded and moved over, gave Amanda space to clamber onto the swing. "You can use me as a pillow if you want," Amanda said. A grateful smile spread across Gracie's face as she rested her head on Amanda's lap. The creaking chains slowed, the swing steadied, and the two friends shared the silence.

CHAPTER 14

Family Night is ruined by a handful of yogurt-covered raisins.

Dessert is Gracie's weekly contribution, since finding one that Luke can tolerate—one free of dairy, egg, nuts, and sesame—is so difficult. She'd been at the checkout counter with Luke's favorite, strawberry sorbet, when it happened, she tells Tim now from the car. He can hear Luke screaming in the background, loud enough to make him hold the phone away from his ear.

"I can't believe I let it happen. I always make sure he's in front of me so he can't grab candy at the checkout aisle. *Always*. But I dropped my credit card, and it got stuck behind the cash register, and by the time I'd fished it out the raisins were already in his mouth. I scooped out as much as I could, but … wait, hold on … Luke, sit down and put your seatbelt back on *now!*"

He can hear the honking of one car, then two, and of Gracie's voice, suddenly distant. "It's my right of way, you idiot!"

"Gracie! Can you hear me?" He hears clattering, and then her voice is clear again.

"Sorry. I had to put the phone down for a sec."

"I don't want you calling me from the car unless it's an emergency. It's not safe."

"Are you *listening* to what's going on behind me? This doesn't qualify?"

"Does he need an Epi-Pen?"

"No, Dad," she says, in a clipped tone. "He's allergic to eggs, nuts, and sesame, but not to milk. He's lactose intolerant, remember? He needs Lactaid, and I must have left it in my other bag. Honestly, you need to keep these straight if you're going to watch … Luke! Stop kicking my seat! I'm driving!"

Tim hears the sound of rapid *rat-a-tat-tat*s, the sound he heard for the first time two Saturdays ago at the lake. *He must be hitting himself.* The screams continue, and Tim cringes as he pictures Luke striking his temples with his palms. "Gracie, you've got to stop him before he does some real damage to himself. Can you reach your hand back?"

"If I do that, he'll bite it. Hard. I'm doing the best I can." He hears impact, not of an accident but of something colliding within the car. "Luke! I'm driving! What if your shoe had hit me in the head?"

Impact again, but it's different now, steady and heavy, interspersed with Gracie's words. "Luke, you're going to break Keith's window. Put your hands down! *Now!* Wait—what is that on the window? Did you? Oh, Luke, *gross.* That smells." He can hear her rapid breaths. "I've only got a couple of minutes before it gets really bad. I just wanted to let you know that we're not going to make it to dinner. Sorry."

"No, no, no … let us help. Bring him here. Jane can make him some soup or tea for his stomach. He can play with the chess set. That always settles him." He can hear her take a deep breath and hold it, but can't tell if she's trying to calm herself or if she's irritated. After a moment she lets it go, and when she speaks again, her voice is flat, controlled.

"That won't work. I need someone big enough to help me restrain him, not tea. Luke's going to break everything he can get his hands on, and then he's going to hurt himself and anyone within reach until he shits the goddamn raisins out."

"Gracie!"

"Fine, *poops* the *stupid* raisins out. Whatever. I have to go."

"But—"

"I have to *go*, okay? I told Keith I'd call him right back." Her voice cuts out for a moment, and then she's back. "That's him on the other line right now. I've got to take it. We'll be fine," she says, and hangs up.

There's no point in calling her back. She probably won't pick up, and if she does, she'll be frustrated that he's interrupting her. The last thing she needs right now is more distraction. He glances up at the framed photos on the wall to his right, and zeroes in on one of a very young Luke at a fair. Looks like a fair, at least, since the people behind Luke are eating cotton candy and pointing at something outside of the frame, their faces bright. He wonders if he was at the event with Luke, or if it's a photo that Gracie gave to Jane because it's such a good shot. Luke is looking directly at the camera, and his expression is one of pure joy, chocolate ice cream staining the edges of his lips and dripping down his chin. He'd even managed to get a streak of it across his left cheek.

When did it happen, then? When did the boy who could eat ice cream and pose for the camera slip away? How long after this photo did food become an enemy, did communication deteriorate?

He walks over to it and peers closer, and can see now that the line across his cheek doesn't match the chocolate stains around his mouth. It's dark red, not brown. And then he remembers. The Wilston Fair. Luke had scratched his cheek on a wooden railing waiting to pet the goats. No one had noticed until his cheek was dripping blood. There'd been no tears, no cries. "It scares me, Dad," Gracie had said. "It's like he doesn't even feel pain."

The *after* years came next. After the sore throat spread through the school, after the dentist discovered a cavity, after Luke vomited from the flu—then there would be an explanation for the screaming, the broken TV, the holes kicked in the wall, the feces smeared into the carpet and lining his shirt and mouth. At some point, Luke began to register pain, but was trapped with no way to express it. No way to ask for help.

Gracie began writing stories for him, stories with pictures of kids his age holding their stomachs, heads, throats. Any part of the body that could cause pain without evidence. "My tummy hurts," the speech bubbles would say, or "I need to tell Mommy," or simply, "Ow."

It didn't work. The tantrums had increased despite the teachers, behaviorists, therapists, doctors, procedures, and medicines. Gracie would call each time there was a diagnosis—food allergies, lactose intolerance, reflux, impaction, sleeping disorder, anxiety, obsessive-compulsive disorder—and Tim's stomach would drop. "No," she'd say. "This is *good* news. Now we have something to fix. Another piece of the puzzle solved."

But the tantrums morphed instead of fading away. Once one problem was addressed, another one popped up to take its place. "I don't get it," he now remembers saying to her last summer, as they watched Luke scamper around his favorite playground. "How can a kid who can tell you what he wants for dinner, or what he wants to watch on TV, or even where to go to buy a new CD—how can that kid not know how to say 'ow?'"

"Well, knowing where to find good 'wackel music' is a high priority," she said, referring to Luke's distorted pronunciation of *classical*.

He indulged her, allowed her to sidestep the question. "How did he phrase it, again?"

She laughed. "I think it was 'Luke's going Target buying new wackel music with Mommy.'"

Good for Luke. How could you not *buy him a CD after such a huge effort?* "But that's my point. He can speak, even if it's all jumbled up. He can read, he can type, he can even do Google searches! Why can't he tell us about something simple like pain?"

"I don't know," she said, the sunny moment gone. "I think part of the problem is that pain is hard to describe. Think about it. When you go to the doctor, they ask you a million questions, right? 'Is the pain sharp or dull? Is it constant or fleeting? How would you rate it on a scale from one to ten?' He can't answer any of those."

"But why can't he learn 'it hurts' or 'ouch' like you've been trying to teach him?"

She shrugged. "I don't know. Language is hard for him. I'm asking him to do something that's difficult when he's in pain. At his most vulnerable. I don't do calculus when I have the flu."

He took his eyes off of Luke, who was trying to scale a climbing dome, and searched Gracie's face, still in profile. *My child, at* her *most vulnerable, and there's nothing I can do to help.*

"I want to comfort him if he's sick," she said as tried to straighten a piece of wire that had curled up from the bottom of the chain link fence with her foot. "The problem is, I don't always know why he's tantrumming. Being sick isn't the only reason why he does it. So what am I supposed to do? Should I assume he's sick and ignore the tantrum? What if I found out later that he'd felt fine, that he was just being a brat? That he'd pitched a fit because he wanted something he couldn't have, or he was tired, or mad? Then I've just given hugs and kisses for being bad. But what if I do the opposite? What if I punish him, thinking he's fine, and I find out later he'd been sick? That I was cruel when he needed me most?"

She gave up on the wire, folded her hands over the top of the fence and rested her chin on them. "It's hard to win. Sometimes I know why

167

he's acting out, and sometimes I don't. Sometimes I can stay calm and sometimes I can't." She forced a smile. "There are always a lot of *sometimes* and *what-ifs* with Luke."

Sometimes and what-ifs, he thinks now, as he stares at the photo. There are so few absolutes with Luke. Every action of his is examined, interpreted, qualified. *Probably, might, could, possibly, maybe, should, usually ...* these are the words used over and over when deciphering the past and strategizing for the future.

Jane's voice interrupts Tim's reverie. "You and pictures lately."

He smiles, embarrassed, although he knows there's no reason to be. "You make the best ... what's the word? When you put the pictures together and they're out of order but you do it on purpose? Like how the top of this frame doesn't line up with—"

"Collages. You like them?"

"Of course I do! You make our house a *home.* That's one of the things I love about you. You know that."

She hugs him from behind, her arms clasped around his waist, her cheek on his back. "I do. But it's still nice to hear from time to time."

Had he stopped telling her at some point? The entire house was a testament to Jane's domestic prowess. The homemade curtains and quilts, the braided rugs under the sink and in the entryway, the dinners made from scratch every night—had he begun to take all of it for granted?

She looks down at the phone, still in his hand. "Who called?"

"Gracie. She can't come."

"Luke?"

He nodded. "Milk."

"Poor thing. He just doesn't know any better. Guess we should eat, then. Everything's ready." She frowned. "It's Luke's pasta primavera, not yours. If I'd known, I would've made the cream sauce, not the oil, vinegar, and lemon one. I can check the cupboard and see if we have—"

"I'm sure it will be fine. More than fine."

"It does have eggplant from the garden it," she says, speaking more to herself than to him. "They came out wonderfully this year."

He follows her to the table, five places set and plates already filled. "Delicious," he says, his mouth full. Somehow Jane always manages to make every meal tasty, even Luke's allergy-free ones.

She watches as he takes a second bite, then a third, and then begins to scrape the pasta from the plates set out for Gracie, Keith, and Luke back into the pot that rests on a trivet at the end of the table.

"Jane, sit, eat. We'll clean up after."

She hesitates before she sits. "I'm sorry Gracie can't make it tonight. I know how important it was for you." She reaches for the water pitcher, holds the lid at an angle to stop the sliced lemons from escaping.

How much, he wonders, does she know? He hasn't once mentioned the bracelet since last week's dinner, certainly hasn't mentioned the true reason he needs to see Gracie.

She takes a sip, catches the stare that he's too slow to hide. "What? You think I haven't noticed how preoccupied you are? Or how many times you've asked about this evening? 'Is she still planning on coming? Is Keith coming, too? What time? Are you *sure* she's coming?'"

"I'm that obvious?"

"I'm teasing, sweetie. But yes." She stabs a piece of zucchini with her fork, then twirls pasta around it, winding the hanging strand to the top with her knife. She holds it in mid-air for moment, then rests it back down on her plate. "I'm hoping that you'll still share your secret tonight. Even if it's just me."

Hope surges inside him. Why had he assumed that Jane—his kind, intuitive Jane—wouldn't understand? Maybe she already knows, and she's waiting for him to come forward on his own terms. Maybe she'll help him come up with an excuse to see Gracie, guide him in how to explain it to her, and this will all be over. The thought of being able to let the dam burst and allow the truth to come flooding out is so enticing that he feels dizzy.

"Tim, are you all right? Your eyes just rolled funny."

"No, I'm fine. Really. It's not the morning, anyway. I would've known by now."

"But you've been under so much stress lately. Maybe it's causing break-through symptoms."

"Trust me. I'd tell you. We're home, there's nothing I'd be missing today by taking my meds and going to bed early. I just felt light-headed for a minute. Probably hungry, is all. I haven't eaten since breakfast." He dives into his pasta, looks up after a few bites to find her staring. "I know that look. Gracie gives me the same one when she thinks I'm trying to hide it. It's not going to happen again. See? I'm not having any problems talking."

"All right," she says cautiously, after another moment of searching his face for signs. "It's just that you looked like that time when—"

"Jane. You're getting all worked up over nothing." He pauses. "I think I know the real reason why you're so anxious."

"It's not that."

"Of course it is. What time is her flight getting in on Wednesday?"

"Afternoon, around four," she says, with a grudging smile. "We'll beat you home. I'll have dinner ready early so you can grab a quick bite before you go back for Bible study."

"I can pick something up, if that's easier."

"Take out? With my *mother* staying here? I'd never live it down."

"Come on, it's good that she'll be here. Otherwise it'd be my parents, and you *have* to be nice to them."

"Tim! Would you like Gracie talking about you that way?"

"She probably already does. That's the way it goes."

"I guess you're right. I'm glad she's staying, even though it won't be easy. She's fragile now that Dad's gone. She's always been a woman who's been cared for." She puts her hand over his. "Your parents have been very understanding. They're the ones who should be staying with us. And I know it's a financial imposition."

"They'll be fine. I think my mom's only stayed in a hotel a couple of times before. It's an adventure for them. I'm glad they've been forced to treat themselves to a little luxury."

"*Luxury?*"

"Okay, I'll admit that the Best Western isn't a five-star accommodation. But it's clean, it's comfortable, and they'll get a continental breakfast. They'll be thrilled. The one I'm worried about is you."

She rubs her head. "It's only a week. One week of 'judge not, lest ye be judged.'"

"Betty's favorite."

"She tacks it on after every insult. Did you hear what she said about Celia?"

"Celia?"

"One of the neighbors in her building. A sweet lady. She offered to lend Mother a dress for the wedding. Did I tell you her reason for turning down the offer?" She rolls her eyes and mimics her mother's voice. "'Jane, that Celia may have money, but money doesn't buy you morals. I've seen her in that dress, and she looks like a whore. But I'm not judging. "Judge not, lest ye be judged," I always say.'"

"Sounds like Betty."

She looks up at the ceiling. "There's a whole lot of judgment coming my way for a week."

"But she loves you. And you love her."

"I know. Remind me, okay? *Frequently.*" She notices his empty plate. "More?"

"Please."

"Here's the thing that gets to me," she says, as she serves him. "She doesn't even understand the meaning of that verse, because she only quotes the first line. I can't remember the exact wording—I'm sure you can—but Jesus says that you can't say to your brother, 'Take that speck of sawdust out of your eye,' if you have a log in yours, right? Unless you take yours out first, you're a hypocrite."

"Very good."

"So it's actually okay to judge. It's okay as long as you understand that you'll be judged by the same measuring stick."

His breath catches. "And what if the other person no longer measures up?" he asks, hoping that she doesn't notice the slight quaver in his voice.

"Well, then it's your duty as a Christian to point out that person's sin in a merciful way, and to help him return to God. But in the end, there's only so much that can be done. Unless the sinner repents in the eyes of the Lord, he can't be forgiven."

CHAPTER 15

Josephine can hear the TV in the bedroom as she opens the front door. *Wes is back.*

She hangs her keys on the key rack, and drops her bag on the side table. She's still for a moment, assesses her conflicting emotions. Hope, relief, shame, anger, fear—-all of them jumbled within her, jockeying for position. But the feeling that dominates them all is exhaustion. She doesn't have the energy to deal with this now. But she must.

She walks through the kitchen, pours herself a glass of water from the fridge, not because she's thirsty, but because she wants her presence to be known. When he doesn't appear from around the corner, she puts her glass in the sink, untouched, and heads to their bedroom. Wes is still in his work clothes, although he's taken off his suit jacket and loosened his tie.

"So you came home before work this morning," she says, running her hand in a straight line from neck to stomach, pantomiming *tie*.

He turns his attention from the TV to her. "I wasn't trying to avoid you. I didn't know if you'd be home or not."

"Yes, you did. You know I always leave by seven."

He is silent.

She sits on the bed next to him, her back touching his outstretched legs. "I waited for you all day yesterday," she says quietly. "I went to my parents' house for lunch, but besides that, I was here. I didn't know what else to do. You wouldn't answer any of my texts or calls." She turns to face him, but he's switched his gaze back to ESPN, or any one of the countless sports stations he considers essential. "You have every right to be mad at me, Wes. More than mad—furious. I know I didn't handle things well." She gives his leg a gentle shake, as she does every morning, then reaches over him for the remote and turns the TV off.

He doesn't complain, nor does he attempt to turn the TV back on. He remains motionless, and stares at it as if analysts, statistics, and footage are still visible.

She stands in front of the TV, blocking his view of the blank screen. "Wes! It's been two days! We need to talk. You can scream at me, if you want, but please, talk to me."

He raises himself up, his weight on his elbows. "You want me to talk to you? Isn't that something *you* should've done before you stopped taking the Pill?"

"Why do you assume that I did it on purpose?"

"Seriously, Jo. Do you think I'm stupid? It's not like we haven't fought over having kids before."

"It didn't happen like that, I promise."

He cocks his head to the side. *Prove it*, the look says.

She swallows hard. "I forgot to take it once, four or five years ago, and I was so scared that I'd get pregnant. But I didn't. And then it happened again in October, and I didn't get pregnant again. But that time, when I got my period I felt sad, not relieved. And then ... I see how good you are with Reid and Owen. You love to play with them, and you've always said you want kids—"

"Playing with Rob's kids is totally different!" He sits all the way up, punches the mattress, and then falls back down, his arm covering his eyes.

"But every time you see them, you say they're such great kids, some day we'll have some of our own."

"I know what I said, Josephine!"

She stops, chastened. She hears the ticking of the clock, the whirring of the air conditioner, the tinging of the light bulb that will soon blow. The meaningless sounds that fill the emptiness where his words belong.

He runs his hand through his hair. "You're right. I *have* said that before, and it's true. But when we're ready, not now. Not this way."

"But I'm thirty-seven, Wes. And I've been waiting for you to be ready for years. We should make the decision, not nature, don't you think?"

"Exactly. *We* should make the decision. But that didn't happen, did it? You made it by yourself. And then you purposefully waited until it was too late to do anything about it."

"It's not too late. I'm still only twelve weeks."

"You're pushing it pretty damn close."

She swallows hard. "Is that what you want?"

"I don't know what I want!" he says, throwing his hands in the air. "No, I take that back. I do know. What I want is a choice, and you've taken that away."

"You don't have to be a part of our life if you don't want to. I'll understand."

" 'Our life?' You and the not-yet-a-baby are an 'our' already? So I guess I do have a choice: deadbeat dad or roped-in boyfriend."

Her voice is shaky, smaller than she wants it to be. "Aren't we more than boyfriend and girlfriend, Wes?" The question hangs in the air for a moment, and then Josephine plunges forward before he has the chance to answer. "I love you, Wes. And yes, I want a baby. But it's more than that. I want a baby with *you*. Trust me. Please."

"Trust you? How can I trust you?"

* * *

The insomnia hit before Josephine was even halfway through her first year of residency.

She'd managed to keep up with the frenetic pace during the initial summer months, but by Thanksgiving the exhaustion had begun to catch up with her. The white noise from the TV in the on-call room did little to mask the constant bustle of the hospital, but falling asleep wasn't the problem, anyway. It was *staying* asleep that her body seemed to have forgotten how to do. Even if she was lucky enough to avoid being paged for a couple of hours, she'd bolt upright on her own, her mind racing about the never-ending cycle of patients to be worked up and admitted; medical plans to be ordered and carried out; lab work and films to be reviewed; routine surgeries to assist with and complex ones to observe; med students to supervise; discharge plans and summaries to write. And somehow she was supposed to find time to study for ABSITE as well.

Coffee. I've got to give up coffee. It'd be worth suffering caffeine-free call nights if she could salvage her nights at home, where sleep had become elusive as well. Wasting hours in the dead of night, watching infomercials and dreading the morning—it had to stop.

Quitting cold turkey didn't stop the night awakenings, as she'd hoped, and resulted in pounding headaches. None of the typical sleep remedies were helpful in the middle of the night. What was she supposed to do, take a warm bath and drink herbal tea at three in the morning? Even melatonin hadn't been able to cure her fractured sleep.

Diphenhydramine came next. What harm could come from an over-the-counter sleep aid? She'd be able to manage every fourth night on call if she could force herself to sleep at home. But the next day her dry mouth and tight throat would make her wonder if the couple hours of sleep she'd gained had been worth it.

With every passing week, her exhaustion grew, as did the sickening dread of falling asleep in the OR. Too embarrassed to confide in Evan or a senior resident, she relied on scattered pieces of advice that she'd over-hear from interns and nurses. "Eat before surgery," "drink just enough to stay hydrated," "wear light clothing under your scrubs"—these were the proactive strategies mentioned the most, but she'd already learned these as a med student. Now that that the punishing call schedule had set in, she needed in-the-trenches tactics. "Shift your weight," she overheard in the locker room. "Never lock your knees." "Keep your feet wide apart." "Lean onto the table." Those that were struggling the most relied on pain. "Bite the inside of your cheek." "Scrape your tongue under your front teeth."

It happened, as she'd feared it would, during a routine gall bladder removal. Not a long surgery requiring hours of retracting in a frozen posi-tion, but during a quick, straightforward laparoscopic cholecystectomy.

The darkness deserved some of the blame. There were no bright, overhead lights to keep her alert. But the bigger culprit was boredom. Driv-ing the camera was so excruciatingly dull that she felt her eyelids growing heavy within the first couple of minutes of the procedure.

It must have been slight, the loosening of her grip. She came to with a jerk, could feel her hands clamp down on the camera before she was fully conscious. A wave of adrenalin coursed through her body, and a bitter, metallic taste filled her mouth. She could smell a sour odor wafting up from her armpits, and she flattened her arms against her sides to conceal the smell.

Had anyone noticed? The surgeon hadn't reprimanded her, hadn't even glanced her way. Neither had the anesthesiologist or the senior resident. But the OR nurse—were those crows' feet around her eyes, or smile lines? There was no way to tell with a surgical mask covering her mouth. If there was a smile underneath it, then what kind? A supportive, *I've-been-there* smile, or a mocking, *you-can't-hack-it* smirk? She held her breath and stared at the OR nurse, demanded a response.

A wink! She felt giddy with relief. *Thank God.* But then, a second thought: *This can never happen again. Ever.*

She needed better drugs. She needed temazepam.

I thought I'd found the solution, she thought a week later, as she closed her textbook and tossed it to the other end of the couch. *If only I'd known.* She stretched, and then glanced at the time displayed on the cable box. It was past nine thirty already, and Evan, due over to her apartment by seven thirty, still hadn't arrived.

She hadn't expected him to make it on time. He'd matched to Barnes-Walker General, after all, known for its grinding pace. Matching into programs only a half hour apart had been a pleasant surprise, but despite their proximity, they rarely saw each other. Once or twice a month at best, even less time than they'd had together in med school.

She stretched out on the couch, turned on the TV and flipped through the channels. How could there be so little worth watching when hundreds of channels offered twenty-four hour programming? She felt her eyelids closing, and considered giving in to sleep. She needed it; she was on call tomorrow. But being woken up by Evan and then not able to fall asleep again would put her right back in the pattern she'd just broken. She forced her eyes open, sat back up and opened her book again. Might as well get back to making good use of the time.

She was only a couple of pages in when she heard him at the door, fiddling with his keys. She walked over to let him in, grasped the doorknob just as the deadbolt unlocked.

"Hey," he said, giving her a perfunctory kiss, then passing her to peer into the fridge. "Crazy day. *Days*, actually. I'm exhausted. And starving." He shuffled the fridge's contents around, searching. "Wow. You really don't have a lot of options here. Looks like a take-out kind of night. Chinese?"

He switched his search from the refrigerator to the pile of takeout menus in the drawer under the phone. "What's the name of that place again? The one with the purple menu?" He flipped through the pile, and pulled out a yellow one instead. "Sushi! That's what I'm in the mood for. How about Yoshida?"

"I don't think sushi's a great idea for me right now."

"I know, it's late. Sorry about that. I should've called from the car, but I was still so keyed up. I needed to decompress, have a couple of minutes where I didn't have to think about anything, you know?"

"No, it's not that. I'm nauseous, that's all."

"That sucks. Hope you haven't caught what I had last week. Man, I was puking nonstop. Spent a whole day doing floorwork hooked up to an IV pole." He looked down at the menu again. "Now I've really got a craving for it. Okay by you if I still get it?"

"Yeah, sure."

"How about I order you some plain white rice?"

"Whatever, fine. But I need to get to bed on the early side, and I really need to talk to you about—"

"Just give me a second to order," he said, as he dialed. "I haven't eaten all day. I'm starting to feel like I might pass out."

"Evan—"

He held a finger to his lips. "Hi, I'd like to place an order? One triple roll combo—tuna, yellowtail, and … " He ran his finger down the list. "California, I guess. And a side of white rice, and a Coke." He pantomimed *drink* to Josephine, who shook her head no. "And that's it." She could faintly hear the voice on the other end of the line, and then Evan again. "Great, see you in fifteen."

He picked up his keys, felt in his back pocket for his wallet. "Back soon, okay?"

She said nothing. Had he heard a word she'd said?

"What?" He looked confused for a moment, and then offered a conciliatory smile. "Sorry. You wanted to talk." He looked down at his watch. "How about you come with me, then? Parking's tough there, so we should—"

"I'm pregnant."

"Funny. I get it, I wasn't paying attention. I said I was sorry, didn't I?"

"I'm serious, Evan."

He studied her for a moment, searched her face for a hidden smile. "But you have an IUD."

"Did."

"'Did?' When did you have it removed?"

"Tuesday."

"You called in *sick*?" He looked horrified. "You're going to see that on your end-of-rotation eval. I know a guy who failed because he took two days off for tonsillitis."

She held in a laugh. *That's how twisted life is for us now. He's more upset that I might violate the doctors-are-superhuman code than by an unexpected pregnancy.* "No, it was my post-call day. My OB/GYN squeezed me in."

She looked down, noticed that she'd been drawing circles on the counter with her finger. "It failed," she said, trying to sound matter-of-fact. "I'm the lucky less than one percent."

"Is it ectopic?"

She shook her head, could feel her chin begin to tremble. "I wish it was."

"*What?* Are you crazy?"

"Don't you see? Then it wouldn't be up to me. The pregnancy would have to be terminated." *Terminated.* The word was clinical, detached.

"I don't get it. Did you have the IUD removed because you wanted to make sure it would be a safe pregnancy, or because you were hoping the procedure would *end* the pregnancy?"

"I don't know. I just wanted it out because it didn't work, so what was the point?" Her throat felt tight, sore from the pressure of holding back tears. "There's more."

"*More?*"

She swallowed. "There's been some … exposure." She concentrated on a hangnail, ripped at the flesh until she drew blood. "I didn't know I was pregnant when I was taking it."

"Taking what, Josephine?" His tone was suddenly neutral, and she wondered if this was the Dr. Evan Blake that his patients knew.

"Well, a lot of caffeine on call nights. *A lot.*" She watched his face pale, but continued before her courage failed her. "And diphenhydramine, on some of my nights off." She took a deep breath and held it for a moment before she let the final two words escape. "And temazepam."

Splotches of red emerged from beneath his pallid neck and cheeks. "You took them all together?"

"Not on purpose."

"So that's a yes." He began to pace in fits and starts. "Who gave you that script? You can get in serious fucking trouble for that."

"I'm not an idiot. I went to my PCP."

"And?"

"And I told her that I'd be traveling for a week or so."

He was pacing now. "A week. Why did you stop there? Why didn't you ask her to give you enough to finish your whole internship?"

"That's not fair! I just—I needed help, Evan. I fell asleep during a lap chole."

The pacing came to an abrupt halt. "Were you assisting?"

"No. Driving the camera."

"So when you say 'fell asleep'—do you mean you hit the ground?"

"No! Are you kidding? I mean I nodded off for a couple of seconds."

"That's it?"

"What do you mean 'that's it?' "

He shrugged. "It's not like you face-planted into an open abdomen. It happens sometimes."

"To you?"

"Lots of times. I kind of like the three-second super nap."

What? Her greatest fear, the one she'd been too ashamed to share with him, hadn't fazed him in the slightest. He actually looked forward to it. "Well, it was the first time it'd ever happened to me, and it freaked me out. It happened last Thursday, and I was so stressed about it that I couldn't even sleep post-call on Friday. So I called my doctor, and I got lucky—she had a cancellation."

"But you're on q4 call right now! How did you expect to function?"

"Last weekend was my golden weekend, remember? I had Friday, Saturday, and Sunday night to sleep. The only time all month that I had a post-call day right before it."

"So why did you take both? What did you need the diphenhydramine for if you had temazepam?"

"I got cold feet. I took the diphenhydramine at eight, hoping I wouldn't need the temazepam. But I woke up about three hours later, so I took it. And it worked! So I used the same combo Saturday. Sunday I dropped the diphenhydramine and only took a half dose of the temazepam since I knew I'd be on call again Monday. So only two times with both."

He rubbed his face with both hands. "Have you looked into temazepam?"

"Of course," she said, trying to keep the irritation out of her voice. This was a lot for him to take in, but honestly, did he think she was too stupid or lazy to do a little research? "In rats, there was an increase in fetal resorptions and rudimentary ribs, and in rabbits, exencephaly and rib asymmetry or fusion."

"Humans, Jo."

"There was a surveillance study in Michigan of about a hundred and fifty newborns who were exposed to temazepam in the first trimester. Six developed major birth defects. Two had cleft palate, which was the only defect noted that might suggest temazepam exposure. Same as any other benzo."

"And?"

"And what?"

"*Come on.* What studies are there for taking the two drugs together?"

"I could only find one animal study, with rabbits. The drugs were administered to controls separately and in combination to a third group. There was no mortality when they were given separately."

"*Mortality?*"

She bit her lip. "When the two were given together, eighty-one percent of the babies were either stillborn or died shortly after birth. The exact mechanism for the interaction couldn't be defined."

"Any reported cases in humans?"

"Just one. A woman had a stillborn baby after taking fifty milligrams of diphenhydramine followed by thirty milligrams of temazepam an hour and a half later. The case report is what prompted the animal study."

"Josephine—"

"I know. But I took the medications three hours apart, so there was less diphenhydramine in my system by the time I took the temazepam. And I only took fifteen milligrams of temazepam, not thirty."

"You may have taken less, but you took it during your first trimester, for Christ's sake! How far along was the woman in the case report?"

"Term."

"And you?"

"Just under eight weeks."

He rubbed his eyes. "Look, I don't see how—"

"How about a pros and cons list?" She searched for a scrap of paper. She couldn't let his words be said aloud.

"Seriously? There aren't enough cons for you?"

"Please, Evan."

He shook his head in frustration. "You need more? Fine. Here's another: you'll have to quit your residency."

"Not necessarily. I checked into maternity leave. I'm out of luck because I don't qualify for FMLA since I've been working for less than a year. But I could take my vacation time—"

"Two weeks? You might not be able to take them back-to-back. Even if you could, it's not enough time. What if you need a C-section?"

"I could take a leave of absence."

"An *unpaid* leave of absence. How's that going to work?"

"My parents could help out financially. The problem is I'll lose my health insurance."

He threw his hands in the air. "That's a bit of a snag in your plan then, isn't it? You're not even looking at the bigger picture, Jo. Even if we can cobble together some plan for the first weeks afterwards, what happens then? How are we going to take care of a baby?"

"We'll have to do day care."

"Where are we going to find a daycare that's open ninety hours a week?"

"We'll get a part-time nanny for after hours."

"Do you have any idea how much that costs? My sister complains all the time that she spends half her paycheck for day care. And she earns a lot more than we do."

"Maybe I could switch into path. The hours are much better."

He rolled his eyes. "Path. Please."

"I don't know why you're such a snob about it. I think—"

"When are you due?"

"The end of July."

"Perfect timing. You'll have to work your ass off this year—super-safe for pregnancy, by the way—so that you can lose it and start your residency all over again. *If* you can find a spot. And what month does that new year begin? That's right, July! I'm sure a path program would love to accept a resident who bailed out on surgery and is going into labor the first week."

"Maybe the program director would let me finish out the surgical year doing research. Then I can start up path late, after I have the baby—"

"Josephine, are you actually considering continuing this pregnancy?"

"I'm just trying to look at all the factors."

"Really? Cause it seems like there's a big one that you've left out."

But she'd thought of all the possibilities, hadn't she? What had she missed? She looked at him, confused.

"Your sister?"

"But you've never even met Amanda."

"You've told me enough. She's mentally retar—*challenged*. How is she going to support herself after your parents die? She'll be your responsibility."

He's right, she thought, dumbfounded. He'd considered the implications for Amanda before she had. It wasn't new, the knowledge that she'd be Amanda's caretaker at some point, but it had always been abstract and far in the future, an easily shelved obligation. Amanda's needs had never influenced any of her decisions before.

"What if there are a ton of medical expenses, Jo? How are we going to pay those bills?"

"We could ... I mean *I* could, umm ... "

He folded his arms as she failed to come up with an answer. "See? Are you really willing to give up your career for a fetus that you may have severely harmed? Wait—I take that back. It's not even a fetus yet. It's still just an embryo."

Embryo. Not baby, embryo. Remember that. It's the size of a bean right now. It has a tail. It has transparent skin. It weights four-hundredths of an ounce.

"You keep talking about 'the baby' as if it's a cooing, smiling six-month-old. And you could end up having that baby. But you could also have the infant that we've both seen in the NICU—the one whose time on Earth is spent suffering."

A stifled cry escaped her as she thought about breathing tubes, ventilators, IV lines taped to fragile bodies in incubators. "The temazepam risks alone are still very low. And the combo—I just can't believe that I'm the only other woman this has happened to. There'd be more in the literature if the interaction was so dangerous."

"It's pretty hard to completely dismiss an eighty-one percent fatality rate. Even in animals."

She began to sob. Horrid, strangled sounds that worsened the more she tried to tame them. He pulled her close, and she could feel the rhythmic pulsing of his heart as her ear pressed against his neck. Her nose was running, and she wiped it with the back of her hand as she let out an embarrassed laugh. They held each other for several minutes, her face pressed against his shirt collar, slick with her tears and snot.

He broke the silence. "Look … this isn't what either of us envisioned having a child would be like, right?"

"This isn't what I want," she said, and the words that she'd been smothering came spilling out. "I was supposed to finish my residency first. I was supposed to take prenatal vitamins and eat organic food, not insomnia meds and whatever's left in the vending machines!" She scanned the room for tissues. "I guess guys don't think about these things."

Evan was silent for a moment, and when he spoke again, the anger was gone from his voice. "No, I have. Somewhat. I guess I always wanted to go into surgery because it's exciting, but also because I'd be able to earn enough to support my family while ... " He swallowed hard, and she felt the rise and fall of his Adam's apple against her ear. "While my wife stays home to take care of the kids."

His words blindsided her.

He didn't love her.

I'll find a way to transfer into path, she wanted to say. *Please, Evan. I'll make it happen, I promise. And then I'll have normal hours and we can make it work.*

But there was no point. He'd already written her out of his future, or maybe she'd never had a place in it to begin with.

She pushed backwards out of his embrace, patted his shirt dry as best she could. "Should we bother with the pros list?"

"I don't have any," he said. "Do you?"

CHAPTER 16

"Have you seen this?" asks Craig, peering into Tim's office. He holds up a paperback book. "Don Geary dropped it off yesterday. He thought it might be something we'd like to discuss at Bible study."

Tim sets his book down, opens a desk drawer and reaches inside a box that's been labeled *bookmarks* in flowing cursive. He pulls out a sapphire-colored one, lined with ribbon and dusted with sparkle sand. It's triangular rather than ruler-shaped, and holds the page in place by grasping its top corner rather than by resting flat on it.

"This way you don't have to worry about them slipping out," Jane said when she gave him the box, modestly waving away his thanks. "They're a cinch to make. I found these real cute envelopes at Hobby Lobby, and then I just cut the corners off, added the zigzag at the base with my pinking shears, and decorated them."

He saves his place with it, then pushes his book aside and examines Craig's paperback. The cover photo is of a well-dressed man in his late forties, looking straight into the camera and offering an ecstatic smile that reveals his gums and disconcertingly white teeth. He's surrounded by his family, five children and a rail-thin woman with platinum hair that doesn't match her dark eyes or brows. Tim rolls his eyes at the staged photo of Ryan Harper, pastor of Creekview, the megachurch half an hour away from Loring Point. "I know, I should've gotten to it by now. It's already been out for a year, right?"

Craig grins. "This is a new one."

"With the same title? Is this part two?"

"The last one was *Reach Your Potential Through Him*. This one is *Exceed Your Potential Through Him*."

"Have you read it?"

"Yep."

"And?"

"Pretty much the same as the first. A lot of pep talk and the occasional quote from Scripture. Weak on depth and context."

"You told Don we'd discuss it *tonight*?"

Craig shook his head. "He's not coming tonight. He was hoping we'd have a chance to read it over the next few weeks. Let him know if we thought it'd be worth integrating into our weekly group." He pauses. "I'm concerned, Tim."

"Why? Nothing wrong with offering some inspiration. We'll just avoid the fluff and provide fuller biblical exegesis."

"That's not why I'm concerned."

"Then why?"

"We're going to lose some people. And it's my fault."

"What are you talking about?"

Craig fiddles with his watch, slides it back and forth over his wrist without adjusting the loose band. "Both of Don's kids are in youth group. Both of them went on my trip to see the Bryson Brothers play at Creekview."

"Craig, please. We're not going to lose our entire congregation because fifteen high schoolers went to a concert. Kids don't choose where the family observes. Their parents do."

"Exactly. I was so caught up in getting the kids involved that I never thought beyond the concert. I knew they'd think Creekview was cool— thousands of people, lights, screens, the whole deal, right? But I never thought they'd like it so much that they'd get their parents interested, too."

"But Don's not leaving. And so far only a handful of members have even expressed an interest in Harper's book." He waits until Craig meets his gaze. "Don't be so hard on yourself. What's great about our church is that it's small enough for us to know everyone by name. You can be dazzled at Creekview, but you can't get the sense of community that we have here. Most people are smart enough to see the value in that."

Craig offers a fleeting smile. "You're right. I'm overreacting. But still," he says, looking at the book, "maybe we have something to learn from Harper. Maybe there's something to be said for pep talk preaching."

"Is that a real phrase? You're making me feel old."

"No, I made it up. But it fits," Craig says, laughing.

"I've always done my best to inspire through Scripture. Are my sermons that dull?"

Craig's eyes open wide in surprise. "No! I didn't mean that at all. I'm sorry, I'm being unclear. Here's the thing: we *both* start our sermons with Scripture and then segue into relevance to daily life. Maybe we should try it the other way around. Start with the cheerleading, so we don't lose people's attention, then tack on the study at the end."

"Why leave it for last? Study is more important."

"I know it is. But maybe we need to guide our flock to it in a different way. Creekview is bursting at the seams, and our congregation has been dwindling for close to a decade."

"I don't know if 'dwindling' is a fair word. Sure, we've lost some families here and there, but … "

"Look, I'm not trying to compete with them. But even if we think our way is better—even if we *know* it is—it's not reaching people. I think the flip-flop approach is worth testing, and I'm willing to do the fluff part. You're the senior pastor. You should handle the interpretation of the Word."

"That's generous, Craig, but if we did, we'd share the honor, of course." He scratches at the stubble that's beginning to peek through on his jawline. "To be honest, I'm not sure I can do it. I've never preached in generalities before. Specifics are what I do. To preach without supporting with chapter and verse would be—"

The answer.

It would be the answer.

His body intuits this before his mind. A merciful coolness spreads throughout his body, even before logic springs into action. A balm, healing him from deep within.

There'd be no need to rationalize contradictions or justify immorality. No need to defend the God who condones the beating of slaves, the stoning of disobedient children, the raping of women, and the destruction of entire cities. All of it, gone. He could pick the good and leave out the bad. He could share the biblical lessons that he still believes in, God or no God. Sharing with the poor. Aiding the sick. Loving your neighbor. Acting with humility. He could live this life. He could keep his family, his friends, his church.

"—a challenge," he says, surprised by his own words. "It would be a challenge. You know what? Let's try it. I'll leave the biblical hermeneutics to you, and I'll concentrate on the life coaching."

Craig looks shocked. "Are you sure? Because I wasn't trying to—"

"I know."

"But like you said—we should share the honor."

"Sure, at some point. But this was your idea, so you should take the lead. Let's start this way, and see where it takes us."

Craig shakes his head. "Wow. This conversation did *not* go the way I expected it to."

The phone rings, and Tim glances at the caller ID. "It's Jane," he says aloud, for Craig's benefit.

Craig points to himself, and then to the conference room.

"Meet you there in five," Tim says, as he picks up the phone. He can hear the fatigue in her voice as she asks him to stop for chamomile tea on his way home.

"It has to be Twinings," she says. "We've already been to three grocery stores, and all we can find is Celestial Seasonings or Bigelow. Mother's napping now, but apparently she needs it tonight or she won't be able to sleep."

"I think skipping the nap will help her more than a cup of tea later."

"But that would be a *rational* decision."

He chuckles, enjoying this rare flash of sarcasm from her. "Hang in there. Only five more days of mother-daughter time left. Find out which store has it, and I'll pick it up. I'll be home between nine-thirty and ten."

He leans back in his chair, allows himself a minute to collect his thoughts. Finally. Months upon months of agony, of plotting and strategizing, and out of nowhere, the answer appears, unbidden.

The passing of the baton, he supposes. Yet it's so different from how he imagined it would be. He calculates how many years he worked with John, then Ed, assigns years to events until he has a clear timeline. Six with John before he left to work with Terrence Binterman. This he knows immediately. The dates are hazier with Ed, require subtraction, but after a moment he settles on thirteen. Close to two decades of mentorship in all.

He'd intended to provide the same for Craig, considered it his duty, but now it seems that his role as teacher will be cut short. Eight, closing in on nine years. It will have to be enough.

It occurs to him that his assumption that Craig *wants* a lengthy mentorship might be flawed. After all, it was he, not Craig, whose life circumstances had precluded him from going to seminary. It was he who spent decades immersed in books to compensate for his inferior formal education. And now, after a lifelong quest for knowledge, he must disregard all that he's learned.

He thinks of Ed, of how kind he was in sharing his education rather than using it to guard his seniority. How Ed lent him his books and papers, helped him as he struggled through syntax in Hebrew and Greek. How Ed had nurtured within him skill in parsing and translation, and opened his eyes to reading Scripture from a historical, theological perspective.

He still misses Ed from time to time, misses the sense of stability and family that colors his memories of their years together. Because with Ed came his daughter, Lisa, just Gracie's age, and his wife, Carol, who introduced Tim to her best friend. To Jane.

When he separates those years from the end, he can still look upon them fondly. The years when he was blessed with the older brother he'd always wanted, when his daughter gained a close friend and he a new wife. But the end can't be ignored for long, because it too began with Ed's family. It began with Brett.

* * *

Tim had set out to be a different kind of pastor from the get-go. True, he was married, but he was just out of college. Surely the high schoolers would find it easier to relate to him than to John.

He was determined to make youth ministry more than a *have-to*, as it had been for him. He'd hated it, and had only gone because his parents hadn't given him a choice. He could still remember his introduction to it, in ninth grade. He'd been instructed to collect the names of neighbors unattached to a church, and offer them his services, free of charge, in the form of mowing, painting, or cleaning. "This is what Jesus would have done," he was coached to reply, when suspicious questions arose. "Please come join us for Sunday services at nine o'clock." It was humiliating, and boring to boot.

Soon after he had been sent with three others to a nursing home. It too was an act of service, he was told, a way of bringing people into the church by leading through example. But the air inside the home was stale and sour, a combination of urine and bleach. What was he supposed to talk about with bedridden ninety-year-olds? Was he expected to try and save their souls before they died? And who was watching the example he was setting? Staff? They already knew far more about caring for the sick than he did.

Looking back, the missing ingredient was easy to identify: joy. The pleasure of helping others hadn't been enough for his teenage self. He'd hated going. It must have showed, too, because despite four years of out-reach, he hadn't been able to bring one person closer to Jesus.

But another four years later, he found himself living across the country, married, and the head of youth outreach as an associate pastor. He knew that his first event had to define him as different, and, hopefully, cool. Service *was* a necessary part of ministry, but he had to find a way to keep self-conscious teenagers comfortable.

The car wash had been Shayla's idea. "You'll get a whole lot of people lining up for it," she'd said. "I bet Wal-Mart would let you use their parking lot. It'd get them more customers. Plus, there's safety in numbers. If the kids are grouped, the shy ones don't even have to say anything. Just make sure each group has a talker in it."

"But do you think they'll have fun?"

"Are you serious? A car wash means water fights. You think all those hormone-crazed, purity-pledged boys won't jump at the chance to soak the girls?"

She'd been right. It had been a huge success, with long lines of cars that led to new faces at church over the course of the next month. Spurred on by this victory, a new event was quickly organized. Thirst Outreach, as Shayla called it, began on a blistering Saturday at Wakefield State Park. Two tables were set up, one at the exit to the largest jogging trail, and one at the exit to the bike path. Chilled bottles of water, decorated with labels bearing the name and address of the church, were handed out along with tracts filled with verses from Romans, Ephesians, and John. A risk-free approach for the faint of heart.

As the years passed, and he developed a set schedule, he began to hand over the organization of social events to volunteers, typically college grads who had moved back to Loring Point. He'd felt awful for delegating, but his responsibilities under Ed were far greater than they had been under John. It was even becoming difficult to find time to lead religious discussion at youth group meetings.

It was Jane who'd eased his guilt, although she'd wounded his pride in the process. "Gracie's friend Abby has an older brother who just started youth group," she'd said one evening, after Gracie had gone to bed.

"That's right—Tyler, isn't it?"

"Yes."

"Hard to believe that Gracie's in middle school. I can remember seventh grade."

"Can you, Tim?" Her brow was knitted. "Sweetie, we both know thirty-four is young. But to a high-schooler, you're ancient. Can you imagine how embarrassing it'd be for Gracie if she were to hear through Abby that Tyler makes fun of you?"

"Tyler makes fun of me?"

"No, no, no. This is just a hypothetical." She lowered her voice, even though Gracie couldn't hear her. "Haven't you noticed that she closes the door when she's on the phone now? That she rolls her eyes at us when she thinks we're not looking? Maybe ... maybe you should think about letting go of youth group altogether." She paused, then added: "The sooner the better."

He'd taken her advice, and by the following year, had formalized an internship program with Norton Roth, a nearby Bible college, placing his involvement with youth group at a bare minimum. When Gracie began youth group in her freshman year, his only connection during the school year was a supervision meeting with the youth group leader once a week and an evaluation once a semester.

He had to admit that having a college student working for course credit injected creativity into a program that had been showing signs of stagnation. Parker, Loring Point Fellowship's first youth group leader, improved programs that hadn't been tweaked in years. Why not take Movie Night—free pizza and a movie in the youth room for those who brought along a friend who hadn't yet been saved—and add a charitable component? Let the students pick a charity as a group, he'd suggested, then require them to bring a donation. A canned good for a local pantry, an article of clothing for a shelter, a book for an underprivileged school library.

Parker also deserved the credit for devising ways to use sports as a method of sharing the good news. A slam dunk competition was his first venture, which only required an adjustable hoop, a busy park, and a rented microphone for a short message in between rounds. Next was a 5K in support of the runner-up charity from Movie Night, the Boys and Girls Club. T-shirts sporting "LPF Cares for Kids" were worn by each runner.

Of course, not every semester brought him a Parker. But every couple of years a kid like him would emerge. Sometimes a youth group leader, sometimes a youth group member, but always confident and engaging—

everything most adolescents are not. In Gracie's junior year, that person was Brett.

Brett's family had moved from North Carolina to Texas when his father was offered a large promotion. They chose to settle in Loring Point, even though it meant an hour and a half commute for his father, so that Brett would have a cousin to help him adjust to his new school.

"Poor kid, moving right before junior year," Ed had said to Tim. "It won't be easy on him. But Mike couldn't turn down the opportunity. At least Brett will have Lisa to show him around."

But according to Gracie, Brett had had no trouble making friends. "He knows all the guys already because of football," she'd said with a shrug, when Tim had asked.

Brett quickly rose through the ranks of popularity at youth group as well, in large part due to his organization of a post-game party at church. Every Friday night, Loring Point Fellowship had more people than the youth room could hold, resulting in a spillage of teenagers into the parking lot behind the church. Carrie, that fall semester's youth group leader, made sure that photos of events were plastered on the walls of the youth room and hallway, and Tim made sure that a quick message was given at the end of the night, along with an invitation for all to join for worship on Sunday morning.

"Fantastic, the number of people he's brought in," he'd said to Gracie over dinner one night.

"I guess. Whatever. Can I be excused? I still have to finish chem homework."

He'd nodded and looked at Jane, puzzled, after Gracie had closed her bedroom door.

"Carol told me that Lisa's been spending time—I mean, *hanging out* with Miranda Kessler quite a bit," she whispered. "And she hasn't been inviting Gracie to join them."

"What does that have to do with Brett?"

"Think about it. Miranda Kessler is *very* popular."

"So?"

She shook her head in exasperation. "You don't understand how high school girls operate."

"You're right. I didn't then, and from the sound of things, I haven't learned much."

"Why do you think Miranda suddenly wants to be friends with Lisa?"

"I don't know. Maybe because ... "

She jumped in rather than watch him flounder. "Because of Brett. Brett's popular and cute." She stopped for a moment, then corrected herself. "Not *cute* anymore. That was junior high. It's *hot* now. Anyway, Lisa seems to be moving up in the world by association, and she's not bringing Gracie along for the ride."

I might not understand teenage girls, Tim thought, as he flipped through a stack of outreach questionnaires at church the next day, *but I do understand how to witness.* There was no way to ignore the distressing truth: Gracie was a terrible evangelist. Month after month, Carrie would hand him a stack of questionnaires, each filled out by a youth group member. The columns marked "person" and "contact information" were just as full on Gracie's papers as they were on her peers, yet "came to service?" and "number of times" were usually blank. Gracie hadn't written "yes" under "requires further outreach/prayer from pastor" once.

For Tim, calling those in need of salvation was a pleasure rather than a chore. There was no greater joy than helping the lost become children of God. But he understood why Gracie hadn't asked for his help. What high school girl would want her dad to swoop in and take charge of such a delicate social situation? Maybe she felt unsure of herself, and didn't want to be upstaged by him. But more likely, he thought with some discomfort, she was embarrassed by him. She was a teenager, after all.

But why was Gracie so poor at spreading the gospel? Her questionnaires showed that she'd introduced herself to plenty of people, and if that was the case, then why wasn't she able to connect with any of them? It certainly wasn't due to a lack of biblical knowledge. Had she forgotten to share with others the way faith had shaped her life? Had she listened to their responses and then followed up with the right questions? Could it be something as simple as a case of nerves?

He'd written off her freshman year to being new, had been understanding during her sophomore year as well. But she was halfway through her junior year. She should've developed *some* skill in witnessing by this point. Now he had no choice but to find a covert way to intervene.

"Let's pair the kids up," he'd said to Carrie at their next meeting. "Let them mentor each other. Might be easier for them to ask each other questions than us. Who do you think would work well together?"

"Courtney and Jake are the most obvious twosome," she'd said, after a moment's consideration. "She's very outgoing and able to start up conversations with people, and he tends to get flustered. Plus, they've been going out since freshman year."

"Courtney? I thought *Lisa* and Jake were an item."

"Nope. Although I'm sure that would make Lisa very, very happy."

Tim smiled. Lisa had always been an open book. Her furtive looks to Gracie when they were caught drawing with Jane's lipstick in first grade; her flushed cheeks when she discovered that she hadn't been invited along with Gracie to Leigh-Ann Carson's sleepover in fifth; her beaming smile when she and Gracie went to the mall unsupervised for the first time in seventh. All still vivid in his memory.

"Why don't you put her with Gracie, then?" He knew that Lisa's evangelizing skills weren't much better than Gracie's, but the words had slipped out. Maybe some forced time together would help them hash out their differences. Such a shame to see their longtime friendship strained over something as trivial and fleeting as high school popularity.

Carrie blinked several times, and then cleared her throat before responding. "We could. But I think it might work out well to put Gracie and Brett together."

So I'm not the only one who's noticed how much help she needs. Brett was by far the most talented of the group. He could feel his cheeks strain as he struggled to keep his smile from receding.

"It doesn't have to be Brett," she said, backtracking. "Maybe Connor, or Haley? I just thought that she and Lisa—"

"No, Brett is fine," he said, interrupting before she was forced to point out that neither of them had much to offer the other in terms of guidance. "There's no way to go wrong with him."

What a blessing Carrie's suggestion turned out to be, thought Tim a year later, and he smiled at the thought of the inadvertent role they'd played in sparking Gracie and Brett's romance. *And now Senior Prom has already come and gone.*

Easter had fallen early that year, at the very end of March, and Tim had forgotten about the dance until Gracie asked him for money for shoes a week beforehand in mid-April, a month earlier than normal due to a last-minute change in venue. Lisa was supposed to lend her a black pair, she'd told him, since her dress was pale pink and would need a neutral shoe. But this plan had been thwarted when Carol refused to buy Lisa new shoes and told her that she'd have to make do with what she had.

He had to admit that he'd be hard-pressed to find anyone he approved of more than Brett, and that he'd been spoiled by having such an upstanding suitor for his daughter. But Brett would be moving to Florida after the summer, and Tim would be left with no choice but to worry about faceless college boyfriends with suspect motives.

He heard laughter in the hallway outside of his office, and looked at his watch. Youth group meeting in ten minutes, and he'd be running it. He sighed. Mid-May—the end of Norton Roth's internship program for the academic year—was always a tough readjustment. No youth group leader until the end of August.

"Catch up in a sec," he heard Brett say to the others from outside of his door, followed by the turning of his doorknob. "You wanted to see me?" he asked, standing in the threshold.

"Yes, come in," Tim said, motioning for him to take the seat across from him. "Gracie told me about your football scholarship. Congratulations!"

"Track. Gracie told you football?"

Didn't she? "I thought she did, but maybe I just assumed that when I heard her say 'scholarship.' I didn't even know you ran track."

"Yeah, track's my sport. I'm nothing special at football."

"Come on. How many touchdown passes did you catch this season? I'm guessing over twenty."

"Twenty-three," Brett said, with an easy smile. "But I'm not tall enough or big enough to be a wide receiver in a Division One school. And I'm definitely not good enough to win a scholarship to one."

"But apparently you are."

Brett smiled again, this time a broad, self-assured one, tempered by a modest shrug. "I guess."

Some people just have it. That inner confidence, that sure-footedness. How had this kid been able to sidestep self-doubt, the hallmark of adolescence? No wonder why people were so drawn to him.

"Well, FSU is lucky to have you. I have to admit, I was hoping you'd stay local. I'd have loved for you to lead youth group in the fall. Your talent in bringing people into the church is ... well, it's exceptional."

"Thirty-four new members."

"Really?" The number surprised him, both in its size and specificity. He hadn't thought it was that high, but then again, he'd never counted.

"Yep. And that's not even including people who were saved at outreach events, but didn't come to church afterwards. That'd put me at forty-nine, which is kind of a bummer, because I really wanted to beat fifty."

"Hold on—people confessed their sins, prayed with you, accepted Christ—but then never showed up at church?"

"Yeah."

But that's backwards. The goal is to get people to church, get them excited about becoming a part of a Christ-like community, and then hope that they're willing to confess their sins and accept Jesus as their Savior. "So what reasons did they give you for not coming?"

"What do you mean? They didn't come, so how would I know?"

"I'm talking about when you followed up with them."

"Oh. I thought that part was optional. I mean, you can kind of tell if someone isn't that into it, so when that happens, I just put my energy into people who I think I can convince."

Convince? Tim winced at the word. "I think 'guide' is more appropriate."

Brett seemed unfazed. "Okay, 'guide.' Same thing."

No. It's not the same at all. "Brett. If I've left you with the impression that witnessing is simply convincing people to recite the Sinner's Prayer, then I've mislead you. The goal is to connect the newly saved to a community that can help them learn to live according to Jesus' teachings. Does that make sense?"

"Sure. So … are we done? I promised Jake I'd catch up with him before youth group, and looks like we're already late," he said, pointing to the wall clock.

"Actually, no. Regardless of the confusion about follow-up, the fact is that you saved forty-nine souls. And since you won't be here next year, I was hoping you could tell me the, umm—"

The secret. What is the secret?

"—the types of questions you asked, the testimonials you shared. Maybe you found particular sections of Scripture to be more effective than others?"

"Naw, none of that. I just figured out what it was that they needed to hear. Everybody has something they need to hear, right?"

Something they need to hear to help them realize that they're in need of salvation? Something they need to hear to help them make the jump from unbeliever to child of God? He waited for further explanation, but none came. All Brett offered was another shrug, and another smile.

All summer, Tim tried to find an opportunity to casually revisit this conversation with Brett. But how? It was humiliating. He should be answering Brett's questions about how to share the gospel, not the reverse. But as the months passed, his thoughts turned to Gracie. Just three more weeks until she would be leaving for college. It was hard to believe that she was only two years younger than he and Shayla were when they first met.

It was Ed who told him the shattering news, on a blistering afternoon in early August. The heat enveloped Tim as he left church, and although he could feel sweat prick his upper lip as he walked to his car, he felt chills shoot up his spine and into his neck, making him shudder as if he had the flu. But illness wasn't to blame.

It was anger.

He arrived in his garage without remembering the ride, having spent the trip immersed in his warring thoughts while his body performed the functions of driving. He paused near the door, key out, but then, instead of going inside, pulled out his creaking lawn mower and wheeled it to the backyard.

The last thing the lawn needed was mowing; the grass was patchy, and had taken on the brittle consistency of hay in spots. Separating the house from the lawn were Jane's flowerbeds and pristine vegetable garden, making the division of labor in the household clear.

He unattached the bagger, since the large hole near its bottom did little to contain the cuttings, then waited as the mower's sputtering developed into a steady hum. It was better to have to pick up the clumps afterwards, anyway. Suddenly he needed to move—needed some outlet for the frenzied energy that had begun to boil inside of him. He wouldn't even use the sweeper, he decided. He'd rake instead, and let the work and sun beat it out of him.

Jane stepped onto the front porch as he was dragging the second bag of cuttings to the side of the house. "You didn't pick up your phone," she said, frustration and concern coloring her voice. "I was worried."

"Sorry."

"Carol called. She told me everything."

He looked up at the sky. "Where's Gracie?"

"In her room. I can't get her out."

He wiped the sweat from his forehead with his arm, then walked into the house to Gracie's room, Jane trailing him. His throat was dry from inhaling bits of airborne grass and fumes, causing him to cough several times as he knocked on her bedroom door.

"Gracie, let me in." He could hear muffled sounds on the other side of the door, but couldn't make out any words. *She must be under the covers.* "I can't hear you, Gracie. What did you say?"

"I said, don't come in."

"We have to talk. You know that, or you wouldn't have locked me out." He waited for her to respond. "Gracie, if you don't open this door, I'll have Jane get me a bobby pin so I can force it open."

"Go ahead."

"Jane, would you please go get me a pin from your sewing kit?" he said, his words formal and loud for Gracie's benefit. He could hear her breaths, forced and uncoordinated. *She's trying not to cry.* "Just tell me, please," he said, his voice ragged with thirst. "Is it true? Are you—are you pregnant?"

The whimpering stopped. "Who told you that? Carol or Ed?"

"Ed. So it's true?"

Heaving sobs racked her, ones he hadn't heard from her since Shayla died. How could she be so careless with her future? How could she care for a child when she was still one herself?

He took a deep breath. "Who's the father?"

The noises came to an abrupt halt. "I thought you said Ed told you."

"I'll tell you what he said when you let me in."

He heard the pop of the knob unlocking, and he opened the door slowly, gave her time to climb back into bed and pull her comforter over her head again. Pushing her legs aside, he perched on the edge of her bed. "Ed said that Lisa told him—told Carol, actually, who then told him—that Brett says he isn't the father."

She let out a bitter laugh. "So that's why Courtney wasn't mad about Jake."

"What does that have to do with anything?"

"Lisa's had a crush on Jake *forever*. And he's been going out with Courtney since ninth grade. And then on Saturday, Lisa and I were supposed to go to the mall together, but when I called her she said she couldn't go because she had plans with Jake and Brett. They weren't even going to tell me about it."

He saw Jane hovering in the doorway, and looked at her helplessly. *What is she talking about?*

She peeked out from under the covers, flashed him an irritated look that said *do I have to spell this out for you?* "Courtney is the most popular girl in the *whole school*. And she's *way* prettier than Lisa. And now Jake's hanging out with Lisa without Courtney, and she's not even mad about it?"

He tried to keep his frustration from showing. "Gracie, you can't ignore the problem anymore. I don't have the patience to hear about who-invited-who-where now."

"Don't you get it?" she said, sitting up and throwing the covers off of her. "Brett doesn't want to get stuck here. You think he doesn't know that his parents would force him to marry me?"

"But Lisa … "

"Lisa has to pick sides!" she yelled. "If she tells the truth, then she's calling her cousin a liar."

"But why would Jake and Courtney get involved?"

"How do I know? Maybe they believe him. Maybe Jake's protecting his best friend. Brett needs Lisa on his side, and everyone knows her dream come true is for Jake to notice her."

"What are you saying? That Brett bribed her with a couple of dates? That's a very serious accusation you're making."

"That *I'm* making? What about Brett? What about what *he's* saying about *me*?" Her eyes widened in disbelief at his silence, and her voice dropped to a whisper. "You don't believe me?"

"I don't know what to believe! You lied about being pregnant for … for I don't know how long, and now you're feeding me some paranoid conspiracy theory. I don't know what to think."

"I never lied." She looked up at Jane. "Do *you* believe me?"

He held his hand up to Jane, cutting her off. "But you kept it a secret. That's a lie of omission, and don't tell me that you don't know that. I raised you better than that." He turned away from her and kicked the door into the wall.

Jane stopped the door as it rebounded towards her, and stepped into the room. "I believe you, Gracie. And your father does, too. He's just surprised."

" 'Surprised?' That's not the word I was thinking of. What are you going to do about college, Gracie? How are you going to support this baby? You have no idea how much kids cost."

"I'll get a job."

"Oh, you'll get a job, will you? *Great.* How much money do you think you'll make with just a high school degree? And who'll take care of the baby while you're earning this *enormous* salary that you somehow think is coming your way? I didn't sign up to be a parent again, and neither did Jane. How could you have made such a stupid, irresponsible decision?"

Gracie turned away from him and curled into a ball, her forehead resting just below the windowsill. *Calm down*, mouthed Jane, as she moved next to Gracie and smoothed back her hair from her face. But he couldn't. He was too filled with hurt and hatred for what she had done to herself, to him, to their future.

"It's not only you this affects, Gracie. How do I explain this to everyone? I'm supposed to be an example for the community! How are Ed and I going to lead the church together when it's Brett's word against yours? What am I supposed to do, sue my co-pastor's nephew for paternity? I can't begin to understand how you could've gotten yourself into this position."

"Why is this all my fault?" she whispered into the wall. "Why is none of this Brett's fault? You didn't even bother to ask me my side of the story."

His rage vanished; his breath caught. *Does she mean? No. It can't be. No.* "You can tell me anything, Gracie." *Please, no. Not my little girl.* "I'm sorry, I was wrong to yell. I'm on your side. I'm always on your side. But I have to know. Did he ... ?" The word couldn't be spoken. "Did he force himself on you?"

She turned towards him, looked at him with contempt. "I knew you'd say that. Because those are the only two choices, right? You're raped or you're a slut."

"Gracie! I will not permit that kind of language in this house."

"Oh, I'm not allowed to say that word? Because Brett uses it all the time now when he talks about me behind my back."

"But he didn't ... hurt you?"

"Not that way."

He kneeled next to her bed, afraid to touch her. "Why then?" he asked, after a moment.

"He said that he loved me. That nothing could keep us apart."

Her words slammed into him, and the pain was fresh again. He ached for Gracie, for Shayla, for what had happened to his family the day she was taken from them for no reason. He'd been a fool, hadn't he? He'd thought that he'd been able to fill the hole Shayla's death had left in Gracie. He'd done all he could to make her feel safe, and it hadn't been enough.

It hit him, then. The realization that he wasn't the first to figure this out. The words, delivered with a self-assured smile and a modest shrug, came back to him.

Everyone has something they need to hear.

CHAPTER 17

Josephine crosses the bridge that connects the main hospital to the medical office buildings, and everything stills. The echoing footsteps, hallway chatter, squeaking wheelchairs and supply carts silence as the door slams behind her. Without the mechanical noise of slide staining machines and centrifuges, or the electronic beeps of bar code scanners and timers, this section of the hospital—the wing that doesn't wake until nine o'clock appointments begin—feels foreign.

It's been so long since she's been here that she has to read the signs hanging from the ceiling in order to navigate the maze of corridors that lead to Eddie's office. She smiles, thinks of how horrified he'd be if he knew that the entire pathology department refers to him, the legendary

Dr. Edward Chase, by this nickname. Once she made the mistake of calling him "Edward" instead of "Dr. Chase" in front of the OR team, thinking it the collegial yet respectful choice, and he grimaced and ended their conversation with a curt "Thank you, Dr. Wallis."

She throws her half bagel into a hallway trashcan. Quarter to six is too early for whole wheat. *Too early for the lab to be open, too, and Eddie knows it.* The OR schedule lists his last procedure of the day at one o'clock, so there's no reason why they can't meet afterwards in the OR, just two floors down from the lab. This is a power play, pure and simple. Payback for the pathology department's recent requirement that tissue be delivered to the lab by nurses rather than picked up by pathology interns.

She weaves through narrow hallways, ignores the blue and yellow arrows that lead to adjacent buildings, and follows the red ones until she reaches the Sutter Breast Center. The door to Eddie's office is open, but he's facing away from her, typing.

She clears her throat. "Dr. Chase?"

"Dr. Wallis," he says, without turning or motioning her in. The typing continues in fits and starts as he reviews the chart in front of him. He stops after several intolerable minutes, and Josephine straightens from her slumped position against the doorway, expecting him to turn towards her. Instead, he pulls a medical journal from his bookcase, searches the table of contents, and flips to an article.

Josephine's jaw tenses. *What a prick. What can he possibly want to talk about that couldn't be done by phone or email? Thirty years later, and the whole hospital still has to kiss up because he cured Martin Sutter's daughter.*

Melanie Sutter's case was one of hospital lore. It had been cherry-picked for Dr. Chase, then an intern, because it was an obvious diagnosis, and he was hardly the shining talent of the department. No one knew the depth of Martin Sutter's pockets—or where Dr. Chase's true talent lay—until two years into Melanie's remission, when the hospital's board of directors announced that Mr. Sutter would be financing a comprehensive, state-of-the-art breast center.

"Excuse me, Dr. Chase? I was told that you have a concern that you'd like to bring to Path's attention?"

He stands and offers her a cordial smile, but no apology for keeping her waiting. "I do indeed, Dr. Wallis. Thank you for coming by. Nice to get out of the lab every once in a while, isn't it?"

Please. You're not doing me *a favor.* "It is. I do have to get back, though, so—"

"I'll get right to the point then. It seems that my colleagues are getting lab results for axillary lymph node dissections more quickly than I am. Dr. Marthan, Dr. Hingham, and I typically operate on the same days, yet their patients are consistently scheduled for chemo and radiation first. If someone in pathology has a problem with me, the professional course of action would be to address the situation with me directly. My patients shouldn't have to pay for some childish vendetta regarding tissue transport."

"I'm sorry that you've come to that conclusion, Dr. Chase, but I can assure you that that that's not the case. Your colleagues aren't getting ALND results any faster. They're not waiting for results because they're not sending us nodes. They've stopped performing the procedure in patients with specific profiles."

His jaw slackens in surprise. "But ALND is the standard of care following a positive sentinel node biopsy."

Does the man not speak to anyone in his department? She feels a twinge of guilt for exposing that everyone has written him off. "It's been a relatively recent change," she says, to soften the blow. "It seems that the tide is changing for early stage breast cancer patients who are clinically node negative."

"I'm aware of the ACOSOG Z0011 findings," he says, a pinched expression on his face.

"Of course you are! I didn't mean to imply otherwise. I only know of the study because Dr. Marthan suggested I read it. It seems to suggest that removing ten to twenty nodes isn't worth it if it's not going to change the course of treatment. Why risk lymphedema, numbness, and shoulder pain if we already know that positive sentinel nodes require radiation and a combo of chemo and hormone-blocking treatment?"

"Because the cost of being wrong is too high. You seem to have forgotten is that it is the responsibility of this department to be vigilant in the determining the extent of the metastasis."

No shit, Sherlock. "Right. So three or more positive sentinel nodes would necessitate complete ALND. But in patients with only one or two positive nodes, the study found no difference in survival outcomes between patients who had sentinel node dissection plus ALND versus those who had sentinel node dissection alone."

"A wise physician notes when a study only reaches half of its targeted accrual, Dr. Wallis. Wouldn't you agree?"

Josephine struggles to keep her expression pleasant. "She also notes the reason *why*. The event rate was lower than expected."

"Don't be shortsighted. There wasn't complete follow-up information in close to twenty percent of the subjects. And the patients were only followed for six years."

"True. I pointed that out to Dr. Marthan. He said that he considers it adequate follow-up, because local recurrence in the axilla tends to happen quickly."

"Dr. Marthan has been practicing for less than ten years. His judgment is still … maturing. ALND has been the standard of care for over a hundred years, and continues to be. In any case, I don't need to justify my decision-making process to you. This is a discussion that the *department* needs to have." He motions towards the door with a dismissive gesture. "I have quite a busy day ahead of me. I'm sure you do as well." He gives her a brusque nod, and then turns back to his computer.

Josephine can feel her heart pounding as she retraces her steps down the hallway, bothered by his feeble arguments even more than his condescension. Had he mentioned concern over the false negative rate, or altered lymphatic flow due to aging, she could have understood his position. Even a dismissal of intra-operative consults in general—an "I don't like frozen sections"—she could give him that, because they *are* misinterpreted more than permanent slides. Some tissue does get depleted or lost when it's trimmed in the cryostat. But no, he'd given her a "that's the way it's always been" response, which smacks of either insecurity or a lack of intellectual curiosity, neither being worthy of—

Nausea surges within her, and she stops short, unable to think of anything but keeping what little there is in her stomach down. She swallows several times, tries to wash down the bitterness in the back of her throat. *Should have forced down that bagel.* She fishes in her pocket for the ginger-flavored hard candy that everyone raves about on pregnancy message boards, and pops one in her mouth, even though they don't work. At least it will get the sour taste out of her mouth.

It seems unfair, that her body reminds her of Wes every time she's able to put him out of her mind. He'd been back for more clothes again, left his dirty ones in the hamper and picked up replacements while she was at the hospital. It had stung the first time, knowing that he'd either gone in to work late or left early in order to avoid her, but this second go-round is testing her patience. *I get it, Wes, you want to hurt me. But you can't avoid me forever.*

But so far, forever has only been five days, she reminds herself. And who is she to judge? Denial is an easy crutch, and she leaned on it for months. It's not Wes's fault that she waited until time was at a premium.

She thinks of her mother, of the countless times that she's accused her of burying her head in the sand, too blinded by self-righteousness to see that she was guilty of the same. *Not the same, actually. Worse. Last Sunday proved that.*

* * *

Her parents' house had smelled of angel biscuits and peach jam. She'd gotten her bearings after driving past Bobby Crayton's house, and made it to the house less than five minutes later. She let herself in without knocking, snagged a biscuit and drenched it in jam before she dropped her bag onto the countertop. She was starting on her second one when she heard the lock turn.

"Where's Mom?" she asked, mouth full, seeing that her father was alone.

"Josie!" he said, as he gave her a kiss. He pointed to the biscuits. "You beat me to them. I was thinking about those biscuits the whole sermon. How'd they come out?"

She gave him a thumbs up, still chewing.

He chuckled and headed back to the bench in the mudroom to untie his dress shoes, and then threw them in the closet rather than placing them in the designated wicker baskets inside. "Mom and I took different cars. I can't take the half hour of chit-chat after the service. She'll be home in a bit."

Perfect! Time alone with the rational parent. "So Dad ... " she began, when he returned to the kitchen. "I need your help. I know this is hard to hear, and that Amanda's still your little girl, but ... you know, she's getting older, and she ... ." She waited for him to jump in and save her from her sudden regression back to flustered teenager. Isn't this why they'd wanted her to come by yesterday, anyway? To talk about Amanda?

"She what?"

Spit it out already, Josephine. " I think we need to consider the possibility that she'll become sexually active, now that she's going to be on her own. Mom's not going to want to hear it, especially from me. But I think we need to be proactive."

She expected that he'd look embarrassed or irritated, but instead, his brow had furrowed in confusion. "What on God's green earth are you talking about? Amanda gets those shots every three months. Has for a long time now."

"What? Mom's okay with that? *Mom?*"

"It was her idea," he said, frowning. He stared at her for a moment, and then shook his head sadly. "I've never understood it. Why is it that you give your mother so little credit?"

"Come on, Dad. You know how Mom is with Amanda."

"Amanda is where she is today because of your mother, not me. She's always pushed her to reach her potential. Always had to talk me into it, too."

"Like getting a job as a *lifeguard?* Hasn't she noticed that quick decision-making isn't Amanda's strong suit? It's ridiculous."

"Of course it is. We knew she'd fail. But what's better: to have Mom and Dad tell her no, or to let her figure it out by herself?" He paused, then smiled at Josephine's surprised expression. "See what I mean? Amanda's ready to live on her own now—something we'd never thought she'd be able to do—because of all of these years of preparation with Gracie. I was dead set against it when she first brought it up."

"That was Mom's idea?"

"Who else's?"

"I just assumed it was Tim's."

"*Think,* Josephine. Gracie was trying to support a baby and all she had was a part-time job at the mall. Cash was real tight. Why would Tim suggest she take on rent when she could live at home for free?"

"I guess I just didn't think it through," she said, stumped. "Gracie wanted to go back to school, and Tim didn't have enough time to babysit. And he knew that Amanda and Gracie both wanted to live on their own, and that Amanda loves kids, and that Mom would be there to help all the time ... "

"But Mom *isn't* there a lot. That's the whole point. She was there when Gracie needed to go to class, helping Amanda learn how to be a responsible babysitter. Otherwise, Gracie was helping Amanda with cooking, grocery shopping, money management, in exchange for free rent and babysitting. We turned over Amanda's housing stipend to her and paid for the remainder."

How had she missed it? All these years that she'd gone about her own life, thinking of her sister only when convenient, her mother had been quietly building Amanda's. "But ... but Mom told me the set-up was to help Gracie with Luke. That we owed Tim because he always made sure that Gracie looked out for Amanda all those years they were in school together, and that this time it was Gracie who needed help. Mom never asked me to teach Amanda how to ... I would have, I just ... " She shook her head in disbelief. "I didn't know," she said helplessly.

"You weren't supposed to, Josie. You need to live your own life. Helping Amanda become as independent as possible is Mom's responsibility, my responsibility—not yours."

"But I want to help. She's *my* sister, not Gracie's. It's hard to visit during the week, but I take her to the lake every Saturday. I try. Maybe it doesn't seem ... I can rearrange my schedule, if you tell me what—"

"Don't feel guilty. It's much better that Amanda learn from her friend than the big sister she can never measure up to. It makes sense, for now. But once Mom and I are gone, Amanda *will* need you more. Isn't it better if you both haven't grown to resent each other by that point?"

She nodded, looked down to hide the tears that had sprung to her eyes. "I thought mom wanted me to come visit alone yesterday because she wanted to talk about Amanda."

He waited for her to meet his eyes. "Oh, honey. She wanted to spend time with you and *not* talk about Amanda."

* * *

Even now, four days later, Josephine feels ashamed of her foolish ignorance. She wipes the light glaze of sweat on her forehead, tries to swallow the saliva that fills her mouth, and knows. She's not going to make it.

The arrows that direct to the bathroom point to the far end of the corridor. She fights against the next heave, frantic for a trash can, and sees one four doors to her right, in the corner between the red building and the hallway to the yellow one. She pushes in the engraved "thank you" flap, and tries to aim into it, the smell of ashes and rotting food causing her to retch even more.

She wipes the vomit from her face and hair, assesses her poor aim. The trashcan and carpet are riddled with spit and the smell of bile. She looks up at the plaque on the office next to the now defiled trashcan. Women's Care of Cutler, it reads. And beneath: Phyllis Reardon, MD, FACOG; Henry Schulman, MD, FACOG; Lauren Abernathy, MD, OB/GYN. She smiles. *At least I puked outside the right office.*

She returns several minutes later, armed with moistened paper towels from the bathroom, and begins the cleanup. She uses far too much soap in her effort to rid the smell, and has to go back and forth to the bathroom several times to rinse with wet paper towels and blot with dry ones. Maintenance will come by before opening, but some attempt has to be made in the meantime.

She double-checks the plaque. She's seen the names on requisition forms, but thankfully doesn't know any of the doctors. This time, though, she notices a swirling design beneath the names, a large lowercase *e*, with a smaller inverted one inside the bend of the larger one. So much better than the logos she sees on most OB/GYN office doors: profiles of stick-figured women dancing, outlines of pregnant bodies, *O*'s with plus signs attached to the bottom, tying the OB/GYN credential to its matching gender symbol. Why the need to cutesy up the office? It's a medical practice, not an interior decorating firm.

It's strangely familiar, though. From an ad in a magazine, maybe? Her OB/GYN's waiting room is stacked with them: *Pregnancy, Fit Pregnancy, Pregnancy & Newborn, Parenting, Today's Parent.* Who knew there were so many? And how is it that there are enough toned, glowing pregnant women out there to even model? *There should be a magazine brave enough to put a bloated, nauseous woman on the cover. That's a magazine I'd buy.*

Josephine looks down at the mess that she's somehow managed to worsen. She tried, at least. She checks her phone. It's six nineteen; the coffee shop will open soon. She follows the arrows back to the connector, in search of a muffin and apple juice.

* * *

Gracie had refused to have Jane take her to her first prenatal visit. "You'll need to find a way to go," Ellen said, when Josephine returned her call several days later. "I know you're busy, but she needs to have someone with her. She hasn't been yet, and Tim and Jane don't even know how far along she is."

"Gracie's *pregnant?*"

"Yes. That's what I just said. So in terms of scheduling, Jane said—"

"Who's the father?"

"I don't know."

"You didn't ask?"

"They didn't offer, Josephine. I don't think now is the time to pry."

"But how are they going to tell everyone at church?"

"I don't think they've gotten to that point yet. The first step is to get her to a doctor."

"Listen, I want to help, Mom, but I can't just up and leave the lab whenever Gracie schedules an appointment. Can't someone else go?"

"And who would that be?"

Good question. Josephine struggles to think of another person in Gracie's life who is both a peer and an authority figure.

"I thought you said that hours would be easier in pathology."

"Well, easier, yes, but second-year residents don't exactly make their own hours."

"That's why I told Jane to make an appointment with a practice by you. You can meet her on your lunch break."

"I don't have a lunch break, Mom. It doesn't work like that."

"There's a nine forty-five on Thursday at the one that Gracie's primary care recommended by you, and an eleven o'clock next Friday. That one's at a satellite office, though. So I'll tell Jane to take the nine forty-five? I know this doesn't give you a lot of notice, but I'm sure if you explain the situation to your ... oh, I can never remember the order of all the doctor titles. Attending? No—Fellow? Senior resident? Whoever your boss is, just find a time when he's not busy, and explain why it's imperative that you go to this appointment. I'm sure if you're respectful, and offer to stay late, he'll let you take a couple of hours off."

Not a chance, Josephine thought the following Friday, as she sat waiting with Gracie in Dr. Reese Malloy's office. *Gracie's lucky that today's my day off.*

After a perfunctory knock on the door, Dr. Malloy entered the examining room, and Josephine tried to veil her surprise. Dr. Malloy looked nothing like she'd expected. It was a commanding name, one that should belong to a rugged pilot or a decorated general. Certainly not to the plump woman now seated to her right, with shorts coils of gray hair and grandmotherly glasses. *Unbelievable. Me, of all people,* she thought, remembering the disappointed looks she'd received from surgical patients who'd assumed the words *male* and *better* somehow went hand in hand.

Dr. Malloy looked up from her chart at Gracie, seated on the examining table, legs dangling over the edge. Her hospital gown was tied in the front, just below her collarbone, and she'd carefully arranged the paper sheet she'd been given around her stomach to keep the unattached sides from splaying open and exposing her. "So, Grace… I understand this is your first prenatal visit?"

Gracie nodded, eyes fixed on the waxed vinyl flooring below her.

Dr. Malloy turned to Josephine. "And you are?"

"A friend."

"I see." Dr. Malloy studied her for a moment, then looked back at Gracie, who had yet to acknowledge Josephine.

"Of the family, I mean. A friend of the family. Obviously we're too far apart in age to know each other from school." She let out a nervous laugh.

"I see," Dr. Malloy repeated. "Grace, you're comfortable with your … friend … being present at this appointment?"

Gracie shrugged her shoulders.

"Because if you're not, that's fine, but you'll need to—"

"It's fine."

Josephine felt her face flush. *What the hell, Gracie? I'm doing you a favor. It's not like I can't find better things to do on my day off.*

"All right, then," Dr. Malloy said. "Your pregnancy test is positive, so the first order of business is to determine the due date. Do you remember the first day of your last period?"

"Umm … I don't remember the *day*, but it was before prom. Maybe two weeks before?"

Dr. Malloy placed a calendar on Gracie's lap. "When was prom?"

"April twentieth. I got it over the weekend, I remember. So the sixth or seventh, maybe? She looked up, finally, a confused expression on her face. "Why?"

"Because the weeks of a pregnancy are counted from that date." Dr. Malloy turned towards her desk and pulled out a pregnancy calculator. "Do you have intercourse regularly?"

Gracie looked horrified. "No! Just that one time. I promise."

"I'm not here to judge you. I'm here to find out how far along you are, and to help you determine the best course of action. So tell me: is your cycle regular?"

"Yes."

"How many days apart?"

"Twenty-eight. Isn't everyone's?"

"Not everyone, no." Dr. Malloy turned the red arrow on the pregnancy calculator until it lined up with April sixth. "January eleventh. That makes you one day shy of seventeen weeks."

Gracie's eyes widened in surprise. "But I don't understand," she said, looking at Josephine. "Because it was just that one time. And that was fifteen weeks ago, not seventeen."

"A pregnancy is forty weeks," Josephine explained. "Forty weeks from the first day of your last menstrual period, or thirty-eight from conception."

"But that doesn't make any sense. How could I be pregnant if I had my period?"

"You weren't. But more women remember the first day of their period than the date of conception, which can be harder to pin down, so doctors take that date, and then count out forty weeks instead of thirty-eight."

Dr. Malloy looked at Gracie intently. "How do you feel about the pregnancy?"

"But it was just that one time!" Gracie repeated, bursting into tears. "He said that that it never happens the first time."

"And you believed him?" Josephine asked, shocked. *How could you have fallen for that line? It's one of the oldest tricks in the book!*

Dr. Malloy shot Josephine a warning look, one that said *now is not the time*, and she stopped, heeded the unspoken reprimand.

"Well, maybe ... I don't know. It just happened so fast. I didn't have time to think about it." She wiped away her tears with the back of her hand, and bit her lip to stop it from trembling. "I'm supposed to be going to college in a couple of weeks!"

Dr. Malloy passed Gracie a box of tissues. "I think it's best to do a physical exam now, and an ultrasound to confirm the due date and determine the viability of the pregnancy. Would you prefer to be alone during this portion of the visit, Grace?"

"Yes."

Josephine was ushered back towards the door by Dr. Malloy, and then the curtain between them was yanked closed. She could hear the rustling of hygienic paper as Gracie was told to lay back, and an explanation of changes in the breast and uterus during pregnancy. Next came the metallic squeal of stirrups being pulled into position, along with the question: "Have you had a pelvic exam before?" Rustling again, as Gracie was instructed to move closer to the end of the table, and then the *click-click-click* of the speculum being adjusted. "Relax your legs, let them fall apart," Dr. Malloy coaxed. "Don't be nervous, just let them fall wide." A nearby door slammed, and chit-chat filled the corridor and muffled Dr. Malloy's voice, but Josephine could still make out the phrases "placental position," and "crown-rump length." Then, a squirt of gel, a steady *whoosh-whoosh-whoosh*, and, embedded within, a softer, faster one. "One-forty," Josephine heard. "Right on track." The sound of static next, followed by "How about I turn the screen toward you?" and then a detailing of the chambers of the heart, the shape of the head, the spine, abdomen, arms, legs, hands, and feet.

"This is a healthy pregnancy," Dr. Malloy said to Josephine, after she was allowed back in ten minutes later. "No fetal abnormalities were detected. The size and position of the placenta is normal as is the volume of amniotic fluid. The size of the fetus corroborates the due date we've estimated. I wasn't able to determine the sex due to positioning."

Josephine looked at Gracie, who had covered her eyes and was crying in a familiar rhythm—one sob, two breaths—and suddenly Gracie was a little girl again, stretched out on the kitchen table, coloring. Josephine felt an unexpected, piercing need to protect that girl, and with it, anger. Anger at Dr. Malloy for pressuring a vulnerable teenager to see images of a baby she didn't want; anger at the unnamed father who'd somehow managed to get off scot-free; anger at Tim for preaching abstinence, a strategy all too often bundled with failure and shame.

Dr. Malloy shifted her weight in her chair and looked back and forth between the two of them, finally settling on Gracie. "Let's talk about your options. I'd be happy to monitor your health as well as the health of the baby for the duration of the pregnancy. You could choose to raise the baby, or, if you decide that you aren't ready, you could consider adoption. There are many wonderful families desperate for a child, and there is no greater gift to give. I can connect you to people who can better explain the process to you, if it's of interest."

Choking sounds escaped Gracie, and she twisted away from Dr. Malloy and Josephine as best she could while still seated.

"Isn't there a more pressing option that we haven't discussed yet?" asked Josephine pointedly.

"Of course," Dr. Malloy said, her tone clipped. "The third option is termination. How old are you, Grace?"

"Eighteen. A couple of weeks ago."

"Then you are of majority. In Texas, at least one parent must consent to a termination of the pregnancy if the woman is under eighteen and not married. By waiting this long, you've given yourself the option of deciding independently. However, if you choose to follow this route, your time is *extremely* limited. The law is not past twenty weeks post-fertilization. That being said, no physician in this practice will perform an abortion past sixteen weeks. I can connect you to clinics that will, though. Is this option of interest?"

Gracie didn't respond. Dr. Malloy glanced at Josephine, and then continued. "The law requires that an ultrasound be performed at the abortion provider's facility, so if you do decide to visit a clinic, there will be a repeat ultrasound. You'll have to listen to a description of the fetus again, and you'll be given the option of hearing the heartbeat. You'll meet with a counselor, be given pamphlets describing the procedure and its risks, and then you must wait twenty-four hours prior to scheduling. The counselors will also discuss financial considerations with you. Is there anyone in your family who would be willing to help you pay for the procedure?"

"My dad's a pastor. My grandfather, too."

"I see."

"But it's your choice, Gracie," Josephine said. "Not your dad's, not Jane's, not John's. *Yours.*"

Gracie shook her head. "It's not an option."

Relief registered on Dr. Malloy's face for a split-second, and then her expression returned to neutral. She turned to the plastic display on the wall to her right and selected several brochures. "These three will give you more information regarding adoption," she said, handing them to Gracie, "and this one will give you information regarding termination, should you change your mind." She reached into her pocket. "Here's my card, in case you would like me to follow you further. A pleasure to meet both of you. Feel free to take a couple of minutes, and Grace—please leave the gown in the bin behind you."

Now, thought Josephine, as the door closed. *Now is the time to tell Gracie what happened to me.* About that week and a half, closing in on two years ago, that she'd spent vomiting and sobbing, despising herself for doing what she knew she must. About the brief moment as she was being wheeled from the OR afterwards, when consciousness ruptured the haze of anesthesia, and she discovered that the guilt, shame, and self-loathing that she thought would be awaiting her, ready to suffocate her, were nowhere to be found. The only emotion she had felt was relief. Pure, utter relief.

But she didn't speak, because Gracie's situation couldn't be compared to hers. Gracie had a *baby* growing inside of her, not a half-inch-long embryo. A healthy baby. She waited too long, had allowed shame and time to conspire against her.

Gracie turned her back to Josephine, slid off the examining table and pulled her underwear and athletic shorts on without taking off her gown. She pulled her sports bra from inside the crumpled folds of her tee shirt, laid it flat on the chair, and finally let the gown fall. Josephine couldn't stop herself from looking. From the back, there was a definite thickening of her waist, but not enough of a change to draw attention.

I wouldn't do it now, if I were in her shoes. But what would the reason be? It just seems wrong at this point? What a pathetic argument. Twenty weeks, sixteen weeks, eight weeks, conception—where was the line? In Tim's eyes, in Jane's eyes, it was always a sin. Always murder. Gracie forfeited the right to determine her own future at fertilization, when a single diploid cell—just one out of the tens of trillions of cells that composed her—confiscated all of her power.

Gracie reached over to the chair she'd rested her bag on, giving Josephine a side view. Whatever bump she had was camouflaged by the oversized tee she'd put back on. Josephine looked away so she wouldn't be caught staring. "I didn't know you didn't want me to come, Gracie. Jane thought that—"

"I know why Jane wanted you here," she said with disgust.

"Come on, Gracie. You think Jane asked me to pressure you? If that's true, then I've done a pretty bad job of it. You needed to see a doctor, and you wouldn't let her come, so she asked my mom to see if I would. She loves you."

Gracie's lip trembled. "Jane wants to make sure I don't embarrass the family even more than I already have. And your mom is her best bet for making sure I don't. I guarantee you she asked your mom to say something to you."

"Listen, I don't know what Jane said to my mom. But I *can* tell you that my mom didn't try to talk me into anything. I promise. Even if she had, it wouldn't have worked. I don't need her to make decisions for me."

Gracie looked pointedly at Josephine. "Exactly." She folded the pamphlets resting on the chair, and shoved them into her bag. Dr. Malloy's business card came loose and fluttered towards the ground.

Josephine caught it mid-air, handed it to Gracie, and turned to the door. She'd done her part today, had helped Gracie the best she could, and what had she gotten in return? Nothing but misplaced resentment. She walked into the busy corridor, thinking of how to say goodbye, then doubled back when she noticed she was alone. Gracie was in the same spot, studying the card and tracing the letters with her finger.

"Coming?" Josephine asked, trying not to show her irritation. She waited for a nod, then turned and walked out the door into the hallway again.

"It's not two *e*'s, like I thought," Gracie said as she followed, her words muffled by the hallway bustle. "It's a mother holding a baby."

CHAPTER 18

"We're a table short," Jane says to Tim, as she appraises the folding tables and chairs that he's set up in the backyard. "I knew it! I knew three seventy-two inch tables wouldn't be enough. What was I thinking, listening to that kid at the rental store?" She readjusts chairs, frowns as the metal legs clang against each other. "Look at this! They barely fit. Everyone's going to be completely packed in! You need to call them and have them send over another."

"Jane, I doubt they have spare delivery vans parked at the store. They're probably all scheduled for the day."

"We only need one more table. You can pick it up."

"I don't know if it'll fit."

"It will."

"Just because you want it to doesn't mean it will."

She gives him a disapproving look. "Then get a kid's table if it doesn't, and we'll sit the four children together. That'll free up enough space."

"Four? Who are the other three?"

"Dylan, Maddie, and Livy. Keith's nieces and nephew."

"I don't think Luke will sit with three other kids he doesn't know."

"Miss Nicole is coming. From school. She can sit with him."

"That's not fair to her, then. She'll have no one to talk to."

"They're kids, not aliens, Tim! Besides, she's not coming out of the kindness of her own heart. She's working." She shakes her head. "But that's beside the point. We've got a problem here, and we have time to fix it if you get going now and stop coming up with excuses not to."

He knows that he's being argumentative, but he can't help it. He's spent the morning tying up loose ends at church for Craig, the afternoon running last-minute errands for Jane, and he's tired. The smell of beef brisket smoking on the grill, cornbread cooling on the counter, and sweet potato casserole baking in the oven has tempted him for hours now, and what he'd like to do is pile a plate high and rest, not hassle over tables.

He sighs. Jane won't let him touch any of the food yet, anyway. "It's three forty-five. By the time I get back with a new one, set it up and switch all the chairs and plates around it'll be five fifteen, maybe even five thirty. It's tight."

"I can make that work. I'll do all the last-minute cleaning, make sure Mother and I are ready, and then you can take a quick shower at five thirty. We'll be at church by six, no problem." She sees him waver, and presses further. "Please, sweetie? I just want Gracie's rehearsal dinner to be perfect."

I should've put my foot down, he thinks an hour later, as he struggles to angle the much-needed folding table out of his car. How had they made it seem so effortless at the store? He abandons this approach after several unsuccessful minutes, tries to free it by brute force instead, which results in it slamming into the driveway as it dislodges. He examines it to find a chink missing at the outermost curve of the circle, and a crack extending from it to the table's center. *Shoot. Now we have to buy the piece of junk. At least we can cover it up with a tablecloth.*

The tablecloth! He'd forgotten to pick up a matching one. *Jane's going to kill me.* He freezes, the table still on the ground, as he considers the best way to tell her. The sound of a car pulling up and parking behind him interrupts his strategizing, and he turns to see Ellen.

"Need some help?" she asks, walking towards him.

He points to the damaged table. "I left the tablecloth at the store."

She looks at the table, makes a face. "Want to borrow one of mine?"

"No, we have one. But it won't match the other ones that we rented."

"A-ha. Well, I, for one, think that's a good thing. Now Gracie's table will stand out as special," she says, smiling. "At least you can present it to Jane that way." She turns, and pulls two platters covered with tin foil from the floor of the backseat. "Just bringing by the cobblers. One peach and one blackberry, as promised. They're vegan, so Luke can have some. There's no egg glaze on the crust, so they don't look as pretty as I'd like them to, but I think they came out all right."

"Thanks, Ellen. I'm sure they're delicious," he says, as she passes him a platter.

"Can you handle the other one, too?"

"Sure." His left arm wobbles as he tries to balance both, though, and she snatches it back before it falls.

"Let me take one. I don't want to interrupt Jane, so I'll just drop this off on the counter and head out."

"No, please. Jane can take a break. Stay for a little."

She glances at the cracked table, and then back at him. A smile spreads across her face. "Because she can't get upset in front of me, right?"

"Okay, you caught me," he says, with a guilty smile.

"Sneaky. I'm surprised. Or should I say impressed?"

"I like to think of it as a concerted effort to preserve marital harmony."

"I see. Then I'm happy to be your cover."

He walks up the steps and across the porch, Ellen behind him, catching the screen door for her with his foot. He hears a muffled cry, and turns to see her dabbing delicately under her eyes with the tips of her fingers. "Are you all right?"

"Fine, fine. Must be my allergies acting up."

"At the end of July?"

"Mmm-hmm," she says, as a teardrop lands with a *plink* onto the tin foil covering the pie. She flicks it away with an embarrassed laugh, and then rubs the streak that's left behind until the tin foil gleams again.

So Jane was right. Throughout the entire wedding planning process, she'd reminded him, over and over, to be careful not to hurt Ellen's feelings. "Ellen may never have a wedding to plan, or grandchildren to look forward to," she said. "Amanda can't care for a child. And Josephine's no spring chicken." The fourth time that Jane brought the subject up, he told her that she was being too dramatic. He'd officiated several weddings that Ellen had been invited to over the past couple of years, and there had been no trace of jealousy or sadness in her face. *But this isn't just any wedding.*

She wipes another wayward tear, smudging mascara across her cheek. "Did you mow today? Sometimes freshly cut grass—"

"Ellen, come on. What is it really?"

"Look at me," she says, shaking her head in disgust. "Ruining this beautiful day. Honestly, you'd think by now I'd be used to it."

"Used to what?"

She sighs, then offers him a weak smile. "To watching her get left behind." She pauses, and when she speaks again there's a vulnerability in her voice that he hasn't heard since she asked him for Gracie's help on the school bus so many years ago. "Gracie's a grown woman. I know you can't tell her what to do. But I hope you'll remind her to keep in touch with Amanda."

"I won't have to remind her. Besides, she's only moving twenty minutes away."

"I know, I know. But people get busy, and it's so easy to drift apart..."

"You forget about Luke. Haven't you noticed that he's not shy about letting people know what he wants? We both know how much he adores Amanda, and I can tell you right now that he's not going to tolerate too much time passing in between visits."

"True," she says with a chuckle. "He's got impressive self-advocacy skills."

They lapse into silence, but instead of turning and walking into the house, he asks, "Do you know Laura Salk?"

She shakes her head.

"She's new to church. She has a grown son who is—who has some of the same issues as Amanda. She comes every week, and we pray for him. For little things, like learning how to keep track of time better, or how to ask for help when he gets frustrated." He blushes. "I misspoke. Those things aren't little for her family. But what I mean is, you don't have to have a horrible health scare to join prayer group. People go for all sorts of different reasons."

It's a knee-jerk reaction, to suggest prayer group, but he's surprised to find that he doesn't feel guilty in recommending it. He can't pinpoint why, but he finds himself hoping that she'll say yes.

"That's a lovely offer, Tim. I'll think about it." She looks down at the platter, adjusts the tinfoil that has buckled up on one side. "You know, I've never told you, but I've always been in awe of your unwavering faith. I've always had more of a—well, I guess the only way to explain it would be a better-safe-than-sorry approach." She sees his quizzical look, and continues. "I've had moments of weakness, where I've doubted. I'm embarrassed to even admit that, especially to you, but it's true. For me, observing has been more about covering my bases than anything else. If God is real, then you're guaranteed an eternity in heaven, and if He's not, then nothing lost, right?"

With those words, Tim feels something shift within him and click into place. Like a kaleidoscope, the colors and shapes of his world, once murky, become defined as they morph into a new arrangement, a new truth. One so indisputable that suddenly it's difficult to remember what was there just a moment before.

But there is a cost. An enormous one.

He thinks of all the time he's devoted to his faith. He's searched for truth, hid from it, and wrestled with it, but not once has he considered the price. If he were to add it all up—the studying, writing, preaching, witnessing, praying—what would it translate to? Years? Decades? What if he'd chosen, instead, to spend a fraction of that time studying books about autism with the same dedication that he'd given the books of the Bible? Would he have gained insight into Gracie's struggles, learned how to help her better? Would he have figured out how to forge a stronger relationship with Luke? What if the billions of believers throughout the course of history had done the same? What contributions to science, to literature, to humanity, could have been made that were not?

Fear. He's paid handsomely in fear. But now, for the first time, he feels that fear transform into anger. Ever since he can remember, he's been told he was born a sinner, that Christ had to die to pay for his sins, that accepting this was the only way to avoid being tortured in an eternal lake of fire. But why was questioning God such a sin? Why could God forgive people murder, rape, abuse, but not doubt? He thinks of the words of James, words he knows by heart: "If any of you lacks wisdom, you should ask God, who gives generously to all without finding fault, and it will be given to you. But when you ask, you must believe and not doubt, because the one who doubts is like a wave of the sea, blown and tossed by the wind. That person should not expect to receive anything from the Lord. Such a person is double-minded and unstable in all they do."

But if God created man with intelligence, why would He be so opposed to us using it? All of His other creations use the gifts He has given them. Birds use their wings to fly and fish use their fins to swim; wolves are blessed with their sense of smell and owls with their hearing. Why should he, who has dedicated his life to spreading the gospel, be punished for acting in the same manner as all of His other creations? If He is omniscient and benevolent, why would He torment us by giving us such large brains and then condemning us for using them?

Ellen's voice interrupts his thoughts. "Tim? I've offended you, I can tell. I'm sorry—I didn't mean to be disrespectful."

Clarity. It's bursting from within now, unstoppable as an avalanche, and suddenly he wants the pies, the tables, and Ellen to disappear. He wants to linger in the moment, wants the avalanche to pick up speed, erase the remnants of fear in its path and deliver him to a place where he can finally be at peace.

But there is no time right now, and so he wills himself back to the conversation. "No, I'm not offended at all. Just preoccupied. Would you mind if we talked more after dinner? I want to give you my full attention, and—"

"Of course! Terrible timing on my part. Let me let you go before Jane gets too anxious." She places the pie on the porch steps. "See you in a bit," she says, and heads back to her car.

He hears the squealing of the front door, swollen from the heat, and turns just as Jane opens it. "Thank goodness you're back! Gracie just called."

He hands her a pie. "From Ellen. They're vegan." He follows her into the kitchen. She places it onto the countertop absently, with no mention of Ellen's thoughtfulness.

"You've got to go pick her up, right now. Luke, too."

"What?"

"Keith's stuck at the airport. His brother's plane is running half an hour late."

"We could ask Ellen."

She looks at him as if he's lost his mind. *Ellen?* No. Gracie needs to be at the church before her guests arrive. And Ellen is always fashionably late, as they say."

"But the table … "

She clasps her hands together in excitement. "They had one? Which size?"

"I can't remember the dimensions. But it matched it up to the sales slip." The cracked table and the forgotten tablecloth seem unimportant now, and so he adds, freely, "I forgot the tablecloth, though."

"That's all right. We'll just use one of ours. Make Gracie and Keith's table stand out as special."

He grins. Ellen had been right. "Good idea."

She looks at the time on the microwave. "Okay, here's the plan: you get the table assembled in the back, grab a quick shower, and head over to Gracie's. I'll take care of fixing all the place settings, and then Mother and I will meet you at church. Sound good?"

* * *

"Where's Amanda?" Tim says to Gracie, as he pulls up to the entrance to her apartment building.

"She left half an hour ago. Josephine picked her up."

"Music," Luke says, before either he or Gracie have closed their car doors after them. "Music, Grandpa."

"What do you want, Luke?" asks Gracie. "Radio or CD?"

"CD." But before Tim is able to load one, Luke changes his mind. "Radio."

"Okay," Tim says, pressing a pre-set station.

"CD."

"Luke," Gracie says, glancing at Tim in frustration. Her jaw is set, but her voice remains neutral. "Which one? You need to pick. CD or radio?" He notices that Gracie has reversed the order of choices for Luke. She does it to make sure his answer is reliable, she explained several years ago. If Luke isn't paying attention, he defaults to echoing the last option. If he picks *CD*, then it's a real choice.

"CD," Luke says, and Gracie smiles in relief. Luke is occupied.

"You swapped them. The choices. Right?"

Gracie gives him a look of surprise. "Way to go, Dad. I'm impressed."

"See, I pay attention." He looks in the rearview mirror at Luke, who is loosening his seatbelt from the top, in a fluid motion to avoid it locking, so he can bend forward to tap the floor with his hand. He intersperses the repetitive floor taps with taps on the window. Gracie seems either unaware or unfazed by it, he can't tell which. "So why did Josephine pick Amanda up so early?"

"They had to go pick up Jack. Amanda's boyfriend."

"I know who Jack is. The kid with the baseball cap. I've met him a few times."

"He's not a kid."

"I didn't mean it like that. I think of you as a kid, too." They lapse into silence, and he fiddles with the volume and the air conditioning vents to fill the time. They're alone, finally, yet now it's too late, his two chances stolen by a bracelet and a few yogurt-covered raisins.

"So I'm glad we have a minute to ourselves, Dad. I should've talked to you about this a long time ago, but I thought it might be a touchy subject, so I put it off." She glances at him, then fiddles with her engagement ring, turns it in circles around her finger. "Anyway, I want to know who you think should walk me down the aisle: Granddaddy or Pop-Pop? I was thinking

Pop-Pop, since he's a direct line to you, but I think Granddaddy might be hurt. What do you think about both, one on each side?"

Even though he knows that Gracie has chosen him for the greater honor, it feels like a punch in the stomach. "But Gracie, *I* want to be the one to walk you down the aisle. I should be the one to give you away. How about letting Granddaddy lead the ceremony?"

If I don't marry her, there is no lie.

It's an after-thought; his suggestion hadn't been a strategic move. Why hadn't he thought of this before?

If I don't marry her, there is no lie.

"He's prepared, don't worry. I asked him to be my backup. You know, in case I don't feel well."

"Granddaddy knows?"

"Well, not *why* I might not be feeling well. It wouldn't be a problem by the afternoon, anyway. But it's better to be prepared."

"But Dad, marrying us is way more important than walking me down the aisle."

· "But think about it from Granddaddy's perspective, Gracie. I think it'd be really meaningful for him, and you know how much he likes to be in charge. I'm just as happy to walk with you. Happier, actually."

She pursed her lips in defiance. "I don't care about Granddaddy's perspective. It's *my* wedding, not his."

Luke lets out a quick shriek, and then covers his hands with his ears.

Gracie turns and checks on Luke, then whispers, "I got too loud, that's all. Sets him on edge. You can put your hands down, honey," she calls over her shoulder. "Everything's all right. Mommy will be quieter."

Luke doesn't respond; instead, he hums, louder and louder, to drown out the volume that only exists in his mind. She unbuckles her seatbelt so she can turn and lift his chin, force him to look in her eyes.

"Look at me, Luke. You're okay. Grandpa's not mad, and Mommy's not mad." But Luke is unreachable now, has retreated into his own safe world. He closes his eyes, and clamps down on his ears harder, his hums drowning out her voice. "Luke, enough!" Gracie yells, and he stops for a split second, looks at her in surprise. But anxiety, shrouded in anger, grabs hold of him next, and he screams.

"I wanna break it. *I wanna break it*!" He grabs a CD case lying on the seat next to him, cracks the plastic cover in half. He throws the shard, hitting Tim in the back of the head, and then covers his ears again.

"Luke! Stop it!" Gracie yells, as she wrestles with him, tries to pull his hands down and bring him back to the world they both share.

"Gracie! Turn around and put your seatbelt on now."

"Fine," she spits out, as she loosens her grip on his arms. Tim isn't sure if she's frustrated with Luke's behavior, ashamed of her own, or embarrassed that she's been caught. "I shouldn't have done that," she says, after a moment. "It never works, anyway." She reaches into her pocketbook and pulls out a Ziploc filled with fluorescent triangular magnets, passes them back to Luke. She readjusts her shirt as she swivels forward, and then turns her necklace so the clasp is behind her neck again. She's quiet for a moment, and then asks, "Why don't you want to marry us? Is it Keith?"

"No, not at all! Keith is a good man, and he'll be a wonderful husband and father. You have no idea the number of prayers I've said, asking God to send you someone just like him."

"Then why?"

He sighs. This careful selection of words, this constant analysis of what to expose and what to hide——he is so very tired of it. "I want your marriage to be holy, Gracie. Untainted. Besides, I've presided over ceremonies many times, but I've never given my daughter away."

"What are you talking about, Dad?" She doesn't raise her voice, for Luke's sake. But he can tell by the way she emphasizes each word that she hasn't missed his first reason.

Suddenly, the weight is too much to bear. He's carried it for too long, and he's too weary not to give in and rest, regardless of the timing or consequences. It is simply too much. "I don't believe, Gracie," he says, his throat burning as the shameful words demand to be heard. "It's the worst possible time to tell you. Selfish, even, for me to tell you now. But I can't marry you if it means casting a shadow on your wedding." He can feel his throat constricting, his body barring him from speaking any more incriminating words.

Her eyes open wide. "You don't believe ... in *God*?"

How can she be so slow? he thinks, irritated, and then he scolds himself for his impatience. *This is completely out of the blue for her. Give her time to process.*

But time is limited now that he's taken the plunge. Soon she'll turn away. "Not anymore. It's hard to even say those words. Now isn't the time, I know, but I can explain." He looks at the dashboard clock. Ten minutes left. Ten minutes until they reach the church. "I'm sure it seems sudden to you, Gracie, but it's taken me a long time to get to the truth."

"The truth?" She turns and looks back at Luke in a controlled motion, as if checking in on sleeping baby. He's calm again, testing the strength of his magnets. "So let me get this straight: you're telling me that everything you've ever taught me is wrong, but because you've changed your mind, I need to, too?" She looks at him with contempt. "Why is it that everyone has to agree with what you believe? What makes you think that *you*—of all of the people in the history of the planet—are the one who's discovered the truth?"

Her words shock him. He'd prepared himself for outrage, for rejection, but not for this puzzling accusation. Arrogant? If anything, he's struggled with a lack of confidence, not an overabundance of it. "I just want to help people, Gracie," he says, rather than striking back. "You more than anyone else."

She looks out the window, watches the scenery pass. "You know, Dad, I bet I could be really good at witnessing. I know who to approach, how to steer the conversation, which verses to quote, how to counter objections—all of that. But I don't think it's my place to tell other people what to believe. That's why I pretended to be so bad at it in high school."

His jaw slackens in surprise, and she laughs. "You had no idea, did you?"

"I didn't," he admits. *And because I didn't, I set her up with Brett.* He wonders now if Gracie knows the part he played in the pairing. And then the sickening realization hits: he'd unwittingly laid the groundwork for her seduction. What course would her life have taken had he not interfered? Would there even be a Luke?

"Who else have you told?"

"No one."

"Are you going to?"

"I have to. It's not fair to expect you to keep *my* secret."

"She's not going to take it well," she says, eyes cast downward.

"I know. But I have no choice. How can I spend my life with her knowing that she wouldn't accept me if she found out?"

"It's not that hard, actually. I speak from experience."

"Are you talking about Keith?"

She nods. "And you."

"But I'll *always* accept you," he says, stunned. "Always."

"Right," she says with a smirk. "You don't think you would've tried to make me change my mind if I told you I didn't believe? You wouldn't have quoted Scripture day and night until you wore me down?"

She's right. I would have. "But it would have been from a place of love, Gracie. Out of a fear that you'd go to hell for rejecting God." He sighs. How is it that he finds himself rationalizing a reaction that he dreads facing? "I wish you'd told me that you'd lost your faith, Gracie. No, wait, let me change that—I wish I'd made you feel that you could."

"I haven't lost my faith."

"But you just said that you pretended to be bad at witnessing. That you've kept something hidden from Keith and me."

A faint smile hovers over her lips. "I believe in God. Just not in the same way you and Keith do. Or did, in your case. I don't believe in a virgin birth and a resurrection. But I do think there's a higher power, a force, something greater than us that binds us all."

"But Keith doesn't know."

She shakes her head. "He won't understand."

"Then how can you marry him, Gracie?"

She looks in the backseat at Luke before she answers. "Keith loves me. But more importantly, he loves Luke. Do you have any idea how hard that is to find? He has more patience than I do."

"But do you love him?"

"I love him enough."

"Gracie, you shouldn't feel pushed into marriage because you need help."

"Look who's talking," she says, with a snort.

He stifles the urge to reprimand her for being disrespectful. He has no right to. He dissected her engagement first.

"Look, Dad, I have no problem with gray. I've lived in it all my life. You're the one who's new to it." She pauses, looks at him for a moment before speaking. "I still want you to marry us. But Keith wouldn't. And I can't start our marriage by dishonoring our wedding. So if walking me down the aisle is the answer, that's what we'll do."

CHAPTER 19

It's an unnerving feeling, a Sunday without church. Tim's only had a handful of them in his life, a sprinkling of days throughout the years when symptoms have forced him to make early morning calls to Ed or Craig. Even though it's already the afternoon, flashes of urgency still jar him, as if he's misplaced his keys or wallet.

He follows Luke on the winding path to the lake, grateful that Josephine has agreed to meet with them on a Sunday. Between the rehearsal dinner, wedding, and today, he's monopolized her entire weekend. He'd assumed she'd cancel when the flu kept Wes from making it to both events. She'd even left the reception early because of it. But this morning she called and assured him that plans were still on.

I should've let her off the hook, he thinks, with a twinge of guilt. But keeping Luke entertained, even for a day and a half, is a daunting task. Luke can't sit still for more than five seconds, even though he used to be able to amuse himself with books and TV.

This morning, he and Jane awoke to the sound of Luke's relentless crisscrossing of the house. iPad pressed against his ear like a boom box, Luke rapped the pictures on the wall and the archways above him, jumped on the beds and couches, and walked across the glass coffee table. Jane, usually in charge of breakfast, left Tim to make do as she shadowed Luke, attempted to engage him with movies, books, and games. Her pleading chatter backfired, though, and ended with Luke biting his wrist, kicking two large holes in the wall, and throwing the iPad across the room. She'd turned towards the kitchen, jaw set, and returned five minutes later with two pieces of toast in a Ziploc for Luke and keys for Tim.

"But nothing's open yet. Where are we going to go?"

"Gracie brought his scooter. Go scoot around the neighborhood."

"That makes no sense. Why would I want to make him go *faster?*"

"Take a walk, then," she'd said, as she closed the door.

The gap between them begins to widen now, and Tim, already tired from their morning scooting, struggles to keep Luke in view. He watches as Luke scampers along the path, giggling, and marvels at the purity of his grandson's delight. Luke is nothing if not genuine. Veiled intentions and white lies are outside the realm of his understanding. A smile from Luke is motive-free.

He can't wait to get to the lake and let the water work its magic. Gracie tells him it's the constant, gentle pressure of the water that Luke finds soothing, since his body has trouble managing sensory input. But even though she's used the term a thousand times, he's still not sure what she means, or why everything has to be explained through the filter of autism. Most kids love to swim. Isn't it possible that he likes it just because it's fun?

Today they'll stay at the lake as long as Luke wants. He needs to keep the boy busy, and Luke clearly finds the water ... what's the word Gracie uses? *Organizing*. Yes, that's it. Luke finds the water organizing, whatever that means.

They've always left within a couple minutes of Josephine and Amanda, since Luke has a habit of drinking the water and eating the seaweed when Amanda's not there to distract him. But Gracie has told him not to bother trying to stop Luke today. "He's going to be anxious without me, and he's eaten far worse. Trust me. Just make sure to take him to the bathroom every fifteen minutes for a couple of hours afterwards, or he'll have an accident. Pack extra clothes."

Luke's scurrying slows to a prowl, and then he veers off the trail and beelines towards a medium-sized boulder. "Luke, wait," Tim calls out of habit, hands cupping his mouth. He surveys the boulder, estimates the potential injury from a fall. At least it's surrounded by grass. But what if this time Luke twists an ankle, scratches his leg, gets a bump on the head? A shiver runs through him despite the suffocating heat, and he breaks into a jog as he thinks of Luke's thirst-triggered tantrum on this same walk two weeks ago.

He maneuvers around the uneven terrain, a faint nausea stirring as he switches his gaze back and forth between the potholes in the dirt and Luke. *Please, please, please don't let him fall. I won't be able to handle him by myself.*

But Luke, once a clumsy kid, climbs the boulder with ease, and is in the midst of descending by the time Tim arrives. Luke slumps backwards onto him, and he staggers under his grandson's weight. He cries out as Luke lands on his foot, but Luke, unaware of the pain he's caused, runs towards the lake, leaving Tim to rub his toe and catch his breath.

Sweat trickles down the side of his face, and he wipes it with his t-shirt sleeve. This hyperactivity, is it new? Jane had said at lunch that she'd never seen Luke so wild or destructive before. That she'd been shocked by the sudden change. But is it sudden?

He wonders, now, if Luke's behavior has actually been going downhill for a while, and if Gracie has just been shielding him from it. After all, whenever Luke comes to visit, she and Keith watch him like a hawk, steer around calamity by clearing fragile items from shelves before they can be thrown, redirecting him when he gets frustrated, blocking him from climbing on furniture. When did that start? He doesn't remember him needing constant supervision when he was six, seven years old. It occurs to him that the only time Gracie lets him stay alone with Luke, with the exception of today's mini-honeymoon, is on this walk to the lake. Where Luke can climb, jump, and run as much as he wants. Where he can burn off some of his boundless energy, tire himself out even before he swims. Had Gracie chosen this lake *because* of the trail?

What he knows for sure is that the Luke he clings to, the Luke who tickles and hugs, shows himself less and less often. There is a force stronger than Tim, than Gracie, than schooling, therapy, or medication that is pulling Luke away, an undertow that has gripped him.

As always, the *why* can only be hypothesized. It could be because of the new medication his neurologist has prescribed. An interaction with his allergy or GI meds. An undiagnosed allergy. Frustration with his own limitations. A desire to have more control over his heavily-scheduled, monitored life.

The questions multiply. Why hasn't Gracie talked to him about it? Has she been too scared to give voice to the terrifying thought? Deluded? Or does she not want to discuss it with anyone but Keith? Up until Friday night, he would have scoffed at the idea of her hiding information about Luke from him. *But it turns out that Gracie's just as good at keeping secrets as I am.*

He thinks of the years he's spent praying for Luke, even as he grappled with the question of whether prayer works. The problem, he's found, is that that there's no way to judge, because the ground rules are rigged. If your prayers are answered, then He has listened and smiled upon you. If they aren't, then you're either unworthy or unable to comprehend His plan. It's a no-lose proposition for God.

He's defended prayer countless times, without much effort. Faith is an easy argument. The only one he can think of that manages to convert its greatest flaw into an asset. No evidence? It's God's way of testing you. Prove your devotion by turning a blind eye.

He's counseled his flock, answered what he thought was every possible question about prayer. "How should I pray, Pastor Tim?" "With others or alone?" "How often?" "How do I know if He hears me?" "Why are my prayers unanswered?" But not once has he been asked the one that sprouted within him the day he met the Muslim man, the day he first had a glimmer of a world outside his own: why do people pray to *different* gods? Because if there's only one god, then shouldn't He have a much better batting average than all of the fake ones? Shouldn't people have figured out by now who the real god is if only one of them can answer prayers?

His thoughts are interrupted by Luke, who has turned and is now running back towards him. He pats his backpack from the outside, listens for the crinkle of the paper bag holding Luke's snack. *Better to offer it before he gets too hungry.* He puts his bag on the ground, pulls out his thermos from the side pocket.

But Luke isn't hungry or thirsty. He stops short in front of Tim, then turns and faces away again. He takes several tentative steps forward, looks back to see if he's being followed, then giggles and takes a few more.

Tim smiles. *Chase. He's asking me to play chase.* "I'm going to get you!" he says, clenching his hands as if they were claws and stamping his feet. Luke squeals and runs away, picking up speed each time he looks back and sees Tim pretend to attack.

He turns back to his thoughts as Luke slows to examine a stick. *What purer prayer could there be than one for the health of a child?* He wonders what Josephine must think when she finds cancer in a child's tissue, how many prayers must be spoken every day in her hospital alone. But if God really does answer prayers, then she's wasting her time consulting with surgeons and oncologists. She'd be smarter to discuss test results with pastors, rabbis, and imams.

Yet his suggestion that Ellen join prayer group had been genuine. He'd always credited unexpected recoveries and happy endings to divine intervention, sparked by the group's shared love of the Lord. But yesterday, when he looked at the filled pews as he walked Gracie down the aisle, the rows of family and friends that have intertwined throughout the years to form the tapestry of his life, it dawned on him: it's the presence of *community* that heals, not the presence of God. Sometimes human intervention is enough.

Luke throws the stick into the brush, then stumbles as his foot slips out of his sneaker. He shoves it back in, crushing the sole and pushing the tongue forwards rather than opening the Velcro, and is off again, nearing the final bend in the path. Tim grimaces, imagines how uncomfortable it must be to walk, let alone run, that way. But Luke has no idea how to tie his shoes, and, from the looks of things, isn't faring much better with Velcro. Again, Tim's mind fast-forwards to the future. What if he never learns how to put his shoes on right? Who will help him with them when he's fifteen, thirty, sixty?

Gracie has never discussed Luke's future with him. "You're the grand-parent, not the parent," Jane has cautioned him, every time he's asked her whether he should broach the subject. "Don't overstep your bounds."

He's deferred to her over the years, heeded her advice and bitten his tongue. *But Jane doesn't get it. Because when you come right down to it, she doesn't love Luke.* He doesn't hold this against her. He understands why. But Luke's future doesn't gnaw at her in the middle of the night the way it does him. It doesn't pick at her insides until she's hollow.

He doubts Gracie has even set up a will. "She'll figure it out," "let her get past this rough spot," "all in good time"—these are the excuses Jane has made for Gracie time and time again. And so Tim has turned to

God for guidance. But now he's tired of being polite and tired of being powerless. Luke will *never* be able to support himself. So where will that money come from? What will Luke do with his days as an adult if he can't get a job?

If her solution is to marry Keith, then she's playing a risky game. What if they divorce? What if they have children, and money gets even tighter? What if Keith's life is cut short, like Shayla's?

There must be agencies that can help. Surely they could guide her in applying for financial support, direct her to community programs, connect her with other families. If Gracie hasn't looked into them, then she needs to start. *And if she needs a shove—if I have to be the bad guy—then so be it.*

He rounds the final bend in the path, and Luke, who was out of view for a moment, is in sight again. He can see Josephine and Amanda at the lake's entrance. There is a man with them, his back to Tim. He's on his hands and knees, spreading out a towel for Amanda, who is bent over rubbing sunscreen on her legs. He's of medium build, wearing striped board shorts, a t-shirt and—the giveaway—a navy baseball cap. It must be Jack. Josephine told Tim at the reception that she had to remind him to take it off during the ceremony.

The man turns as Josephine waves to Luke, and as he does a shock of sandy-colored hair falls across his forehead. So it isn't Jack. It's Wes.

Of course. It's Sunday, not Saturday, so no soccer. But wasn't Wes sick? Even if it was just a twenty-four hour bug, Josephine should've asked if it was okay for him to come when she called. What if Wes is still contagious? Luke getting the flu would be disastrous.

Josephine waves and makes her way towards the trail, her steps cautious as she navigates around pebbles and shards of crushed shells. It's her mother's careful high-heeled pace, not her usual determined one, and he chuckles at the thought of how much the comparison would bother her. Amanda turns to follow her, tossing the sunscreen tube onto the towel and rubbing the excess into her arms as she walks. Sidetracked by the streaks of cream on her shoulder, she strays to the right of Josephine, and it's then that Luke spots her. He stops, jumps several times in excitement, and then makes a slight diagonal shift in direction in order to line up with her. Tim checks if anyone else is walking on this final stretch of the trail between Luke and Amanda, but the path is clear.

"Over there," he calls, pointing to an open spot between Amanda and the brush at the edge. She nods, and directs Wes, several steps behind, into the spot to form a human barrier. He sighs in relief. *Thank you, Josephine.*

He can relax now if he wants, but for some reason he finds his pace quickening. His knees ache as he runs, and the hot air that he sucks in irritates his throat, but he doesn't stop. The uneven trail flattens, becomes paved, and suddenly he's chasing Gracie, not Luke. Gracie going to see her friend down the street.

Beyond his blood, beyond Gracie and—he can only hope—his parents, of all those he has loved and trusted, the Wallises will be the last ones standing. Death had stolen Shayla, and its aftermath had snatched John and Lillian; an unexpected life had taken Ed; and soon God will claim Jane, Craig, and the community of people he'd once believed to be his brothers and sisters in Christ.

Yet the fear is gone. Fear of being alone, fear of his own inadequacy, fear of the whims of the divine—for the first time in close to thirty years, it is gone. He'd rebuilt his life, twice, desperate for a level of guidance that only God could provide. But faith, the spiritual remedy for despair, could no longer offer comfort once he found himself unwilling to let an emotional argument trump a reasoned one. He'd tried to suppress the truth, disguise it, even contort it, but ultimately, it had overcome him, tethered itself to him. *Like Luke's magnets.*

He's been alone all along. He just hasn't known it.

The back of his throat is raw, burnt by the scorching air, and he tries to breathe through his nose instead. He fights the dizziness and the shooting pains that run up his calves as his feet strike the pavement. His chest aches, batted about by the rhythmic contraction of his heart and expansion of his lungs. His mouth is open again, and somehow he's inhaling and exhaling at the same time, but that can't be, that's not possible … and he's gaining on Gracie, his strides effortless, and now he's gliding, the pavement is ice now, and the jarring impact is gone, he's free—but then he's falling, his right leg is stuck—why won't it glide?—and then he's on the ground, the taste of dirt in his mouth.

It is a path again, not pavement.

He spits out the dirt, can hear Luke's giggles over the sound of his breathing again. He sits and rubs his ankle, then stands, puts his weight on it gingerly. A band of dull pain runs along the bridge of his foot, but his leg doesn't buckle. He takes a cautious step, then another. Even though his breath is still coming in jagged spurts, he starts to run again. One foot in front of the other, one foot in front of the other, one foot in front of the other, as he leaves behind heaven and hell, passivity and uncertainty, and strides towards the only life that is guaranteed.

He is ready.

"Luke," he says, beaming, his hurried footsteps spraying gravel and dust. "Luke, I'll be right there."

A Note from the Author

While the situations and characters of the novel are fictional, the medical studies referenced within it are factual. The following research bears citing:

Briggs, G.G., Freeman, R.K., Yaffe, S.J. (2008). Drugs in Pregnancy and Lactation: A Reference Guide to Neonatal Risk, Eighth Edition. Philadelphia, PA: Lippincott, Williams & Wilkins.

Giuliano, A.E. et al. Axillary dissection versus no axillary dissection in women with invasive breast cancer and sentinel node metastasis: a randomized clinical trial. JAMA. 2011; 305(6):569-75.

Kargas G.A., Kargas S.A., Bruyere H.J. Jr., Gilbert E.F., Opitz J.M. Perinatal mortality due to interaction of diphenhydramine and temazepam. N Engl J Med. 1985; 313:1417–8.

In order to stay true to the timeline of the novel, only research that was published prior to the book's conclusion (July 2011) was considered.

I did manipulate the timeline in regard to Texas abortion law, as significant change occurred when House Bill 15, The Woman's Right to Know Act, was enacted in September 2003. The characters of Josephine and Gracie faced their decisions earlier—2000 and 2002, respectively—but I chose to allude to the current protocol to better reflect today's reality.

House Bill 15 instituted the requirement that women undergo pre-abortion counseling, and that written materials be provided to them. Of contention is the booklet's assertion that abortion is tied to increased risk of breast cancer. The National Cancer Institute, American Cancer Society, and American College of Obstetricians and Gynecologists do not support this claim.

In 2011, the law was expanded to require that women undergo a sonogram by the doctor performing the procedure, regardless of whether one has already been performed by a referring physician. The heartbeat must be made audible, and the image of the fetus must be displayed on the screen and described in detail. A mandatory twenty-four hour "reflection" period between receiving the sonogram and undergoing the procedure was instituted as well.

In 2013, House Bill 2 placed further restrictions on abortion, and in 2014 the bill was amended to require that abortion clinics be licensed as ambulatory surgical centers, causing many to shut down.

Acknowledgments

Enormous thanks are owed to Daniel Burgess, for his perceptive and constructive editorial comments; Teddi Black, for her artistic rendering of my vision; Rachel Haims, for her medical clarifications and early interest in the novel; and Sarah Gracombe, for her literary expertise and forty years of friendship.

For her tireless support and unwavering interest in my writing, I thank my mother, Diana Levinson.

My deepest gratitude goes to my husband, Derek Navisky, whose suggestion to throw away my initial convoluted plot allowed this book to be born. In return for this sage advice, I resolve to restrain myself from poking fun at his book selections in the future. His faith in me and steadfast devotion to our family—including our very own "Luke"—is a gift that I'm thankful for every day.

Made in the USA
Middletown, DE
13 December 2015